EVIDENCE OF EVIL

SILVER AND GREY
BOOK 2

MARY LANCASTER

ARE YOU SIGNED UP FOR DRAGONBLADE'S BLOG?

You'll get the latest news and information on exclusive giveaways, exclusive excerpts, coming releases, sales, free books, cover reveals and more.

Check out our complete list of authors, too!

No spam, no junk. That's a promise!

Sign Up Here

www.dragonbladepublishing.com

Dearest Reader;

Thank you for your support of a small press. At Dragonblade Publishing, we strive to bring you the highest quality Historical Romance from some of the best authors in the business. Without your support, there is no 'us', so we sincerely hope you adore these stories and find some new favorite authors along the way.

Happy Reading!

CEO, Dragonblade Publishing

Additional Dragonblade books by Author Mary Lancaster

Silver and Grey Series
Murder in Moonlight (Book 1)
Evidence of Evil (Book 2)

One Night in Blackhaven Series
The Captain's Old Love (Book 1)
The Earl's Promised Bride (Book 2)
The Soldier's Impossible Love (Book 3)
The Gambler's Last Chance (Book 4)
The Poet's Stern Critic (Book 5)
The Rake's Mistake (Book 6)
The Spinster's Last Dance (Book 7)

The Duel Series
Entangled (Book 1)
Captured (Book 2)
Deserted (Book 3)
Beloved (Book 4)
Haunted (Novella)

Last Flame of Alba Series
Rebellion's Fire (Book 1)
A Constant Blaze (Book 2)
Burning Embers (Book 3)

Gentlemen of Pleasure Series
The Devil and the Viscount (Book 1)
Temptation and the Artist (Book 2)
Sin and the Soldier (Book 3)
Debauchery and the Earl (Book 4)
Blue Skies (Novella)

Pleasure Garden Series
Unmasking the Hero (Book 1)
Unmasking Deception (Book 2)
Unmasking Sin (Book 3)
Unmasking the Duke (Book 4)
Unmasking the Thief (Book 5)

Crime & Passion Series
Mysterious Lover (Book 1)
Letters to a Lover (Book 2)
Dangerous Lover (Book 3)
Lost Lover (Book 4)
Merry Lover (Novella)
Ghostly Lover (Novella)

The Husband Dilemma Series
How to Fool a Duke (Book 1)

Season of Scandal Series
Pursued by the Rake (Book 1)
Abandoned to the Prodigal (Book 2)
Married to the Rogue (Book 3)
Unmasked by her Lover (Book 4)
Her Star from the East (Novella)

Imperial Season Series
Vienna Waltz (Book 1)
Vienna Woods (Book 2)
Vienna Dawn (Book 3)

Blackhaven Brides Series
The Wicked Baron (Book 1)
The Wicked Lady (Book 2)
The Wicked Rebel (Book 3)
The Wicked Husband (Book 4)
The Wicked Marquis (Book 5)
The Wicked Governess (Book 6)
The Wicked Spy (Book 7)
The Wicked Gypsy (Book 8)

The Wicked Wife (Book 9)
Wicked Christmas (Book 10)
The Wicked Waif (Book 11)
The Wicked Heir (Book 12)
The Wicked Captain (Book 13)
The Wicked Sister (Book 14)

Unmarriageable Series
The Deserted Heart (Book 1)
The Sinister Heart (Book 2)
The Vulgar Heart (Book 3)
The Broken Heart (Book 4)
The Weary Heart (Book 5)
The Secret Heart (Book 6)
Christmas Heart (Novella)

The Lyon's Den Series
Fed to the Lyon

De Wolfe Pack: The Series
The Wicked Wolfe
Vienna Wolfe

Also from Mary Lancaster
Madeleine (Novella)
The Others of Ochil (Novella)

CHAPTER ONE

S OLOMON GREY HAD leased a pleasant house behind the Strand, from where, impenetrable fog permitting, he could look out and see the bustling River Thames. It was not a fashionable address, but he did not entertain, and it was located within easy distance of his main office and the charities that took up the rest of his time.

At eleven o'clock on a sunny September morning, Solomon sat in his large study, which was also his sitting room, a map of the world spread open before him on the table by the window. The wicked delight of truancy that had assailed him during his first day away from the office had lost its charm. Today, he felt restless, and the notion had come to him that he might like to travel purely for pleasure, merely to appreciate the art and architecture of the world's capitals, and the beauty of unfamiliar scenery.

When he heard the knock on the street door below, he paid no attention—he had a servant to repel boarders—until his study door opened and Jenks, his manservant, announced, "Mrs. Silver, sir. I believe she has an appointment with you."

Solomon started to his feet. Since he had quite expected to be alone, he had not troubled to don coat or necktie, so he was hardly fit to receive visitors. Moreover, he doubted he would ever be fit to receive this particular visitor.

Constance Silver glided into the room behind Jenks, a breath-taking blast of beauty and fresh air.

"Solomon," she said affectionately, holding out both gloved hands as she sailed toward him. "How delightful to see you again!"

She was right, damn her. It was delightful, only surprise held him speechless and distinctly disadvantaged. This was not how he had planned to meet her again.

"Will that be all, sir?" inquired Jenks, who must have at least suspected that Constance had no appointment, but had clearly decided his master deserved this treat.

"Yes," Solomon said, unaccountably flustered, for he had no choice but to take Mrs. Silver's hands in a brief hold and give a very sketchy bow. "No. Tea, if you please."

"Goodness," Constance murmured as Jenks departed. "All this and hospitality, too. How are you, Solomon?"

For an instant, her eyes searched his face, and he realized this was the first time since her arriving that she had actually looked at him directly. She was not as confident in her welcome as she had appeared, and he had the flattering idea that she did actually care how he was.

He found his voice. "Flabbergasted," he said. "How on earth did you find me?"

"Oh, it's easy enough to find anyone if you know the right people," she said vaguely. "I did try at your St. Catherine's office, but they told me you were not expected there, so here I am."

"Please, sit down." He indicated the more comfortable chairs by the fire, but she had moved to the table and his map.

"Are you planning a trip?"

"I'm thinking about it."

"Just thinking? Then you don't sail within the next fortnight?"

"I don't need to. Why?"

"I have a proposition for you." Her eyes danced, and he knew she was teasing him with her choice of words but inviting him to share the joke.

Was that relief flooding through his veins? That the odd friendship they had found still existed, despite their not seeing each other for almost three months.

"Should I apologize for lying to your servant?" she asked, disposing herself gracefully in an armchair.

"Probably. You could just have sent up your card. I would have received you in more formal attire."

She eyed him. "Please. We both know he would not have let me in."

"He did let you in. I'm not quite sure why, since I doubt he believes in your appointment any more than I do."

"He probably thinks you are too isolated. Why aren't you going to work, Solomon?"

"I am perfecting the art of delegation."

"So that you can travel with a clear conscience?"

"Something like that."

A smile flickered across her long lips with their extra-fascinating upward curve. "You are bored."

He was saved the necessity of answering that by the arrival of Jenks carrying a tea tray. A coat hung over one arm. After placing the tray on the low table between the chairs, Jenks handed the coat to Solomon, who shrugged into it as casually as he could under Constance's amused gaze.

Jenks departed as impassively as he had entered, and Constance began to pour the tea without being asked.

"Tell me your proposition," Solomon said, sitting down at last, aware of a spurt of excitement that might have been to do with her mere presence, or with what she had come to say.

"I have a friend who is afraid she will be accused of murder." She handed him his cup of tea the way he preferred it, with neither milk nor sugar.

"Is she guilty?" he asked. It was not unreasonable to inquire. Constance lived among the *demimonde*, owning a discreet and expensive brothel in Mayfair. Wealthy and powerful men were rumored to frequent her establishment.

"No," Constance said. "Lizzie would not hurt a fly, let alone a living person. I want to prove her innocence."

"By discovering who *did* commit the murder?"

"I thought you might like to help." She sipped her tea as gracefully as any Mayfair lady. "Considering how successful we were at Greenforth Manor this summer. And two heads are obviously better than one."

Was she giving him too many reasons? She must have known he would not be eager to poke about among the unsavory lives of her women and their clients.

"Who is she? Who is the victim?"

"My friend is Elizabeth, Lady Maule," Constance said, meeting his gaze. "She is the wife of Sir Humphrey Maule, a landowning baronet in Sussex."

He refused to betray as much as a blink of surprise. He should have known.

"The dead lady is a Miss Frances Niall," she went on, "the daughter of Maule's neighbor. Her father is a colonel recently retired from India."

"And why should your friend Lady Maule be accused of killing this woman?"

"Because she was the last person known to have seen her alive."

"But with what motive?"

"I believe they had quarreled. And Miss Niall's body was recovered from the lake on Maule grounds."

"But you don't believe she did it? Why not? How well do you know her?"

Constance sighed. "I thought I would impress you with the respectability of my friends, but I see I will have to be truthful. Lady Maule once stayed in my establishment."

"She was one of your girls," he said neutrally.

Constance waved that aside.

"And this Maule married her?"

"Well, he did not meet her in my establishment," Constance said. "She answered an advertisement to become governess to his children—he was a widower. And they married the following year."

Solomon did not regard himself as a puritan, but this sat uneasily with him. "I take it you engineered this? Was it right to put such a person in charge of children?"

"I believe so. Whores are not all cut from the same cloth, any more than seamstresses or bankers or plantation owners."

"Point taken," he said politely, though he should have known better.

"Liar. What do you think happens to the girls of respectable families who are seduced by the uncaring and disowned? How do you think they live, eat, feed the results of their seduction? They have no character. No one will house or employ a ruined woman, though the man who bears at least half the responsibility walks away without a care in the world."

"Is that what happened to you?" he asked.

"God, no. But it's what happened to Elizabeth. She comes from a gentry family, has the education and the nature to take care of children. She was an excellent governess, and I daresay she is an excellent mother. She should not have this taken away from her by false accusations."

"Is that really likely to happen?"

"She fears it, which is why she has asked for my help. And I am asking for yours, if you can spare a week from your busy schedule."

Solomon sipped his tea and regarded her. Her gaze was limpid and innocent. Too innocent.

"And?" he said steadily.

Constance set down her cup and saucer. "Well, naturally, I wrote back that I would happily go down to Sussex and stay with her while we sorted it all out. I also said I might bring a friend who is good at such puzzles as this. She immediately replied that my friend was welcome too, but that for the sake of respectability, since my friend is male, she told her husband that we are married."

No doubt his jaw dropped at that.

"You must see it from her point of view," Constance said hastily. "All her connections must at least appear to be of the utmost respectability. A woman—even a widow—traveling in the sole company of a man unrelated to her would not be remotely respectable."

He regarded her with fascination. "But an unmarried woman traveling as the pretended wife of an unmarried man *is* respectable?"

"My dear Solomon, even you know respectability is all about appearance, not fact."

"And you are...comfortable with appearing to be my wife?"

She picked up her cup and saucer again and took another sip of tea. "Well, at least we are friends, and we are unlikely to meet anyone we know. The Maules and their neighbors are all very much country people, not London gadabouts. There is a train tomorrow morning."

"I would rather travel by coach."

"It will take twice as long," she objected.

"Then I am prepared to leave this afternoon. I shall call for you at two of the clock."

"In broad daylight?" she mocked. "Mr. Grey!"

He bowed. "Mrs. Grey. Apparently."

ALTHOUGH IT WAS tempting to show Solomon the tasteful, understated comfort in which she lived, Constance elected to spare him the humiliation of entering a brothel and lurked in the entrance hall with her bags. She owed him that much for agreeing to come.

"You stepping out wif someone, Mrs. S?" asked Hildie cheerfully as she flicked her feather duster over the unlit gas lamps. She wanted to be a housemaid.

"No, I'm going into the country to stay with an old friend.

Barbara's in charge while I'm gone, so no impudence."

Hildie grinned. "*Me*, Mrs. S?"

"Carriage, ma'am," said Joseph the footman, striding from his cubbyhole where he'd been watching out of the window. "Bang-up it is, too. Beautiful horses." He hefted her bags and strode out of the house while Hildie opened the front door for her.

Solomon, ever the perfect gentleman, stepped down from the carriage to hand Constance inside. She was sure Hildie goggled from inside, though Joseph was busy stowing the luggage.

"How long are we staying?" Solomon inquired. "A month?"

"Don't be facetious. I shan't know what I shall need until we get there."

"Are you not taking a maid?"

"I doubt the Maule household is ready for Janey."

He climbed back in and closed the door then sat opposite her, with his back to the horses. "Why not?" The horses set out at a brisk trot.

"She swears like a trooper and slaps anyone who gets in her way. I taught her everything I know."

He regarded her with amused disbelief until she entertained him with a few of Janey's more exquisite curses. She was encouraged to see his eyes laugh rather than turn blank with distaste. She stopped before disgust could set in.

"So, explain to me how long we have been married and where we met," he said.

"Oh, I think we have been married only a short while, don't you? That will account for any lack of familiarity with each other. I suggest we met at an exhibition of art, or perhaps a lecture at the Geographical Society?"

He blinked. "Have you ever been to such a lecture?"

"Several. You would be surprised by the breadth of my interests."

"I already am," he said.

She wondered if it was true but refused to look at him to find out. Why had she thought of him as soon as she read Lizzie's letter? Just because they had solved a mystery together in the summer?

No, it was more than that. It had always been more than that. Though he disapproved of her on a level that could never be undone, he had said they were friends. Which was a novelty. She knew many amiable men, but none were friends except Solomon Grey.

After Norfolk, when they had each returned from Greenforth Manor, she had expected him to call on her—a morning call, of course—only he never had. Nor had he written even the tersest note. And when she had run into Lady Grizelda, whose fault it was they had met in the first place, she had heard nothing of him for weeks.

Elizabeth Maule was her excuse.

Oh, Constance was truly concerned for her old friend, but Lizzie was given to panic and exaggeration, so Constance doubted that Lady Maule was truly about to be accused of murder. She was visiting mainly to be sure of her friend's well-being, and to ascertain exactly what was going on in Elizabeth's life. Suggesting a friend come too had been a moment of foolishness she instantly regretted—until Elizabeth wrote back that they must pretend to be married.

Constance had a mischievous soul. And so she had finally sought Solomon out. She hadn't truly expected him to agree, let alone be prepared to sit in a carriage with her for two days and pretend to be the husband of a notorious courtesan.

But it seemed they truly were friends, for here he was. His gaze fixed on her face in the long silence that followed his admission of surprise.

He stirred. "What else have you been doing since leaving Norfolk? Have you been well?"

Truth be told, she was hurt that he had waited ten weeks to find out. But she would never admit it.

"Quite well, thank you," she replied politely, and then went on the attack. "What of you? Are you ill that you are playing truant and planning journeys abroad?"

"No..."

She peered more closely at him, for the denial was not a very firm one. He *looked* healthy enough. His regular, handsome features were not marred by signs of exhaustion or pain. His velvet-dark eyes were clear and bright. He was thin, of course, but it seemed to be the way he was made. It did not denote a lack of physical strength, as she well knew.

She doubted he was ill, and yet he looked away, out of the carriage window, as though to avoid her gaze.

He drew in a breath. "I believe I am...bored."

She blinked. "Bored?"

"It is a sort of sickness of the spirit." He sounded almost apologetic. "Certainly, it is a weakness. Once I have things running as I wish, I tend to lose interest."

"You have no more room for expansion?" she asked in amazement.

"Oh, there is always room. I just have no desire at the moment. In all my businesses, I have good people in place, though I have not given up my oversight. I have just made myself less...necessary."

"While you make a leisurely journey around the world?"

He shrugged. "Perhaps. Certainly while I look for another area of interest."

No, Solomon was not a contented man. Restless, clever, and crushingly lonely, he only ever seemed to be driven toward what made him more alone than ever. Once, she had vowed to show him happiness—an arrogant, overambitious vow if ever there was one. Certainly if he would not stay put, nor even write to her.

"Will you go back to Jamaica?" she asked lightly. *Please say no...*

"Not without reason."

She knew what that meant. His only reason would be news of his lost twin brother, who had vanished without a trace at the age of ten. In the midst of the Jamaican slave revolt.

His gaze came back to hers, self-deprecating, with a touch of humor. "I am searching for inspiration. Perhaps I will find it with your mystery—and help your friend at the same time."

CHAPTER TWO

I F CONSTANCE HARBORED any secret doubts that Elizabeth's manner might have changed toward her, they were swiftly put to rest as Lady Maule flew down the front steps of her home and embraced her friend.

"Constance! I am so glad you are here. How wonderful to see you." Elizabeth drew back far enough to examine her and smiled even more broadly. "You are as beautiful as ever."

Constance examined her friend in turn. Despite the unconventional enthusiasm of her welcome, Elizabeth wore the lady of the manor's garb quite naturally. Though her eyes betrayed the knock her confidence had taken for some years, only a friend could discern it. To others it probably seemed an endearing shyness due to the fact she had so recently been promoted from governess to wife.

To Constance, her friend was healthy, if not quite glowing with bridal happiness. There were lines of worry and strain about her eyes, some shadows that betokened a lack of sleep. No, all was not well with the new Lady Maule.

"Ha," Constance said, smiling. "You are being kind to an old lady. Come and meet my—"

"Husband," Elizabeth interrupted nervously, casting a quick glance at her servants, who were hurrying to remove the baggage from the coach.

Releasing Constance altogether, she thrust out her hand at Solomon, who bowed over it punctiliously.

"Mr. Solomon Grey," Constance murmured. "Solomon, my old friend, Lady Maule."

Elizabeth's eyes widened as she took in the sheer beauty and elegance of his person. Although those things were only part of his arsenal. Solomon had *presence*.

"Welcome to The Willows, Mr. Grey," Elizabeth said formally. "I hope you will enjoy your stay with us. Come, let me show you to your room."

Room. So they really were to be treated as a married couple. Perhaps there would be a dressing room, or even better, separate bedchambers with only a connecting door. Her mischief had come up against reality suddenly, and the idea of sharing a room—let alone a bed!—with Solomon made her unaccountably nervous.

The Willows was a comfortable manor house of indeterminate age and many styles. Full of odd staircases and passages and changes in ceiling heights and wall decoration, it looked as if each baronet had added something of his own over a period of several centuries. Constance rather liked its asymmetrical, slightly chaotic appearance. It seemed to suit Elizabeth and her wild changes in fortune.

"Did you bring servants with you?" Elizabeth asked, leading through the maze of passages and staircases.

"Oh, no," Constance replied. "That would have been even more of an imposition."

"How is Janey?" Elizabeth asked, her eyes dancing just for a moment.

"In good voice," Constance replied. "But showing promise. Do you have other guests?"

"No, just you."

Then perhaps there was space to arrange separate rooms…

Elizabeth threw open the door of a bright, spacious apartment containing a large four-poster bed with brocade curtains that matched the coverings on the chair and sofa before the hearth. The fire burning in the grate added cheerful warmth to an already pretty and gracious room. Like the house, the furniture was of various ages and did not match, but somehow this all added to its charm. A vase of late roses stood on the table before the window.

"This is lovely," Constance said warmly. Solomon's trunk and her bags stood beside the bed, as yet unpacked.

"I'm glad you like it," Elizabeth replied. "And look, it has beautiful views over the park..." She trailed off as they joined her. Her expression had changed to one of anxiety and consternation.

Through the trees, Constance glimpsed an expanse of water—surely the lake where the neighbor had died.

"What happened, Lizzie?" she asked gently.

Elizabeth seized her hand, pressing it hard. "Oh, don't call me that, Constance. I need all my dignity here..."

Trying not to wince, Constance stared at her. "You're not saying that...? Elizabeth, does *Sir Humphrey* believe in your guilt?" How could any marital relationship come back from that?

But Elizabeth was shaking her head tiredly. "He says not. In fact, he is furious at the implication. But I cannot bear this *festering* between us."

Solomon, who had been silent all this time, as he often was, turned from the window to look at her. "Will you tell us about this woman and how she died?"

"Her name is Frances Niall. She lives—*lived*—with her family, over at Fairfield Grange. Her father is a widower, a colonel in the Indian army, recently retired. The family came back to the Grange only a month after we were married."

"Are there other family members?" Constance asked.

"Her brother John. He is younger, only just twenty-one." Elizabeth moved restlessly away from the window. "We see—*saw*—rather a lot of the Nialls. But Frances and I never really liked each other. She thought I was a jumped-up governess, and I thought she was spoiled and sly. We had...words."

"The night she died?" Solomon asked, resting his hip on the window seat and watching Elizabeth's perambulations.

"No, a few days before that, when they dined here. But on Wednesday she sent me a note of apology, saying she regretted her hasty words, and would I like to go for a walk to clear the air between us. I agreed, and she came over that evening. Which was not entirely convenient, for it was already dusk. However, I felt I should appear willing, so we walked around the lake for a little, said pleasant and forgiving things to each other, and then parted."

"Where did she go?" Constance asked.

Elizabeth shrugged. "Home to Fairfield Grange, I suppose. It's an easy twenty-minute walk. The path is well trodden, and she had a lantern."

"Was she alone?" Solomon asked mildly.

"Yes. Well, she arrived with her maid, then once we were both outdoors, she sent Bingham back to the Grange and said she would follow in just a little. So she left the lakeside alone."

"In the direction of Fairfield Grange?" Constance pursued.

"Yes."

"Then what happened to her?"

"I don't know. But apparently she never reached home. Neither her family nor her maid, nor any other servant, saw her alive again. Our gardener pulled her body out of the lake in the morning." Elizabeth shuddered, swallowing hard.

"That must have been awful," Constance said sympathetically, although, like her, Elizabeth had probably seen her share of bodies in London's less salubrious back streets.

"It wasn't pleasant. So terrible for her family. Colonel Niall is devastated. So is John. And the servants. Humph is still quite shocked."

Despite the seriousness of the discussion, Constance almost smiled to hear the endearment of a pet name on Elizabeth's lips. It seemed there was hope for their marriage.

"Did you see her body?" Solomon asked.

Elizabeth blinked rapidly. "No, thank God. My husband did. He helped the gardener drag her out, but she had clearly been dead for hours. The doctor came and confirmed that she had drowned, and by then Colonel Niall was here... It was dreadful."

"Was the magistrate informed?"

Elizabeth gave a watery smile. "Humphrey *is* the magistrate. Like everyone else, he thought it was a tragic accident and Frances drowned by falling in the lake in the dark. Although we have no idea what she was doing back there..."

"I thought she had a lantern with her," Solomon said.

"She did when she left me," Elizabeth confirmed, "but there was no sign of it when they found her body."

"So she might well have fallen into the lake in the dark," Constance said. "I doubt lights from the house, if there were any, would reach through these trees."

"That's what we thought. What we all wanted to think, I suppose, because the only real alternative was suicide, and no one wants to believe such a thing."

"So why has opinion changed to murder?" Solomon asked.

"Because Colonel Niall insisted on an autopsy. He seemed to blame me even then. And Dr. Laing discovered..." Elizabeth swallowed hard, and Constance pressed her hand encouragingly. "He discovered that she had not breathed in any water. She was dead before she entered the lake."

"Couldn't she have hit her head on the way in?" Constance suggested.

"Or on a tree branch or something earlier," Solomon agreed. "Head wounds are strange. She might have keeled over quite suddenly some time after taking a knock."

"Apparently there were no injuries to her body, no signs of heart disease or any other illness, no poison in her stomach. Yet still she is dead, and not by drowning."

"How very strange," Constance said slowly. "But...why would Colonel Niall blame you?"

"Because I am the stranger here. Because I quarreled with her. Because I saw her last. And because he is grief-stricken and lashing out." Elizabeth drew in a breath and smiled with false brightness. "So that is my trouble, and one reason I am so pleased to see friendly faces! You will meet Humphrey and the children at tea, so I will leave you for now to settle in. Tea is in the drawing room."

She marched so decisively toward the door that Constance panicked. She was not ready to be left alone with Solomon in the apparently marital bedchamber.

"Oh, can't you give me a tour of your house, first?" she suggested, hurrying after her friend. "Solomon will be glad of five minutes' peace after my chattering in his ear for two days..."

It was probably true, although he had given no sign of it. After the first hour in his extremely comfortable coach, they had lapsed easily back into their old companionship, a mixture of impersonal conversation, comfortable silences, and banter. They saw the world in different ways, but his were always interesting. Even the night they had spent at a slightly run-down coaching inn had been comfortable, with separate rooms and a private parlor in which to dine.

Certainly, he made no demur at her departure now.

"Come and see my own rooms first," Elizabeth said eagerly. "You will love them."

This suited Constance very well, since she was keen to see how her old friend lived in her private moments. One could learn much from bedchambers.

In this case, however, Constance caught only a glimpse through a door that was slightly ajar. What Elizabeth showed her was a pretty, private sitting room overlooking the gardens at the front of the house. She had some bookshelves, a large sewing basket, an elegant little bureau for letter writing, two comfortable chairs, and a chaise longue. The colors were light and pleasing and very Elizabeth, with a seascape on one wall and a landscape on the other, both in harmonious shades.

"How lovely," Constance said genuinely. "You must be very happy here. Do you have a dressing room, too?"

"No. Humph has that." Elizabeth waved her hand to the ajar connecting door. "That is our bedchamber, and beyond that, his dressing room. I like it this way."

"I can see why." Constance perched on the chaise longue, spreading her fingers over the luxurious fabric. It felt new. "You are truly happy as Lady Maule?"

Elizabeth sighed. "I was until all this happened. It has taken the edge off a bit. The thing is, I know Humphrey is remembering that I am not entirely respectable, though he doesn't want me to guess, and so we are tiptoeing around each other with politeness. Politeness does not come naturally to Humph!"

Constance blinked. "It doesn't?"

Elizabeth laughed, warmth in her eyes. "Oh, I don't mean he is *rude*, but he is downright, says exactly what he thinks, and is inclined to irascibility. I call him Sir Grumphy when he's like that…" The laughter faded from her eyes. "You see why I need your help?"

"Because finding out what truly happened to the dead lady in the lake will make your marriage more comfortable." To say nothing of keeping her from the hangman's rope.

"What of your Mr. Grey?" Elizabeth asked, sitting down beside Constance at last. "I've rarely come across so devastating a man. Is he serious about you?"

"Don't be silly," Constance said dryly. "I told you we were friends, not lovers."

Elizabeth's eyes widened. "Then he did not come to…the establishment?"

"God, no, he is not that way inclined."

"He prefers men?"

"He might, for all I know—which is only that he does not frequent establishments like mine. We met at a country house party in the summer and together solved the nasty mystery of our murdered host. So you see why I wanted you to invite him."

"But he has agreed to pretend to be your husband?" Elizabeth said in some alarm. "I'm so sorry, Constance! I thought my notion was perfect for both respectability and comfort. But is it not incredibly difficult for both of you?"

Yes. "No," Constance replied. "We shall play our parts to perfection." She hesitated, then added, "Though I think it's a mistake, Elizabeth. Secrets rarely improve a marriage,"

"Our kind of secrets do," Elizabeth said bleakly.

WHEN CONSTANCE FLED from their bedroom in Lady Maule's wake, Solomon watched with sardonic amusement. He guessed that her little joke was no longer quite so amusing in the harsh light of a four-poster bed and no dressing room, nor even a sofa. For his part, Solomon was only too aware of those things, especially considering his own reactions to her nearness.

A man would have to be at death's door not to desire Constance Silver. But she was not his lover, she was his friend. And that, as she had perceived several months ago, was the most important thing to both of them.

It didn't stop her teasing him for staidness or puritanism or whatever else she imagined governed his life.

Having sent away the servant who offered to unpack their bags, Solomon unpacked his own, putting his things away neatly and taking up as little space as possible. Then, since Constance had not returned, he left the room with the intention of going to the lake to see what could possibly have caused someone to fall in there in the dark, killing them outright on the way.

As he descended the stairs, he was aware of men's voices below, one of which was loud and angry. The front door all but slammed as he rounded the half landing in time to see a tall man with prominently furious eyebrows stride across the hall.

He must have been around forty years old, characterful rather than handsome, and confident to the point of arrogance. Catching sight of Solomon, he halted and glared at him.

"Damned jackanapes!" he growled.

"I beg your pardon, sir," Solomon said calmly, continuing his descent.

A crack of unexpected laughter greeted this. "Not you! Sorry, damned snooping policemen put me in a filthy temper." He walked toward Solomon, thrusting out his hand. "Humphrey Maule. You must be my wife's Mr. Grey."

They shook hands. "I am, of course, at her ladyship's feet, although I confess it is the first time I have met her. Solomon Grey. Thank you for your hospitality under what I gather are difficult circumstances."

"It's a damnable mess," Maule said frankly. "But I'm very glad Elizabeth has a friend to be with her. Very unpleasant for her, you know."

"Did you say you had the police here?"

"Bloody Scotland Yard," Maule snarled.

"Truly? Who called them in?"

"I did," Maule said bitterly. "I'm the magistrate. Niall is accusing my wife. I need unbiased investigators. But the fools don't know their own place."

"I see."

Maule raised one of his beetling brows. "Elizabeth tells me you and your wife are good at puzzles like these. I must say, I don't envy your familiarity with such matters."

"No," Solomon agreed. "But if our past experience helps, we are glad to share it. Constance is very observant of human nature, sees things the rest of us often do not. And my mind cannot help but worry at puzzles till they're solved."

"Chess player, are you?"

"I enjoy the game."

"Then we'll play later. What do you think of this mess, then?"

"I think I don't yet know all the facts," Solomon said, for he was sure Lady Maule was keeping things back. If she wasn't telling downright lies. "Would you mind showing me the lake? And where the poor woman's body was found?"

Maule shrugged. "Why not?"

It was a pleasant September afternoon, although the heat had gone from the sun. Some of the trees were already beginning to change color, though few leaves were falling. Maule, who seemed to do everything in a hurry, strode around the house to a path that led in the direction Solomon had earlier glimpsed the water from his bedroom window.

"These are the willows the place is named for," Maule said, waving one hand around him. "Some of them are hundreds of years old. Makes it a lovely spot in the summer."

"Or any time, I should think."

The lake was indeed beautiful. Scattered with bright water lilies of such an intense pink they were almost red, it was overhung in places by willow branches, in others open to the sunlight. With dappled shadows and reflected colors, the place had an air of magic that made Solomon think of Arthurian legends and the tales of mischievous spirits his mother had told in his boyhood.

Maule set off around the lake, dodging beneath willow branches. "Cranston, my head gardener, was tidying up the paths first thing in the morning when he saw her floating among the lilies. Just about *there.*" He pointed two or three yards away from the bank. "She can't have moved much, so I think she must have gone into the water around there, too."

It was possible. There was a gap between the trees, and the bank was a little loose. A large tree root poked out of the ground.

"What if she tripped on that, hit her head unluckily hard, and slid into the water?" Solomon suggested.

"That's what I thought, even before the autopsy proved she was dead before she went in. It fits either way, except there is no wound to her head. There should be *something* to show such a serious injury."

"True. Was she dressed?"

"In her nightgown," Maule said, blushing with unexpected bashfulness. "Which was why I thought but never mentioned suicide. Why do you ask?"

"Could she have gone in swimming? *Could* she swim?"

Maule's bushy eyebrows flew up. "I've no idea. Never entered my head. Can't think it likely in her nightgown!"

Solomon shrugged. "It might have seemed amusing to her, then the cold of the water made her heart fail."

"You're clutching at straws. Like me."

"Just thinking aloud. What was she like, this woman?"

"Frances? Charming girl. Or young woman, I should say. She must have been twenty-six or seven."

"But never married?"

"Spent the last five years in India. I daresay her choices were limited."

Solomon nodded, looking up through the trees to gauge how much of the area could have been seen from the house. Only the rooftop was visible. "What was her quarrel with your wife about?"

"Lord, I don't know. Foolish women's stuff. Don't think they took to each other, if you know what I mean, but the idea of Elizabeth lifting a hand to any living creature, let alone killing a neighbor and family friend, is utterly preposterous."

"That's what Constance said."

Those piercing blue eyes met his. "You don't believe us?"

"I don't think any of us are incapable of violence if the circumstances are right. And those are different for all of us. Did you know Lady Maule was going for a walk with Miss Niall that evening?"

"Yes, she called to me in the library when they went out."

"Did you see her return?"

"Yes, she came back about twenty minutes later and said friendship was restored and Frances had gone home."

"Did Lady Maule seem content? Her usual self?"

Maule bristled. "Entirely," he said stiffly.

"I'm not asking to catch you—or her—out," Solomon assured him. "It's the sort of thing the investigation will need to know, either to prosecute or defend your wife." He looked at the ground and the various paths that led away from the lake and began to walk on. "Did you happen to notice any footprints or other marks when you first discovered the body?"

Maule scowled. "No, I'm afraid I was too appalled, concentrating on getting poor Frances out of there."

"Of course... How *did* you get her out? Could you reach her from the bank?"

"No. Poor Cranston went in and pulled her over so that I could catch her and drag her up. Wasn't easy." His voice had gone hoarse, and his scowl almost consumed his face before he straightened it out again.

They walked on. "Can you think of any reason why anyone might have killed her?"

"None," Maule said flatly, without hesitation, and yet for the first time, Solomon wondered if he was lying.

"She was well liked, then? Miss Niall?"

"I would say so. I never heard a word against her, not even from Elizabeth. She was beautiful, spirited, charming. Which might have caused a little envy among the ladies of the neighborhood, but hardly of the kind that leads to violence. In any case, there was no sign of violence of any kind on her body, so how Niall came to believe it was murder is beyond me."

"Then you didn't summon Scotland Yard because you were suspicious?"

"No, more to prove the point to Niall. The inquest was adjourned because no cause of death could be agreed."

"Perhaps the opinion of another doctor...?"

"No need. There were two physicians present. Laing and his apprentice Harry Murray."

"Ah." Around the next bend, Solomon caught sight of a shed. "Do you keep boats there?"

"A couple of small rowing boats." Maule seemed to see his point at once. "If the murderer had taken the trouble to use a boat to move the body, would he not have dropped her farther in to the middle?"

"I expect so. But I was thinking more of a boat hook. From

the position you indicated, her body couldn't have been dropped in from the bank unless it was deliberately pushed farther out."

"We certainly have a boat hook," Maule said, increasing his pace even more.

The hook was easily located in the first left-hand corner of the shed.

"Is that where you normally keep it?" Solomon asked.

"Yes, I think so. What do you expect to learn from it?"

"Nothing much," Solomon admitted. "Mainly I wanted to see if it was clean enough to have been in the water recently."

"Looks it to me," Maule said, picking it up to examine it more closely. "But then, I used it quite recently myself."

"When was that?"

"A couple of days before we found Frances. Must have been about nine or ten days ago."

Something caught Solomon's eye, and he reached out to the iron hook.

"Oh God, what's that?" Maule asked with dread. "It's not her hair, is it?"

CHAPTER THREE

"N O," SOLOMON SAID, managing to pinch it off at last with his fingers. "It's a couple of white cotton threads. What color was Miss Niall's nightgown?"

"White…" Maule swallowed hard. "You're right, then. Whoever did this pushed the body out from the shore with this. Why would he bother? Did he mean to hide her?"

"I doubt it. She wasn't weighed down, was she? I think he meant her to be seen. Too close into the bank and a casual observer like your gardener might not have noticed except from particular angles."

Maule wrinkled his brow in consternation. "Can't see the point. Man must be a lunatic. But then, who else would do such a thing to an innocent young lady?"

Solomon gave no answer. Instead, wrapping the threads in his folded handkerchief, he put them in his pocket. As they left the boat shed, he asked, "Did you row out on the lake alone when you went?"

Maule blushed again. "No, I took the children, and my wife."

"Very proper," Solomon replied.

"You can take yours out, if you wish," Maule said. "I understand you're more recently married than I am. Romantic gestures are always appreciated, if frequently sabotaged by the presence of children."

Solomon smiled faintly.

"Mind you, the lake doesn't seem so attractive anymore,"

Maule said with a sigh. "Come on, let's go and have tea with the ladies. Afraid you'll have to do the penance of meeting my children, too. They have tea with us every day, mainly to give their poor governess a break."

Solomon didn't entirely believe in his reason for the children's presence at tea. And he was proven right when, as soon as they entered the drawing room, three children launched themselves from the table to grab Maule's arm, hand, and leg respectively. Moreover, he did not immediately scold them but hugged them back before scowling direly and pointing to the table. Though they obeyed, the children did not look remotely abashed, let alone frightened.

"Oh, you have met Mr. Grey," Lady Maule said to her husband, apparently used to this ritual. "Come and meet my dear friend, Mrs. Grey. Constance, my husband, Sir Humphrey Maule."

Constance rose to curtsey and offered her hand with the grace she brought to every movement. "Sir Humphrey, I'm delighted to meet you at last. And your delightful family, of course."

"Delightful? Ha!" said Maule, making his children grin again. "Grey, these are our children, Benjamin, Juliana, and Clive."

Benjamin, the eldest, could have been around ten or even eleven, the others a year or so younger. They all stood to bow and curtsey, regarding him with great interest.

It was certainly a lively tea party, although Solomon found the children well behaved. If they stepped over the line from lively to rowdy, Elizabeth intervened with a word that quieted them down. She must have made a good governess, he reflected. Kind but strict, although perhaps not as strict as some parents required. To Solomon they seemed happy children, which he mentioned to Constance when they finally had the chance to speak alone in their bedchamber.

"I think they are," she agreed. "When Elizabeth first came here as governess, she said they were running wild for much of the day and cowed by their father during brief parental inspections. After his first wife died, I don't think he knew what to do with them."

"When did she die?"

"Shortly after Clive was born, so about eight years ago. There were complications from the birth, apparently. A fever. About eighteen months ago, Elizabeth arrived as governess, gradually involving their father more in the children's lives, which seems to have been good for both of them. I suppose it is also how she grew closer to him."

"Then their marriage is a happy one?" Solomon asked, pacing to the window, where his gaze seemed to be drawn inexorably through the trees to the glinting water of the lake. The spots of intense red were like droplets of blood. Foolish fantasy.

"You think it isn't?" Constance asked. She was moving around behind him, putting her clothes away in drawers and cupboards. Next to his.

He shrugged without turning. "I can't make up my mind. He seems devoted, says *my wife* with pride, takes her and his children rowing on the lake. But I don't think he's being entirely truthful."

She stilled. He could feel her turning to look at his back. "You don't like him."

"Actually, I do. He just strikes me as a man with a secret." Reluctantly, he turned to face Constance.

She had put her hairbrushes next to his on the dressing table, along with a perfume bottle and a couple of the mysterious jars that always seemed to accompany a female. It was all disconcertingly domesticated.

"I'm not sure Elizabeth was telling me everything either," she admitted. "She loves him. Of that I am not in doubt. But whether he loves her, whether they are covering for each other... Do you think someone *did* kill that woman? Or was it a tragic accident, as they first thought, and the family is simply lashing out?"

"I don't know. Maule showed me where she was found. Far enough away from the bank that she was unlikely to have slipped into the water. The lake is very still and sheltered. Short of a high wind, the body is unlikely to have moved much. It's possible someone put her in the water, then pushed her away from the bank with a boat hook."

He took the handkerchief from his pocket and carefully unfolded it to show her the threads of cotton. "I found them on the end of the hook, almost unnoticeable."

"Well done," she said, peering at them. She raised her eyes to his face. "So it's possible she was killed elsewhere and dropped in the lake…to implicate the Maules? Elizabeth in particular?"

"Unless the murderer was just trying to hide the body and didn't realize it would rise naturally to the surface."

She sighed. "Why would anyone kill her in the first place? She has hardly been back in the country long enough to have acquired murder-worthy quantities of ill will. They only returned here in the spring, a bare six months ago."

"Elizabeth didn't like her," he pointed out.

"Elizabeth is not particularly secure," Constance said ruefully. "In her position among her neighbors or in her marriage. If this woman was lovely and charming, she could easily feel threatened."

"You think she was jealous?" Solomon asked.

Constance frowned. "Not jealous enough to commit murder, though it could explain her antipathy. She is not quarrelsome by nature, but she will defend herself. She could not have survived if she didn't."

"What if defending herself—or her husband and new family—necessitated being rid of Frances Niall?"

Constance shook her head violently. "No. She would have found another way. In any case, what on earth could one woman recently returned from India possibly have done to threaten a neighbor who probably knew her from childhood?"

"I have no idea. None of it seems very likely, and yet the woman is dead, fished out of their lake, and she did not drown."

"If you are right," Constance said slowly, walking away from him toward the bed, "about someone deliberately implicating Elizabeth in her death, then it has to have been someone who knew Frances had come here to speak to her. We need to speak to her family."

"I suspect that will have to wait until tomorrow. Do you want to see the lake?"

"Yes," said Constance decisively.

➤➤➤✦◀◀◀

ELIZABETH WAS DECIDING between a pearl necklace and a simple gold locket when Humphrey wandered into the bedroom with his cuff links in one hand.

"Oblige me, my love," he said, as he often did.

Elizabeth smiled as she laid down her own jewelry and went to him. She liked performing these little wifely services for him. As she threaded the buttons through his cuffs she asked, "Did you play football with the boys?"

"I did. They put me in goal and thrashed me. Tomorrow, I get my revenge."

Elizabeth reached for his other cuff. "Do you like my friends?"

"Of course I do. He's quite sharp, isn't he?"

"Mr. Grey? Constance says so, but like you, I hadn't met him until today. Then you agree they might help us?"

Humphrey scowled. He did that a lot, bless him, though mostly he meant nothing by it. "Probably more use than those policemen," he growled. "But we shall see." He raised his gaze from the threaded cuff link to her face. "They are...discreet people, are they not?"

"No one is more discreet than Constance. And he must be cut from the same cloth. But I can't see why it matters particularly. If Frances truly was murdered, then everyone needs to know who did it."

"Of course," he said testily. "But when people's lives are probed into, all sorts of things come out, things no one wants to become subjects of gossip."

Her stomach twinged. *"Things?* What sort of things?" When he didn't answer, she said brittlely, "Things like my past?"

"Or anyone else's. Everyone makes mistakes."

"Well, Constance knows all of mine. She does not know yours." It was a childish thing to say, and she regretted it instantly.

He snatched his hand away from her. "What do you mean by that? What exactly do you suspect me of?"

"Nothing," she said miserably. "It is you who can never forget mine." And if he learned the whole truth, that would be the end of everything.

CONSTANCE WAS NOT used to such domesticity, the day-to-day interactions between married couples. Unpacking her belongings and placing them beside Solomon's had disconcerted her in some strange way, which might have been why, during dinner that evening, she imagined some sort of tension had sprung up between the truly married couple in the house.

Not that they were ever rude or even short with each other, but there was no sign of the playfulness or the banter she had seen earlier at tea when the children were present. Since the servants were constantly in and out of the dining room, there could be no discussion of the murder, so conversation was impersonal.

Sir Humphrey, for a self-professed rough-edged country bumpkin, was clearly very well read and knowledgeable on a wide range of topics, from politics to the classics, and Elizabeth had the education to keep up. So did Solomon. It was unusual for Constance to feel at a disadvantage—she had educated herself, first in the necessities and later in pursuit of her own impulsive interests—but in this house and this company, she was all too aware of the gaps. She imagined *ignoramus* or even *dunce* imprinted on her forehead.

So she smiled, observed, and contributed little. Without her beauty and the cultivated charm that she always used as weapons, would she simply be dull?

Unimportant. I am here to help Elizabeth, not lament my upbringing.

Only over the dessert course, when the servants had all departed with the other dishes, did she say, "Tomorrow, would it be possible to call on the Nialls?"

This time, the Maules' eyes did meet in definite if silent communication.

"It would have to be Humphrey who takes you to Fairfield Grange," Elizabeth said. "I am not welcome there."

"And I am understandably reluctant to go," Sir Humphrey said, "considering the accusations Niall has thrown at my wife. Grief cannot excuse that."

"No," Solomon agreed. He glanced at Constance. "I suppose we could come up with some ploy or excuse."

"I'm sure we could," she said heartily.

Sir Humphrey glowered. "No need for that. Niall will admit me. And I shall endeavor not to hit him."

"Excellent," Constance said. "This is delicious, Elizabeth. You must winkle the recipe from your cook, so I can pass it on to mine."

When the women finally withdrew, leaving the gentlemen to their port, Elizabeth asked lots of questions about the girls she had known in Constance's establishment. Many amusing tales came out of that, capped by Elizabeth's humorous anecdotes about the children. Constance almost forgot about the murder, though the anxiety lingered in her friend's eyes.

Elizabeth rang for tea as soon as the gentlemen rejoined them, and after one cup, Constance pled exhaustion from the journey and retired.

"I shan't be late," Solomon said casually. "I'll try not to wake you."

This was ridiculous, Constance thought, as she closed the bedroom door and leaned against it. She was behaving more like a nervous bride than an infamous courtesan—the polite title for her profession. It was not as if Solomon would ever bring himself to touch her, at least not in that way.

But he had kissed her farewell as he left Norfolk in the summer. It had been a very brief, *almost* chaste kiss, and yet it had made her happy. She had taken it as a sign that she would see him again, that their friendship was not over. And yet she had been the one to go to him in the end.

What did he think of that? Did he guess...

Guess what? she asked herself aggressively. *There is nothing to guess.*

And yet that kiss stayed with her months later as she undressed, washed, and donned her nightgown. Inevitably, it was a pretty one of fine lawn and lace. She did not own any other kind. Would he imagine that she wore it for him? That she was trying to seduce him? After all, she had asked him to come with her, knowing they would have to pretend to be married.

No, he had known that part was her teasing. They had agreed on friendship, and Constance had no desire to change that. To be fair, neither had he.

She brushed out her hair, confined it with a ribbon, then blew out all the candles except one, which she decided to leave for Solomon, though he would undoubtedly arrive with one too. By then, she would be asleep.

Please, God.

She was not asleep. She was curled up on her side with her back to the door when she heard it open and close. He moved about the room, rustling and splashing water. Deliberately, she kept her breathing deep and even.

But apparently, he was not fooled. "Constance? Where do

you expect me to sleep?"

"There is only one bed," she pointed out.

"Precisely. If you give me a blanket, I'll sleep on the floor."

Am I so very repulsive? Like the untouchables of India she had read about somewhere...

"It's a big bed," she said lightly. "I promise not to touch you, but put the bolster between us if you're afraid."

"Oh, trust me, I'm afraid," he said, drawing the bolster out from under the pillows.

It felt cold against her back. Then the mattress dipped as he climbed in and lay down. She nudged the bolster further away. He didn't seem to notice. In fact, a few moments later, he appeared to be sound asleep.

⇒⇒⇒⇐⇐⇐

SHE WOKE WITH someone moving around the room. Disoriented, she sat bolt upright, peering into the early morning light in search of Janey and her morning coffee. Instead, she found Solomon in his shirt and trousers, pushing his feet into boots.

"Sorry," he said in his velvet-soft voice. "I didn't mean to wake you."

Very aware she was exposing the low-cut flimsiness of her bodice, she resisted the ridiculous, maidenly urge to snatch the covers up over her bosom. "I'm too used to having coffee shoved into my hands first thing. Is it very early?"

"Not quite eight. I wanted to speak to the gardener who found the body."

"Good idea. I'll come with you."

"Then I suppose I had better speak nicely to the kitchen and conjure you a cup of coffee. Breakfast is not until nine." Boots in place, he rose from the chair and reached for his coat.

She watched him amble off with supreme casualness and absolutely no awkwardness. Which, oddly, made her feel better.

She threw off the covers and dressed as quickly as she could in a dark walking dress with matching jacket and stout boots.

She found Solomon in the kitchen making friends with the cook and the kitchen maid. They all looked so comfortable that she could not resist pausing at the foot of the kitchen stairs to observe them—which was when she became aware of the low-voiced conversation going on in the room beside her that stretched beneath the stairs.

She guessed it was the housekeeper's sitting room, for the female voice was relatively cultured, if indignant, as it drifted through the half-open door.

"...no better than they should be, if you ask me. Looks like that aren't natural."

"His or hers, Mrs. Haslett?" inquired a male voice politely, with just a hint of sardonic humor.

Ah. Constance knew from Elizabeth that Mrs. Haslett was the housekeeper.

"Hers, of course. Too beautiful by far, and too many fine clothes into the bargain. Why would a *governess* have a friend like that?"

The word *governess* was spoken with unexpectedly virulent contempt, causing Constance to linger where she was. Especially since no one appeared to have noticed her. Everyone in the kitchen seemed to be either busy or gossiping with Solomon. Or both, in the cook's case.

"Her ladyship is no longer a governess," the male voice said austerely. "And I'd advise you to remember it. Besides, a governess is still a lady, and there's no reason in the world she shouldn't have wealthy old friends."

A disparaging sniff sounded. "Maybe. But he doesn't even look English to me. Watch those silly girls drooling over him— even Cook, who should know better."

"Mrs. Haslett, you're getting into one of your moods. And I really don't see what you have against her ladyship. She has done wonders for the master, and for those children."

This was better. The man was clearly the butler, whom Constance had glimpsed only once, when he announced dinner last night.

"I suppose you're right, Mr. Manson," the housekeeper said grudgingly. "She just doesn't measure up to the first Lady Maule. No one could, and it breaks my heart to see a mere governess in her place."

"It broke your heart not to see Frances Niall in her place," Manson said dryly. "And if that had come to pass, just think where we'd be now."

"At least the Nialls are gentry," Mrs. Haslett muttered. "And local."

"If you want to seek another post, Mrs. Haslett, I'm sure her ladyship would give you an excellent character."

Another sniff. "I'm not at that stage yet. I suppose she'll learn in time how to put a decent menu together. And I suppose she doesn't skimp on the things that matter. I just wish she'd take more advice."

The housekeeper's voice came nearer, as though she were about to step out of her sitting room, so Constance walked rapidly toward Solomon. Ruefully, she reflected that Elizabeth's life was not free from struggle, even without the murder to contend with. If Mrs. Haslett was as disrespectful to her mistress's face—or before the lower servants—Elizabeth should dismiss her.

Catching sight of Constance, the servants about Solomon largely broke apart. Constance took the proffered cup of coffee from him, fervently saying, "Bless you!" to the cook, who beamed back at her.

She devoured the cupful in a few swallows. "Now I can face the day. Shall we walk?"

"The girl will bring you a cup to your room tomorrow, if you like," the cook offered.

"Wonderful," Constance said with a smile, and followed Solomon out of the back door. "Learn anything?" she murmured.

"Only that they seem to respect their master and mistress,

like their positions, and had nothing at all to do with the poor lady who died. There is also a disapproving housekeeper called Mrs. Haslett."

There is indeed. "What does she disapprove of?"

"Everything, I should guess—certainly me, although we did not discuss it."

"She disapproves of Elizabeth, too," Constance said, "mostly because she's not the first Lady Maule, from what I can gather, but also because she was a mere governess. She would have preferred Frances Niall step into those shoes."

Solomon raised his eyebrows. "Indeed? That is interesting."

"And not very pleasant for Elizabeth. The woman doesn't like us either, probably because we are Elizabeth's friends. The good news is, she appears to be the only one who feels that way. I had the impression the butler had heard it all before and wished she would pull herself together or give notice. Did you learn anything else?"

He shrugged. "The Willows servants are on good terms with most of their fellows at Fairfield Grange, though one is apparently foreign."

"From India?" Constance asked with interest.

"Yorkshire, apparently. They didn't ask where I come from."

Mrs. Haslett did, though Constance chose not to tell him so. "You're Quality, so you don't count."

"I've never been called that before."

"I doubt you ever will be again, so make the most of it. Is that the gardener disappearing around to the front of the house with his wheelbarrow?"

They found him raking the light scattering of leaves from the front lawn and surrounding flowerbeds.

"Good morning," Constance said cheerfully when the man, a red head perhaps in his late thirties, tugged his cap in their direction. "One of the more annoying tasks of autumn." She indicated his rake and the pile of leaves already in his wheelbarrow.

"I don't mind. The boy does it usually, but he's cut his hand and can't work much with it yet. Or so he tells me."

"When did he do that?" Solomon asked.

"More 'n a week ago now, which is why I think he's at it!"

"Must be a nasty cut," Solomon agreed. "You're Cranston, aren't you? The head gardener."

"I am."

"You haven't had much luck around here recently, I hear. Sir Humphrey has been telling us about the poor lady you pulled out of the lake."

"That were 'orrible," Cranston said with a shudder. "And now they're saying she didn't fall in by herself, neither."

"I know you were the first to find her," Solomon said. "So what I want to ask you—"

"Don't see why you want to ask me anything," Cranston said, meeting his gaze with a touch of hostility. The locals were closing ranks.

"No, it must seem a trifle ghoulish to you," Constance said sympathetically. "The thing is, as friends of your master and mistress, we are trying to find out what actually happened to poor Miss Niall, because apart from anything else, you must see this reflects most unfairly on the whole household."

The gardener nodded. "We can all see that, ma'am."

"Then perhaps you'd tell me what tracks you noticed on the ground around the lake that morning when you first arrived to find her in the water." Solomon held his gaze. "Did you see footprints before you raked them over?"

Cranston took off his hat and scratched his fiery head as though to aid remembrance. "Yes, there were a few. But then, her ladyship walked round it with Miss Niall the evening before."

"Round about where you found the body, were there more than two sets of prints?"

Cranston plonked his hat back on. "Hard to tell. They were all tangled and scuffed before I got there." His eyes widened slightly. "I'll tell what I did see, though. A line of wheel tracks, like a wheelbarrow."

"Was that not you?" Solomon asked, glancing at the wheelbarrow behind them.

"No, I didn't take the barrow that morning. Not many leaves, so I meant to just rake them off the path into a pile and get them all at once later on."

"So, when did you last take a wheelbarrow around the lake?

"Not since spring."

Constance felt a twinge of excitement. "Where did they come from? The wheel marks?"

"Lord, I don't know. I never followed them. Everything went up in the air when I saw her floating there among the lilies..."

"From the path that leads to the house, perhaps?" Solomon suggested. "Or to your shed?"

"No, they're on the other side of the lake, aren't they? No, it was toward the other path, the one that leads to the road and down to the village, or up to the Grange."

Solomon pounced. "Toward the path? Did you notice the tracks actually going along that path?"

"No, I never followed them. I had to help get her out, and then I had to go home and change—and if you want the truth, I don't like going near the lake at all now."

"Can't blame you for that," Solomon said. "Thank you. You've been very helpful."

"She was brought here in a *wheelbarrow*?" Constance said as soon as they were far enough away from the gardener. For some reason, the vision inspired fresh pity at the indignity, though it made no difference to the poor woman who was already dead. It seemed...disrespectful.

"I think it's possible." Solomon, of course, sounded perfectly calm. "The main question is, where was she brought from?"

"If it was the path Cranston thought, then it could have been the village or Fairfield Grange or anywhere else on that road. But," she added with more than a trace of triumph, "not from The Willows."

"Why not?" Solomon asked distractedly.

"It's hardly the quickest way from the house. If you had just committed murder, you would not go on a tour of the estate wheeling a heavy corpse."

"No," Solomon agreed. "But you might take a route that offered less likelihood of being seen by a random insomniac in the house."

Constance opened her mouth to object to that, but he forestalled her with a rueful glance.

"Unlikely, I know. But on their own, the wheelbarrow tracks don't rule anyone out. And since they're long gone from the ground, we can't follow them."

CHAPTER FOUR

O VER BREAKFAST, SIR Humphrey offered to take them to Fairfield Grange in the carriage. Constance asked if they could walk instead, since she and Solomon were eager to see what other dwellings might be nearby on the same route.

"How far is it to the village?" she asked, pausing to glance back in that direction.

"Only about a mile."

At the foot of a gentle incline—at least the path that she could see. It would be hard work pushing a dead person in a wheelbarrow up the slope as far as the lake. But then, it would be hard work from any direction. Bodies were not light. On those grounds alone, no one should even be considering Elizabeth.

"Who lives there?" Solomon asked ten minutes or so later, pointing ahead a few yards and to the left.

Constance could not even see a dwelling of any kind, only the hedge at the side of the road. Solomon, of course, had the height to see over it.

"A local character, you might say," Sir Humphrey replied with an odd dryness. "Mrs. Phelps. She's my tenant, with nominal rent, for a tiny farm. She was the village blacksmith's wife, and when he died, a nephew inherited the smithy and threw her out. She had nowhere to go. So we let her have this pocket of land, and she makes it work. The kind call her eccentric. Others call her mad as a bag of frogs."

"What do *you* call her?" Constance asked.

"Madam," he replied.

"Can we speak to her?"

"That's rather up to her, but we can see if she's at home."

As soon as they turned through a gap in the hedge, it was clear Mrs. Phelps was indeed at home. A large woman of at least fifty years, although her weathered face looked more like sixty, was chopping wood in the yard of a small, neat cottage. She swung her axe with such easy and effective energy that the first thought that struck Constance was that this woman had the strength and the muscles to carry anybody's dead body anywhere.

Mrs. Phelps ignored their approach until the log was cut into the number of pieces she wanted, then she straightened, scowling.

"Oh, it's you," she said to her landlord without noticeable respect, though she managed a curt nod. Although she didn't appear to be obviously out of breath, she wheezed faintly. "Morning."

"Good morning, Mrs. Phelps. Just showing my guests around. Going to call at the Grange and stopped to say good morning to you."

"Why?" she asked suspiciously, glowering at Solomon and Constance.

"Curiosity," Constance said at once. "Sir Humphrey told us you run your farm all by yourself. I run my own business, too, so I was interested."

Mrs. Phelps let out a cackle. "You don't look like a farmer to me."

"Oh, I'm not. Don't know the first thing about farming. But you clearly do."

"Ain't about knowledge, it's about hard work, morning till night. Even after dark there's things can be done."

With a leap of the heart, Constance glimpsed a wheelbarrow propped up by the woodshed.

"You clearly make good use of all your time. Might I ask you something? Do you see much activity after dark along this road?"

"Can't see over the hedge, and they can't see me neither. That's the way I like it."

"No, you certainly have privacy here," Constance agreed. Apart from the narrow gap in the hedge. "But you would hear people passing."

"Well I'm not *deaf*," came the aggressive reply.

"Which is why I think you are a good person to ask," Constance said. "Did you happen to *hear* anyone passing—perhaps with a wheelbarrow—last Wednesday night?"

Mrs. Phelps looked at her incredulously. "How am I supposed to remember that?"

"It was the night before they found Miss Niall's body in the lake."

She stared at Constance, then deliberately hefted the axe. "I didn't hear or see nothing."

"Oh. Then you didn't see her pass this way, going toward The Willows at about nine o'clock? Or just before?"

"She had her maid with her. Don't usually when she's floating about."

"Floating about?" Constance repeated as though amused. "Did she do a lot of that?"

Mrs. Phelps smiled sourly. "Ask Jim Cranston about that. It's him found her in the lake like an extra lily."

"Did *you* see her in the lake?" Solomon asked suddenly.

"Course I bloody didn't," Mrs. Phelps said with contempt. "Got far too much to do on my own land."

Constance cast Solomon a quelling glance. "But you did notice her going toward The Willows with her maid. Did you notice either of them come back again? It would have been dark, but the maid would have had a lantern."

"No," Mrs. Phelps said, lining up another large log. "I got better things to do than watch those that got nothing to do with me. I'm busy. In case *you* don't notice." She nodded at Sir Humphrey, though it was more like a glare, and wielded the axe once more.

"Good day, Mrs. Phelps," Sir Humphrey said wryly, and led the way back out on to the path. "Well?" he asked as they moved on. "Did you learn anything?"

Constance drew in a breath. "She has a wheelbarrow and didn't like Miss Niall very much."

Sir Humphrey stared at her. "She doesn't like anyone. Surely you don't think *she* is the killer?"

"Not without a better motive," Solomon said.

Sir Humphrey closed his mouth and rubbed his chin. "I do wonder why she did not at least see the maid going home."

"Probably because she was asleep," Constance said. "If she works hard all day from dawn until dusk, then whatever she says about working into the night, she must sleep like—er...a log."

Some hundred yards further along the road, on the right this time, they came to another house. This was a more substantial cottage, with a front gate and a low garden wall with wrought iron railings, around which was entwined a climbing rose. The front garden consisted of a neat lawn with borders of flowers and pots of herbs by the front door. Ivy grew over the walls in a pleasingly rustic manner.

"Dr. Laing's house," Sir Humphrey told them before they could ask.

"He's the doctor who performed the autopsy?" Solomon said. "Could we call on him?"

Without answering, Sir Humphrey opened the gate and gestured for Constance to precede him. However, when the door was answered by a housekeeper, they were told the doctor was out on his calls.

"We'll try again later," Sir Humphrey said, turning away with a speed that suggested he really didn't want to be there. He found the whole business distasteful. In fact, it spoke volumes for his anxiety as well as his affection for his wife that he was prepared to countenance their investigation at all. He certainly hadn't liked the police poking about, even though he had summoned them for that purpose.

They encountered no further distractions until Fairfield Grange itself. This was a large house, probably about the same size as The Willows, but newer and somehow less imposing.

A morose butler admitted them. It was clear at once that this was a house of deep mourning. The mirrors were covered with black crepe. The servants' shoes made no sound on the floor, even in the intense silence.

They were led up a dark staircase to a large room also swathed in black crepe.

"Sir Humphrey Maule, sir," the butler announced. "And Mr. and Mrs. Grey."

Constance would never get used to that name, she thought as an odd little frisson ran down her spine. No doubt the shiver had more to do with the heavy atmosphere of death and mourning than with her own deception.

"How are you, Niall, old fellow?" Sir Humphrey said, going forward with his hand held out.

Colonel Niall, a fierce-looking man of middle years with military-style whiskers, leapt to his feet as though prepared to be outraged. He swept his gaze over his visitors and beyond—perhaps in search of Elizabeth—and came back to Sir Humphrey slightly mollified. He accepted Maule's hand, briefly.

"My friends, Mr. and Mrs. Grey," Sir Humphrey murmured. "They are staying at The Willows for a few days. This is Colonel Niall."

"How do you do?" said the colonel, flaring his nostrils. "You'll forgive my lack of hospitality. This is a house of mourning."

"So we understand," Solomon said, bowing. "Please accept our sincere condolences on your terrible loss."

"Thank you." Colonel Niall waved his hand. "Please, sit down. I'm sure Worcester will bring tea."

The door opened again and another, much younger man hurried into the room. "Sir Humphrey," he said almost breathlessly.

Constance had the impression he had bolted here from another part of the house upon hearing who the visitors were. Perhaps he had feared his father's rudeness, especially if Elizabeth had been present too, for he shook hands warmly with Maule and greeted Constance and Solomon with something approaching relief.

"The colonel's son, Mr. John Niall," Sir Humphrey said. "John, my guests, Mr. and Mrs. Grey."

"Kind of you all to call. Worcester is arranging for tea. I hope you're well, Sir Humphrey?" John added politely as they all sat.

"Oh, perfectly, apart from the sorrow and anxiety, of course. No point in beating about the bush to friends, so I'll tell you straight out—that's why we've come. Grey here is something of a solver of puzzles, so I've asked him to look into this matter of poor Frances's death."

John's eyebrows flew up in amazement—which was nothing to the reaction of his father, who was turning purple.

"By what right," the colonel demanded furiously, "do you dare involve strangers—"

"By the right you handed to me when you accused my wife of this unspeakable crime without evidence or reason," Maule retorted. "To say nothing of my rights as magistrate. I brought Scotland Yard here at your request, and now I bring other good people who might be strangers to you but are my guests!"

The two fierce men glared at each other. John offered a faint, resigned smile. "Thank God," he murmured. "Tea. Guaranteed to calm the trickiest situation."

"Would you like me to pour, sir?" Constance offered.

A spasm crossed the colonel's face. "If you would be so good," he said with at least an attempt at grace. "In any case, those wretched policemen are useless," he flung at Sir Humphrey. "They hang around here looking important, asking idiot questions. I've told them where to look, but do they?"

"Yes," said Sir Humphrey. "I had to send them away yesterday with a flea in their collective ears."

"What is the point," Solomon asked mildly, "of summoning

the police here to find the truth, if you then refuse to answer their questions?"

"Well said," John murmured.

"Because they're not asking the *right* questions!" Colonel Niall exploded.

"You mean they haven't hanged my wife out of hand yet!" Sir Humphrey growled.

"Investigators," Solomon said, his soft voice in startling contrast to strident tones of the older men, "detectives, if you will, are useful because they are dispassionate. They look into all possibilities in search of evidence, from which they try to discover the truth. No one wants a medieval-style witch hunt of accusation and counteraccusation, do they?" He glanced from Sir Humphrey to Colonel Niall and hurried on, perhaps in case he was assured that this was exactly what they wanted. "However, may I ask you a few courteous questions?"

"Yes," said John before his father could open his mouth. "Please do."

Solomon glanced at father and son. "Did you both know that Miss Niall went to call on Lady Maule last Wednesday evening?"

"Yes!" said the colonel triumphantly.

"But not until the following day," John said, "when Bingham, her maid, told us."

"Bingham being the maid who accompanied her?" Constance asked.

John nodded. "Frances's personal maid."

"Why do you think she didn't tell you where she was going?" Solomon asked.

The father and son exchanged looks. John said, "My sister was something of a free spirit. She did not like to be tied down, and my father would certainly have forbidden her from going out on foot, as night was falling. So she simply didn't tell him. Or me. Worcester knew they had gone, though."

"But he did not tell the colonel?" Solomon pounced.

John gave a sad little smile. "My sister had all the servants wrapped around her little finger. They would do anything for her."

"Was this not rather a dangerous thing she asked of them? To keep her expedition in the dark from her family?"

"It wasn't quite dark when she left," John said, "and besides, it isn't dangerous around here if one keeps to the road and the main paths."

Colonel Niall's face twisted. "Or at least it wasn't until that female—"

Sir Humphrey sprang to his feet, his fists clenched.

"Papa!" John said sharply.

The colonel subsided, muttering beneath his breath, and Maule, red-faced and furious, sat down stiffly on the edge of his seat. Had it not been for Solomon and Constance, he would surely have stormed out, never to darken the Niall doorstep again.

"Very well," Solomon said. "When did Bingham say she came back here?"

"Just before ten," John replied. "She had left the lantern with Frances while she and Lady Maule walked around the lake, talking."

"Talking in a friendly way?" Constance asked.

"According to Bingham. She would not otherwise have left her mistress alone there."

Constance made a note to speak to Bingham herself. And other servants, who frequently had a different view of people from their betters.

"Sadly, I never met Miss Niall," Constance said. "What was she like?"

"The light of my life and everyone else's," Colonel Niall said in a muffled voice. "She lit up the room with her charm and goodness. Everyone loved her."

Constance watched John rather than the colonel during this accolade. A tiny smile flickered across his lips, a little resigned, a little sardonic. Interesting...

"Did you know Miss Niall had quarreled with Lady Maule?" Solomon asked.

"They had an exchange of views over dinner one night," John said, again before his father could speak.

"What about?" Solomon asked.

John's eyes slid away from Sir Humphrey. "The duties of a wife. It was all a little silly, to be honest. Especially since Frances didn't even believe what she was saying."

"Of course she did," Colonel Niall said. "And she was quite right! It is a wife's duty to obey, defer, and submit to her husband!"

"And Elizabeth disputed that?" Constance asked, uneasy for some reason. The idea of submitting to any man was utterly abhorrent to her, but Elizabeth had taken vows of marriage.

"Not in its entirety," John said, shifting uncomfortably and setting down his cup and saucer. "She insisted it was also a wife's duty to tell her husband when he was wrong."

"She was right," Sir Humphrey insisted. "They were both right, and from what Elizabeth tells me, that was the conclusion they reached during their talk by the lake. They both regretted their hasty words—and, in fact, Elizabeth had thought no more about them until she received Frances's note of apology." He glanced at the colonel. "Her *gracious* note of apology."

Colonel Niall sniffed but looked mollified once more.

"It doesn't sound like much of a motive for murder," Constance observed.

"And what would you know of such matters, young lady?" Colonel Niall demanded.

"I am hardly an expert in murder, of course, but I do observe human nature," Constance said before anyone could doubt her respectability. Which amused her on one level.

Solomon regarded the colonel. "Sir, given that we all need the truth about what happened to your daughter, would you grant us permission to speak to your servants, particularly Miss Niall's maid?"

"No, I would not," the colonel said wrathfully. "Those policemen have been pestering them already. I won't have them under suspicion for something they clearly did not do!"

Which was interesting when he obviously had no such compunction about his friend's wife.

"I have no reason to suspect them," Solomon said mildly. "My hope is that they might have witnessed something or someone that will shed further light on the matter. We are speaking to as many people as we can from here to The Willows."

Sir Humphrey looked appalled. He did not have the patience or the stomach for such work.

John said, "It can only help, Papa. I shall supervise such interviews if you wish."

Abruptly, the colonel seemed to lose all his fight. He made a weak gesture with one hand. "Do as you will. None of it will bring Frances back."

Constance rose to her feet. It was clearly time to leave him. "No," she agreed. "I am so sorry, colonel."

Sir Humphrey was looking relieved as he stood with her. Solomon, as impassive as ever, merely bowed and thanked Colonel Niall for his time. John ushered them out of the room and toward the stairs.

"I'm sorry about my father," he said awkwardly to Sir Humphrey as they all moved toward the staircase. "He is just lashing out because Lady Maule is the only person he has ever seen quarrel with my sister. I know it was only a minor disagreement, but he seems to have latched on to it."

Constance latched on to something else—the peculiar wording of John's apology. *Lady Maule is the only person he has ever seen quarrel with my sister.* Did that mean she had quarreled with others her father had *not* witnessed?

"Siblings tend to grow up quarreling constantly," she said, "and yet are the closest of friends. Was it like that with you and your sister?"

"Not really," John said. "Frances is—was—six years older than me. I was always a child to her." He shrugged, leading the way downstairs. "We were not together much. In fact, I was at school in England most of the time she was in India with my father."

"Still, a brother's insight can be helpful. Can you think of anyone who might have wanted to harm your sister?"

"No," John said, shaking his head. "The police inspector asked me the same thing."

"I gather she was a beautiful and fascinating lady," Constance said.

Before John could respond, Sir Humphrey said brusquely, "Look, I have to get back to The Willows. Would you mind awfully if I abandoned you to find your own way home?"

"Not in the slightest," Solomon said.

Through the hall window beside the door, an arriving carriage was visible.

"Drat, it's the vicar," John said in hunted tones. "He means well, but he always winds my father up with his platitudes."

"It might be good for him," Constance said, and John blinked at her in surprise.

"Perhaps," Solomon said, "I'll just go and have a word with the vicar myself."

"I thought you wanted to speak to the servants?" John said with a first hint of irritation.

"I shall join you in the kitchen, if I may, in just a few moments." Solomon was already following Sir Humphrey out the door, no doubt to obtain an introduction to the vicar. "Constance?"

"Of course." She smiled at John. "You don't have to come with me either."

"No, no, it's better if I do," John said hastily, glancing again toward the front door, now closing behind Solomon. A brace of rather pleasing glass lanterns of matching bulbous shape stood on the table there, reminding Constance that the dead woman's lantern had not been found. Although, if she had brought it back here that evening before she died, would anyone have noticed?

As they walked to the back of the house, John said ruefully, "It's an excuse to avoid the poor old vicar, to be honest."

Constance returned to her interrupted question. "Being so beautiful, your sister must have had many admirers."

"She always seemed to," John said vaguely. "She never paid much attention to any of them, though. Except…" With his hand on the baize door to the servants' quarters, he glanced back at the front door.

Constance's stomach twisted. She halted, staring at him. "Except… Not Sir Humphrey?"

"Didn't you know?" John said with surprise. "Frances and Sir Humphrey were more or less engaged when my father hauled her off to India with him. She always assumed she would marry him when she came home."

"Only he was already married to Elizabeth," Constance said slowly. No wonder the two women hadn't liked each other.

CHAPTER FIVE

S OLOMON'S DESIRE TO speak to the vicar was driven more by hope than expectation of learning anything useful. For him, Frances Niall was still a very shadowy figure, eulogized as beautiful and charming and the light of everyone's life, as the dead often were. And yet no one had told him in what way she was charming and clever. Mrs. Phelps had made some off-hand remark about her *floating about* but offered no real criticism of the dead lady.

In fact, even the Maules were reticent. They had given no clear picture of who Frances Niall was, even though they must have known her well.

Right now, Maule had clearly had enough of investigating his neighbors and was anxious to get back to his own life, but he paused long enough to greet the vicar, who had just emerged from his ancient carriage—an amiable-faced, slightly stooped man who might have been any age between fifty or sixty, clean shaven, with white, thinning hair.

"This is a friend of mine, staying at The Willows with us for a while," Maule said. "Mr. Solomon Grey. Grey, Mr. Irvine, our vicar."

"How do you do?" the vicar said civilly before turning back to Maule. "You have just come from our friend the colonel? How did you find him?"

"Oh, you know," Maule said awkwardly. "Struggling and angry. Can't blame him for that. You'll forgive me if I rush off? I have neglected my duties of the day. Good day, Irvine. Grey, I'll see you at luncheon, no doubt."

"A terrible business," Solomon said to keep the vicar with him as Maule dashed off, "the death of Miss Niall."

"Terrible indeed," Irvine said heavily. "I truly cannot credit that any of my parishioners could have committed such a heinous act. I am sure there has been some mistake and it was all a tragic accident."

"I do plan to speak to the doctor about that."

Irvine peered at him in surprise. "You do?"

"Yes. I should say that Sir Humphrey has asked me to look into the matter. He accounts me good at puzzles, which, on some level, this tragedy is. And as you know, Colonel Niall has made some rather hurtful accusations against Lady Maule."

The vicar shook his head. "We all know that is the colonel's grief talking. No one believes it for an instant."

"No one who knows Lady Maule, perhaps. The detectives from London do not know her."

For an instant, the vicar looked anxious. Then he said, "We must trust in God."

"And in his poor tools upon the Earth," Solomon said piously, very glad that Constance was not present to hear him. "You must have known Miss Niall from her childhood?"

Irvine beamed. "I baptized her myself."

"I understand she grew up to be a beautiful and charming lady."

"Indeed she did. Clever, too. Her mind was quick and she was more given to study than most young girls."

"Indeed?" Solomon said with interest. "You mean she studied more than the usual ladylike accomplishments of her class?"

"Yes, and she was very able. The trouble was her chosen subject. Too scientific for her parents' tastes. I blame myself, to be honest, for she used to visit the sick with me, and from that she developed a rather unfortunate ambition to become a physician."

Unfortunate and impossible for a woman of any class... "Did she go on visiting the sick?"

"Not quite so much," Irvine said carefully. "Her parents—very properly, of course—discouraged her from anything associated with medical ambitions. Medicine, you know, *anatomy...!*"

Solomon's lip twitched. He wished Constance were here. Hastily, he changed the subject. "Did Miss Niall attend church regularly?"

"Oh yes. Even when the colonel does not—his attendance fell away somewhat after his wife died—she is there."

"Before and after her stay in India?"

"Of course."

Solomon tried another tack. "She must have been very popular in the neighborhood."

"Oh, yes."

It felt a little like bumping his head against a thick cushion. Apart from the surprise about Frances's former medical ambitions, he still had no real knowledge of her as a person. "Why do you suppose she never married?"

"I can only suppose the right gentleman never asked her at the right time," the vicar said vaguely. "But she was still young. Tragically young." He shook his head.

"Bearing in mind," Solomon said carefully, "how well you must know all your parishioners, can you think of anyone who might *not* have liked her? Who had any reason, however misguided, to harm her?"

"No," Irvine replied without hesitation. "Not one."

Solomon's eyes were drawn beyond him to two men marching up the drive. They had a certain look about them that marked them as strangers, city men in unfamiliar country. The London policemen, no doubt.

"Did she ever confide troubles to you?" Solomon asked, adding hastily, "I understand you could not tell me what those troubles might have been. It would merely help to know if she had any."

"None that I know of. Not since her girlhood."

"Then she was a contented kind of person?"

The vicar seemed doubtful. "I suppose she must have been."

"But she did not seem so to you?" Solomon persisted.

Irvine began to look flustered. "I did not say so, sir. I have no reason to believe she was *dis*contented. Merely that she was...*looking* for something. For God, perhaps."

"Perhaps," Solomon agreed. He doubted he would get much more sense from the man, and the town gents were heading around the house toward the back door. He tipped his hat to the vicar. "Many thanks for your insights, sir. Good morning."

"Good morning," Irvine returned, looking slightly bemused as he continued his way to the front door.

Solomon sprinted after the visitors, catching up with them on the path before they reached the back door. They must have heard his quick footsteps, for they both turned sharply to face him.

"Good day, gentlemen," he said politely, slowing to a halt and touching the brim of his hat. "My name is Grey. Am I correct in thinking I address members of the Metropolitan Police?"

"You are," said the older man. He looked a little downtrodden in a worn overcoat, his expression lugubrious, although his eyes were bright with intelligence. Solomon guessed he was frequently underestimated, and resolved not to make the same mistake. "I'm Inspector Omand, and this is Constable Napier."

"How do you do?" Solomon said. "I wonder if I might have a word? My wife and I are currently staying with the Maules, over at The Willows."

My wife and I It felt very odd saying those words, and not just because they were untrue.

"I heard there were visitors," the constable said, looking him up and down. He was a very different specimen from his superior. Much younger, he was also better and more smartly dressed. He positively reeked of ambition and arrogance, even before he checked out every feature of Solomon's face and allowed his twitch of contempt to be seen. "And you say you are a *guest* of Sir Humphrey? You'll forgive me if I confirm that with his household."

"There is nothing to forgive, constable," Solomon said. He turned back to the inspector. "You will be aware of the rumors, the accusations against Lady Maule? I am trying to help my friends by finding out the truth of the matter."

"With respect, sir," Inspector Omand said as the constable opened his mouth once more, "that is our business, not yours. Do you have information for us?"

"I'm not sure," Solomon said lightly, "being unaware of what you know already. Do you have any reason to suppose Lady Maule's guilt?"

"Plenty." Constable Napier smirked, earning a glance of irritation from his superior, which seemed to pass him by.

Solomon pursued the weakness. "But she has no possible motive."

"No motive?" sneered Napier. "Against the woman who was once engaged to her husband?"

So that was it.

From old business habits, Solomon was used to keeping his expression neutral, whatever surprises were flung at him. "I could more easily understand that as a motive were the boot on the other foot. Miss Niall had more reason to be jealous of Lady Maule."

"We work on evidence, Mr. Grey," Inspector Omand said shortly. "Not supposition."

"I'm very glad to hear it. According to Cranston, the head gardener at The Willows, there was a wheelbarrow track leading to the place where she went into the water. It strikes me she could well have been brought there by such means."

Omand was scowling at his underling, who should, presumably, have found this information for himself, though he addressed Solomon. "And where did these tracks come from?"

"Cranston was too upset at the time to look, but they certainly came from the direction of the path to the road that leads here—and to the village if you turn left instead of right."

"Cranston never mentioned tracks to me," Napier said dismissively.

"Well, you got to give people time to talk," Omand said. "Not bully them so that they only want to be rid of you as fast as possible. You're a clever lad, Napier, but you've a lot to learn. Thank you, sir, for that information. If there's nothing—Hello, who's this?"

Constance had emerged from the kitchen door, easily managing her wide skirts through the narrow space. In her elegant dark-green gown and bonnet and black gloves, she still somehow dazzled like the sun.

He looked hastily away to discover Constable Napier's none-too-friendly eyes upon him. "Has Sir Humphrey *employed* you?" he demanded. "And you think that entitles you to use the front door like—"

"Like what?" Solomon asked softly. "Like a gentleman?"

"Fancy clothes don't change what you are," Napier said with undisguised contempt that finally drew his superior's alarmed attention.

"And what is that?" Solomon asked with interest.

"*Napier,*" Omand barked before his underling could speak the word so clearly on the tip of his tongue. "Forgive my lad, sir. He's naturally suspicious, which comes from the job, but he doesn't yet have the experience to spot a gentleman from a trickster out of twig, if you understand me. Kitchen, Napier—see if you can't learn something this time instead of showing everyone how clever *you* are."

Napier, his face burning with resentment, stalked away so quickly he almost forgot to tip his hat to Constance.

"Inspector Omand, my dear," Solomon said. "Inspector, Mrs. Grey. I see you find it odd that she should use the back door and I the front."

"No, I find the whole situation odd," Omand said. "*Has* Sir

Humphrey employed you in any capacity?"

"Of course not. We are just trying to help."

"I am an old friend of Lady Maule's," Constance said, taking Solomon's arm in the familiar fashion of a wife. "I brought my husband to meet her and discovered this terrible tragedy on their doorstep."

"I see." Omand's eyes were shrewd but not hostile.

"I suppose," Solomon said, "there is no doubt in your mind that this *is* murder and not an accident?"

"We weren't called in soon enough, sir," Omand said regretfully. "Between you and me, there is nothing to prove one or the other. Both would appear to be impossible. Excuse me, sir, madam."

"What on earth was all that about?" Constance asked, beginning to walk toward the drive.

Since she still had hold of his arm, Solomon had to either remove it or walk with her. He chose the latter for any number of reasons.

"Oh, just making myself known to Scotland Yard. He's not much like Inspector Harris, is he?"

"It's the young one who concerns me," Constance said.

No doubt she had heard and understood everything, which annoyed him for some reason he could not fathom.

"He has a large chip on his shoulder," he agreed.

She glanced up at him, frowning. "Does that happen to you often?"

"What?" he asked vaguely, for he didn't want to talk about it. But she spoke again before he could change the subject.

"Reasonless insolence."

He sighed. "It is not reasonless to them. They have been brought up to imagine the skin makes the man. To be fair, he had a dashed good look first."

She curled her lip. "At least the inspector appears to have some sense. *Does* it happen often?"

He should have known better than to imagine he could put

her off. "Not to me. I am not obviously European *or* African, so people tend to view me as they wish. I suspect Napier may have come off worse in some dockside raid or other and acquired another chip for his overburdened shoulder. Did you know that Frances was all but engaged to Maule before she went to India?"

"Rats," said Constance, scowling. "I wanted to tell *you* that. I just learned it from John Niall."

"Napier told me. And he was right about one thing—it does imply a real reason for Elizabeth to be jealous."

"What worries me," Constance said, "is why neither she nor Sir Humphrey troubled themselves to tell us. Why would they keep it from us?"

"To convince us of Elizabeth's innocence."

"I am already convinced. They can't have imagined it would remain a secret once we started asking questions!"

"Maybe they didn't realize we would. Perhaps they envisioned us sitting in contemplation of the few facts until the solution made itself clear."

"Well, now they know. No wonder Sir Humphrey bolted. But if they didn't even tell us that, what else are they keeping back?"

"I suggest we do our best to find out this afternoon. Or at least after we've bearded the doctor. What did you learn from the Grange servants?"

Constance wrinkled her nose. "Little enough. Bingham, Frances's maid, confirmed the story of being sent home from the lake in the dark and never seeing her mistress again. Apparently, Frances was a kind mistress, though Bingham has only been employed since they returned to India. The other servants, some of whom had known her before India, said much the same sort of things. But then, I suppose they would with the dead woman's brother breathing down their necks."

"Did he?" Solomon asked, surprised.

"Did he what?"

"Breathe down their necks," he said patiently. "Was he paying close attention? Coercing them in any way?"

She sighed. "No, not that I could see. But I still doubt they would say anything bad about her in front of him."

"Do you think there is any bad?"

"She does seem a bit too good to be true, doesn't she? Except, I suppose, that the night she died, she sent the maid home without a light. Which makes her thoughtless, rather than bad. Beyond that and Elizabeth's now-understandable antipathy, I see only good."

"She went to church regularly, too."

"Anyone can go to church," Constance said dismissively. "Was she involved in good works?"

"Visiting the sick, at least when she was young, long before she went to India. It gave her a notion to be a doctor, and her horrified parents largely put a stop to it."

Constance showed a spark of interest. "I wonder if Elizabeth knows that?" But her mind had jumped back to more personal matters. "If she was almost engaged to Sir Humphrey before they went to India...why did she go? Obviously, Colonel Niall had no choice but to go where he was posted, but Frances was of age. Why didn't she marry Humphrey and stay here?"

"Was he still in mourning for his first wife?"

"It must have been more than two years since her death. And in any case, if things had progressed so far, would a proud papa, on the verge of making an excellent match for his daughter, take her to the other side of the world at precisely the wrong time? Why wouldn't he have arranged for her to stay with a relative or family friend?"

"I don't know," Solomon confessed. "Such matters are beyond me. But does the breaking of such an understanding not reflect poorly on Maule's honor?"

"You would certainly expect it to cause coolness between the families," Constance agreed. "But it didn't, did it? They saw a great deal of each other, more than Elizabeth was comfortable with. In fact, there seems have been no ill feeling at all until

Frances died."

"Perhaps they were just being terribly polite to each other, but the ill feeling rankled and that is what is now causing Niall's wild accusations against Elizabeth."

"Maybe," Constance said.

"No, I don't believe it either. In any case, it hardly explains the murder."

"I can't help hoping that everyone was right the first time and there was no murder. We need to talk to this Dr. Laing."

WHEN MRS. GREY left the kitchen, using the back door, John Niall gazed after her uneasily. She was somebody well beyond his experience. She had absolutely no right to be interviewing his father's servants, but in the circumstances, the whole household had to appear to be doing everything in its collective power to reach the truth of who had murdered Frances.

It was not the *who* that bothered John so much. It was the *why*.

Blinking rapidly, he became aware that the eyes of all the servants were upon him. Bingham, Frances's maid, had a resentful look about her. Inevitably, she was looking for a new position, with Frances gone. She did not have the ties to the family that most of the other servants did. On the other hand, she was dependent on them for a character to take to her next employer. It was a hold that made him uncomfortable, not least because it could easily expire once she was in her new position.

"Thank you," he said to the gathered servants. "You have been very helpful once more. Let us hope all these unsettling disruptions will stop soon. I'll leave you to go back to your duties."

Bingham went immediately to the stairs, without waiting for the housekeeper's dismissal. Mrs. Lennard—who, with Worcester the butler, had kept the house running with a minimum of staff during the time the family was in India, receiving John for school holidays occasionally—met his gaze with raised brows. Clearly, she felt Bingham was getting above herself. Well, perhaps the girl was owed that much.

Worcester bowed, allowing John to precede him up the stairs.

"You'll forgive me, sir, if I point out that it is not right if our people are required to answer the questions of strangers. Not even neighbors, but the mere guests of neighbors."

"You are right, of course," John agreed. "I don't like the prying any more than you do. But my sister was murdered, Worcester. That is more wrong than anything else."

A thundering on the back door made them both turn back. A chill swept over John that felt almost like despair. The kitchen maid opened the door to the two London policemen, and John almost groaned aloud. Would this never end?

"The truth will out, Mr. John," Worcester said ominously. "One way or another."

"Some truths we need to out," John said, passing through the baize door to the main part of the house. "The rest, for my father's sake—for *all* our sakes—we need to keep amongst ourselves."

CHAPTER SIX

A FTER A SHORT wait in Dr. Laing's pleasant parlor, they were shown into his study, which apparently doubled as an occasional consulting room.

The doctor rose to meet them with his hand held out. "Mrs. Grey? Mr. Grey? I'm Dr. Laing. Do sit down. How can I help you today?"

He was a fair, pleasant-looking man in his early thirties, who exuded an air of confidence and trust. Constance, who had reason to distrust many of his profession, thought his manner no more than ordinary for the owner of a rural practice who no doubt had ambitions toward greater things. Until she looked in his eyes, which were bright blue and curiously intense, almost driven. An interesting man.

She left it to Solomon to answer.

"You may have heard that we are guests of Sir Humphrey and Lady Maule."

"My housekeeper did say. I trust I don't find you unwell?"

"We are both fortunate in that regard," Solomon said smoothly. "Our interest is rather in the lady whose body was found in The Willows lake."

The doctor's expression changed immediately to one of acute sadness, even distress. "Forgive me," he said, an edge to his voice, "if I fail to see your interest in the matter."

"It is not a salacious or malicious interest," Solomon assured him, "nor even a personal one, except in so far as we are trying to help our friends."

"The Maules," the doctor said, relaxing once more, although his expression was still bleak. "I suppose you have heard that Colonel Niall is convinced of Lady Maule's guilt in the matter."

"He told us so himself," Constance said, "though he failed to provide any evidence."

"I would be hugely surprised if there were any," Laing said dryly. "I believe the police from London have found none either. However, I fail to see what I can tell you that might help either Sir Humphrey or his wife."

"You carried out the autopsy," Solomon pointed out.

Laing grimaced. "I did. And not very well. It was fortunate that my assistant, Dr. Murray, was observing, for it was he who spotted what I failed to notice."

"The lack of water in her lungs?" Solomon gazed at him, unblinking. "Forgive me, but how could you fail to notice such a thing?"

The doctor colored. "Unforgivable, I know. I confess I was merely going through the motions. It was so clear that she had drowned—as I thought—and to be frank, I found it upsetting to be carrying out such a procedure on someone I regarded as a friend."

"Ah," Constance said sympathetically. "So you and poor Miss Niall knew each other?"

Laing smiled slightly. "Of course. Mine is the only practice for miles. Everyone in the neighborhood is my patient. But I also dined occasionally at Fairfield Grange. And at The Willows. We even danced once at Mrs. Darby's ball. Do you know Mrs. Darby?"

"Sadly not," Solomon said, while Constance filed the name away for future reference.

"She has the big house about ten miles south of here. She is some kind of relation of the Nialls and held a ball to welcome them back to England."

"I see."

The doctor glanced from Solomon to Constance and back, a small, cynical smile forming on his lips. "Do you? Please don't imagine I was trying to court Miss Niall. For one thing, she was very much my social superior. For another—and much more importantly—she was my patient."

And an ambitious man in a small community would not risk his reputation.

"Forgive the thought," Constance said. "We understand she was eminently court-able."

"A beautiful and fascinating lady," Laing said ruefully. "Such a loss to her family."

Solomon leaned forward on his chair. "Was she ill, doctor?"

Laing hesitated. "You'll appreciate my difficulties in discussing even a late patient with strangers."

"I beg your pardon. Allow me to rephrase the question. To your knowledge, was there any likelihood, or even possibility, of Miss Niall dying of natural causes? Of some illness or condition that was not apparent to those who knew her?"

Laing shook his head slowly. "None that I ever found. I treated her only for minor ailments—and one small injury to her wrist. There were no signs of other illness."

"Have you *any* idea how she died?" Solomon asked.

Laing sighed. "None. There were no marks upon the body, no poisons in her stomach, no enlargement of the heart or other organs, no clots of blood on her brain or elsewhere."

"Had she been in the lake for very long?" Solomon asked.

Laing grimaced. "A good few hours, I would say."

"Can you be more precise? For instance, could she have died as early as nine or ten o'clock the previous evening?"

"She could," Laing admitted with reluctance. "But if you mean could Lady Maule have somehow contrived it while they walked together, I really don't see how. I presume that is what you wished to hear?"

"Yes," Constance said, "but only if it is true. Doctor, you know everyone in the neighborhood. Did anyone dislike Miss

Niall strongly enough to kill her? Did anyone have any reason, however unlikely, to do so?"

"I have asked myself that question many times. And I can truly think of no one. Even if I could, I cannot see how it was done."

"What about Mrs. Phelps?" Constance asked suddenly. "She's a little mad, is she not? And I had the impression she did not care for Miss Niall."

"I know of no one Mrs. Phelps *does* like," Laing said wryly. "And I would say she is eccentric rather than mad."

"She is also astonishingly strong for a woman of her years," Constance said, recalling the effortless swinging of the axe. "It would give her no trouble to load a body into a wheelbarrow, push it up to the lake, and tip it up."

Laing blinked rapidly. "*Wheelbarrow?* You think she was moved to the lake by such means after her death?"

"It is a possibility," Solomon said.

"It is," Laing said slowly. "But from where? Even if it was Mrs. Phelps, I cannot see how or why she killed her in the first place."

"Perhaps she didn't," Constance said. "Perhaps Miss Niall just suddenly died in Mrs. Phelps's vicinity. I have known it to happen for no obvious cause. And then, afraid she would be blamed, Mrs. Phelps could have moved the body elsewhere."

The doctor looked unconvinced.

"Fanciful," Solomon pronounced, "but not impossible. Would you agree, doctor?"

"I suppose I would." Laing sounded bemused, in fact. He seemed to give himself a little shake. "You know, everything I have told you, I already told to the inquest and to the police Sir Humphrey called in."

"I know," Solomon said. "But sometimes, just talking about a situation again, perhaps from a slightly different perspective, brings new memories or ideas to light."

Laing regarded him dubiously. "You appear to speak with

some conviction. Do you often find yourself in the midst of crime?"

"Not often," Solomon replied. "But it has happened." He rose to his feet. "Thank you for your time and your patience, doctor. Good day."

A few moments later, Constance found herself back on the road to The Willows.

"I had high hopes of learning something from him," she said discontentedly. "And I don't believe we did. Do you?"

Solomon shook his head.

Constance frowned. "Do you believe him? That his friendship with Frances was strictly proper for a doctor and his patient?"

"Yes."

She pounced. "Why? By all accounts she was beautiful, charming, fascinating. He is a young man and unmarried. Why would he be immune to her?"

Solomon shrugged. "Possibly because he has trained himself to be."

"Maybe," she said doubtfully, "but why are you so sure?"

"Because he didn't look at you either."

Constance closed her mouth. Solomon was right. She was so used to men looking at her with some kind of desire, or warmth at the very least, that she barely noticed unless she sensed a threat. Sir Humphrey, John Niall, even Colonel Neill had all acknowledged her looks, however silently. Dr. Laing had barely noticed her.

"You are observant," she allowed. "I'll take it as flattery."

"Take it as truth and see what you come up with."

Dr. Darcy Laing drummed his fingers on his desk, thinking over his interview with the very odd Mr. and Mrs. Grey. The woman's insensitivity to disgusting matters like murder, blood, and internal organs offended him. What was her husband thinking of to let her near such discussions?

And what on earth was their interest in the matter? What did they imagine they could learn that the police could not?

A brief knock on the door heralded the arrival of his apprentice, Harold Murray. Recently graduated from the medical school at Edinburgh University, he was gaining experience by assisting Laing.

"Who are they?" Murray asked, jerking his head toward the front of the house, where he had, probably, seen the Greys leaving.

"Guests of the Maules. They seem to have taken it upon themselves to prove Lady Maule's innocence in the matter of Miss Niall's death."

"I wish them luck," Murray said stoutly. "For I can't believe so gentle a creature could possibly have done such a thing."

Laing cast him a tired, twisted smile. "We don't even know what the *thing* was. But you are right. Whatever it was, I am certain Lady Maule is the least likely culprit. It is possible, of course, that no one is to blame. Sudden death for no reason may be rare, but it does happen."

"Oh, there's always a reason," Murray replied. He could be annoyingly pompous for an apprentice. "It's just that we don't always know enough to understand what it is."

"We didn't miss anything, did we?" Laing said. "At least, not after my initial failure."

"That was understandable," Murray said. "Such examinations seem an intolerable invasion when the subject is known to us."

"I'm glad you were there," Laing said.

"I'm beginning to wish I hadn't been," Murray said. "I'm not sure I made things any better."

"Not so far," Laing said heavily. "But if there *is* a killer, we have to find him. Or her."

BEFORE LUNCHEON, CONSTANCE extracted Solomon's promise not to approach Sir Humphrey concerning his "almost engagement" to Frances until she had the chance to speak first to Elizabeth.

This proved to be more difficult than she had imagined. After washing her hands in her room—Solomon was obligingly absent—she went down early for luncheon in the hope of a tête-à-tête. She found Elizabeth easily enough in the bright, comfortable morning room, but she was not alone.

Mrs. Haslett, the housekeeper, sat on the opposite side of the desk, her back to the door, so she did not see Constance enter. They appeared to be discussing menus for the coming week. Or at least Mrs. Haslett was discussing them, explaining in a highly patronizing manner why the vegetables or sauces of the main course did not work together, and how the courses themselves were ill balanced.

Elizabeth, trying to appear patient, looked merely harassed. Yet the look she cast Constance when she noticed her held more shame than irritation. Which was ridiculous. Mrs. Haslett was being needlessly obstructive, merely exercising her contempt for the second Lady Maule. And Elizabeth must have been putting up with this for well over an hour. She probably did so every week. And who knew how many other obstacles the woman put in her way, just because she thought she could?

God knew why Elizabeth was putting up with it. Constance had already had enough. Rather than leaving her friend in private purgatory, she bustled into the room, saying, "Goodness, Elizabeth, I thought you had decided on your menus already? Let me drag you away from this tedium. You know your meals are always delightful."

Elizabeth rose quickly. "Yes, perhaps that is enough for today, Mrs. Haslett. Tell me about your morning, Constance."

Mrs. Haslett, finally dismissed, took her time about departing, collecting all her pen-marked papers together. They reminded Constance of a piece of substandard schoolwork. She waited in silence while the woman walked in a leisurely fashion to the door, as if she still imagined herself victor of the field, and queen of the menus.

"My dear," Constance drawled to Elizabeth, not troubling to lower her voice, "has she truly nothing better to do? I know you have."

A sniff preceded the click of the closing door.

"I do," Elizabeth said wearily. "The woman grows more difficult by the day. Nothing I do, or order to be done, is ever right."

"Elizabeth, you were brought up to run a household! Her place is to carry out your wishes, not dispute the minutiae. *You* taught *me* that."

Elizabeth sighed. "I know, but it isn't that simple. I was the governess and I'm not good enough for Sir Humphrey."

"Again, not her place."

"No, but she has been with his family forever and Humphrey wouldn't like me to dismiss her. I expect all the other servants would give notice too if I did. I thought if I just deferred to her a little, she would be flattered enough to come round to me in the end, but she never gives an inch, never stops..."

No, Elizabeth's marriage was no bed of roses, even before Frances Niall's death.

Constance sat down. "It was a good strategy," she allowed, "and I suspect it would have worked with most people. Mrs. Haslett, however, seems to take every deferment as weakness, and is exercising her petty power to torture you."

"Oh, Constance, it's not as bad as that!"

"Isn't it? If not, it will be in time. Don't put yourself through the business of menus with her again. Send them directly to the cook. There is nothing wrong with any of your choices. You don't have to justify your orders, but if you feel the need, tell her you are reorganizing your time. The woman is becoming a tyrant—don't make yourself complicit in that."

Elizabeth held her head in both hands. "I have missed your common sense, Constance," she said shakily. "I do feel very alone sometimes. And you're right—it is time I exerted my authority. Only if she goes to Humphrey about it…"

Constance reached across the table to remove Elizabeth's hands from her face. "You're afraid he won't support you? If she goes to Humphrey she will merely irritate him, and he'll leave it to you anyway. He *will* support you." She had seen him at Fairfield Grange, facing Colonel Niall.

"Don't let this woman chip at your confidence again," Constance continued. "This house is a delightful home largely because of you. As for Mrs. Haslett," she added with sudden insight, "I suspect some of her behavior stems from her desperation to stay. She sees you as a threat because you stepped out of your place."

Elizabeth raised her head, looking thoughtful.

Constance had no intention of repeating what the housekeeper had said about preferring Frances as mistress. Still, the matter of Humphrey's engagement had to be faced.

"Elizabeth, something else—"

A brief knock interrupted Constance, and Manson the butler announced the serving of luncheon.

Although Sir Humphrey was perfectly polite as they ate, Constance sensed a tension in him. She wondered if he was regretting allowing her and Solomon to stay and investigate the truth of Frances's death. She wondered if Elizabeth was.

They did not discuss the murder, though, and Sir Humphrey excused himself on the grounds of estate matters almost as soon as the meal was finished.

"Would you like to see the garden?" Elizabeth asked.

She had always loved gardening. It was she who had first planted and cared for the kitchen garden in London, even making a pretty, colorful place to sit in the warmer weather.

"I would," Constance said, rising at once. "You have much

more land to play with here than in London."

"Mr. Grey?" Elizabeth said politely as he stood also. "Do you care for gardens?"

"I do," Solomon said, "but I beg you will excuse me until another time. I have letters to write that are growing urgent." He bowed and withdrew.

"Is he bored, or does he really have such matters to attend to?" Elizabeth asked as they made their way to the side door into the garden. It was warm enough not to need coats, and not quite sunny enough to require hats, so they wandered outside as they were.

"Oh, he isn't bored," Constance said, "though I suppose he might be being tactful, so that we can enjoy a tête-à-tête."

Elizabeth veered away from that, asking hastily, "What does he do, your Mr. Grey? Humph said he was in shipping."

"Among other things, but yes. Only...he seems to be taking a step back, delegating the business to others and leaving himself free."

"To do what?"

"Travel, I think," Constance replied. "Though I'm not sure he knows. Still waters run deep in Solomon. And in you, it would appear."

Elizabeth cast her a quick glance. "I don't know what makes you say so. This is the rose garden."

"So I see. It's beautiful and smells heavenly." Constance decided on the direct approach. "What makes me say so is the fact that you never told me your husband was once engaged to marry the dead woman. Or didn't you know?"

Elizabeth sank onto the first bench and closed her eyes. "I should have told you. I just thought it might make things look bad for Humph. And me."

"The *lying* makes things look bad for you and Humph," Constance said severely. "So you did know."

Elizabeth nodded. "He told me about her before he even asked me to marry him. But they were never *engaged*, Constance.

He was seriously considering it, for the sake of the children, because they needed a mother, and the first governess he hired was quite unsuitable. You must understand he grieved terribly when Gillian—his first wife—died. He never expected to love anyone else, and he thought Frances, a well-thought-of lady of good birth and education, would do."

"*Do*," Constance repeated. "I have heard many descriptions of her now. I have heard her eulogized and admired by all as beautiful, good, fascinating, beloved, clever. Yet Sir Humphrey thought no more of her than that she would *do?*"

Elizabeth gave an unhappy little smile. "Well, she was pleasant to look at, and I daresay she seemed a bit of a trophy, so he paid her a *little* attention. But the more he saw of her, the more he realized she had no interest in the children—and she doesn't, whatever wiles she used to make them adore her."

Constance frowned. "Did she do that? In what way?"

"I don't really know. I wasn't there before she went to India, but after she came home, they all goggle at her beauty, fall over themselves to make her smile, to do any little things she wants of them, and she does ask." She drew in a breath. "*Did* ask. 'Bring me a flower. Go and fetch your papa. Go to the kitchen and beg a slice of cake.' She especially liked if they were things I had forbidden them to do, like pull the head off a rose or eat more cake than was good for them..."

At last. "So she was not so perfect." Jealous, surely, at the very least...

Elizabeth shook her head. "Humph had already drawn back from her when Colonel Niall swept them all off to India. Despite the gossip in the village, there was no understanding between them, let alone any formal betrothal. Humph was perfectly free to marry me."

Constance sat down beside her. "Elizabeth. If you want my help, you cannot keep things like this from me. It's as if you're manipulating us to look in wrong directions, and if you do that, we may never be able to find out what happened to Frances. You may live under constant suspicion. Or that police inspector from London might decide it's worth arresting you."

Elizabeth's pale face whitened further. "I'm sorry," she whispered. "I have been so mixed up—at my wits' end, to be honest—that I don't know what to do or say for the best to anyone. Least of all to Humph. I am so afraid he takes all this as evidence of some evil within me…"

Constance grasped her hand. "There is no evil in you," she said firmly. "None whatsoever. So tell me the truth. What did Frances really say to you when you walked around the lake?"

Elizabeth stared at her hands. Constance gazed at her face until her friend slowly raised her eyes to hers.

"What did Frances say to me? She told me she was carrying Humphrey's child."

SOLOMON HAD NO urgent letters to write, but he thought he might use the time alone in his and Constance's bedchamber to write to Jamaica, to make sure his agents there remembered to earn their fees, both on the plantation and in the ongoing, increasingly hopeless investigation into the disappearance of his brother David. Twenty years had passed since the last time he had seen David, ten since, in the wake of his own failure, he had given the investigation over to others—not just in Jamaica but in every port in which he had contacts.

However, it was not David that kept him from concentrating on plantation business. It was this case of Frances Niall, who had died from no apparent cause and for no obvious reason. He found himself gazing out the window, across the pretty countryside and not even seeing it.

An unexpected knock on the door drew him back to the present. "Yes?" he called.

To his surprise, Sir Humphrey entered, scowling direly.

Solomon rose to his feet. "Sir Humphrey."

Maule halted in the middle of the room, glaring at Solomon. "Sorry to interrupt you."

The unexpectedness made Solomon blink. "Not at all. Can I help?"

Maule sighed. "Need a word."

"Then shall we sit and be comfortable?" Solomon indicated the two armchairs on either side of the fire, which was not yet lit.

Distractedly, Maule chose the nearest armchair. Solomon sat in the other and waited for him to speak.

"Dammit, I owe you an apology," he said in a rush. "To be frank, I didn't really believe in your skills of investigation. I only agreed to please Elizabeth, and because I thought she needed a friend to support her. Then, over at the Grange, it struck me I was sending you in blind, as it were, only giving you half the information and making everything you do for us doubly difficult. And in any case, I'm sure you'll find out in far less discreet ways than a little honesty on my part would have achieved." Maule paused for breath, eyeing Solomon with rather touching awkwardness. "Sorry."

Solomon shook his head. "There is no need for apology. If you mean to tell me about your understanding with Miss Niall—"

"There was no understanding on my part," Maule growled. "But it was a damned lucky escape. The more distance I put between us, the more she tried to cling. I kept running into her where she had no business to be—on my land, in the village inn, calling on me without her family. I tell you, I was mightily relieved when Niall hauled her off to India with him."

"Was that why he took her to India?" Solomon asked. "Because she was importuning you?"

"I don't imagine he knew she was. I certainly never told him. Awkward thing to say to a man about his daughter."

"And when she came home again?"

"I hoped she'd be married," Maule said. "She wasn't, but she did seem to have grown up in India. She was the perfect hostess for her father, entertained us at Fairfield Grange and generally behaved just as she ought. And was charming with it." He frowned again. "Elizabeth didn't take to her, though she was always perfectly polite, even during their so-called argument—which was more an exchange of views, at least from Elizabeth's understanding."

"And from Miss Niall's?"

"There was a flash of...venom in her eyes. Elizabeth says she muttered something under her breath, an insult ladies are not supposed to hear, let alone understand." He shrugged. "Frances grew up among soldiers."

"You must have been glad when she sent the note of apology."

Maule hesitated. "I was. Briefly. There's more, you see."

His forearms rested across his knees as he leaned forward, twisting his hands together. Solomon waited.

"I spoke to her that Wednesday afternoon. After I read her letter, but before she called on Elizabeth."

"She came to see you?" Solomon asked in surprise.

"More in her past manner," Maule said. "I was riding over from the far end of the estate when she appeared on the bridle path. I could have sworn she was waiting there for me, as though someone had told her where I was. I had a bad feeling about the whole thing, but I spoke courteously, thanking her for her gracious note to Elizabeth. She said..."

He drew in a breath and his eyes grew fierce again. "This is the difficult part, because I don't want this coming to my wife's ears. Which means you can't tell *your* wife either. But I think you need to know."

"Go on," Solomon said evenly. He had no intention of promising not to tell Constance, and fortunately, Maule did not push him.

He licked his lips as though they had gone suddenly dry. "Frances said... She said I had married the wife I deserved, a whore. That before Elizabeth came to The Willows as governess to my children, she had been a common prostitute selling her wares at Covent Garden. And that if I ever crossed her again, she would tell the world."

Solomon perceived the pitfalls. "What made her say such a thing?" he asked carefully.

"God knows. An unsavory mind coupled with unladylike knowledge and, I can only suppose, a hate-filled jealousy of my wife."

He doesn't know. Solomon realized it from the outrage in the man's eyes. Treading on tiptoe now, he said, "I see. So you did not tell your wife this for fear of hurting her feelings?"

"My wife has certain...tragedies in her past that I will not have raked up with this kind of malicious mudslinging. Of course I did not tell her."

"But you let her walk alone with this woman the same evening?"

"What else could I do? I couldn't tell Elizabeth why I suddenly distrusted Frances. But I...I watched them from the attic. There's a storage area up there, closed off from the servants' quarters, from where you can see over the trees to the lake."

Solomon sat up straighter. "What did you see?"

"I saw them part. Frances took the path toward the road, while Elizabeth came straight back to the house. Which is why I always knew my wife had never pushed her in, whatever Frances said to her."

"What do you think Frances *did* say to her? Was Lady Maule telling us the truth about that?"

"I don't know," Maule said miserably. "She told me the same thing, that they just made up their argument with mutual apologies and parted as friends."

"But you think otherwise?"

"I'm afraid Frances made the same accusations to Elizabeth's face that she had already made to me."

Solomon shifted position. He knew very little about the trust and secrets involved in marriage. "Why would your wife not tell you the truth about what was said?"

"To keep me from worrying."

"Or perhaps nothing untoward was said."

Maule looked beyond him. "Perhaps."

"You don't believe that. Because you are aware of Frances Niall's nature?"

An unhappy smile twisted Maule's lips. "No. Because I am aware of my wife's. She is too careful, too distant around me. There is a loss of…intimacy that speaks of shame and fear of what I might believe of her."

"I see."

Maule's gaze came back to his. "Do you? Do you see that this gives both Elizabeth and me motives for murder? To silence Frances forever?"

"Did you?" Solomon asked.

CHAPTER SEVEN

A LONE IN THE rose garden, Constance contemplated the
beauty of the flowers and the ugliness of human nature. It
depressed her spirits to the extent that she didn't notice anyone
approach until the bench creaked under a man's weight.

"Maule spoke to me," Solomon said heavily.

"Elizabeth spoke to me. Frances Niall was an unpleasant and
vindictive person. But she doesn't seem to have been the only
one. And the worst of it is, the truth provides Elizabeth with a
motive. And Sir Humphrey."

"I know. But what is the truth?"

Constance frowned at him. "That Frances was carrying
Humphrey's child."

Solomon's eyes widened. "Is that what she said to Elizabeth?
She told Maule something quite different."

"What?" Constance demanded. What could be worse than
that kind of betrayal by a husband who was supposed to love her?

"Frances told him than she knew of Elizabeth's past. On the
streets around Covent Garden."

"The truth," Constance said in despair. "Which makes it all
the more likely that she told Elizabeth the truth too."

"Does it? It can't have been mentioned at the inquest, and Dr.
Laing certainly didn't mention it to us."

"Well, he wouldn't, would he? Colonel Niall and Sir Humphrey are both his patients still."

"We need to find out if it was true," Solomon insisted.

"Why on earth would she lie about such a thing?"

"I really don't know, but a rather nasty person is emerging from behind Frances's halo. I don't like her."

"No... I still don't believe Elizabeth killed her."

"I don't see how. Besides which, Maule said he was uneasy enough about Frances's visit to watch them from the attic window as they walked around the lake. He claims he saw them part."

"Do you believe him?"

"I think so. His story matches Elizabeth's, even though they don't seem to have conferred much on the subject."

Constance shifted uneasily on the hard bench. "What if, having seen them part from the attic window, Sir Humphrey followed Frances, and killed her somehow to prevent her telling the world about his child?"

"After he called acknowledgment to Elizabeth when she told him she was back and all was well? It's possible."

"You sound doubtful."

"I am. I don't doubt Maule could have carried her body back to the lake and dropped her in—but she was wearing her nightgown. When did that change happen?"

"If they were having an affair, he might well have had one at hand. Where did they meet? We need to find their cozy love nest."

"I don't believe they had one," Solomon said, irritatingly certain in his manner. "He does not speak of her as someone he loved or had anything but contempt for. I don't think it's in his character, either to have the affair or to kill his lover and his own child."

"People will do anything to maintain the appearance of respectability," Constance insisted. "He probably felt he had enough to cope with if Elizabeth's past was about to come out."

"But he doesn't believe that part. He thinks it was all Frances's malice."

Constance stared at him, then struck the heel of her hand

against her forehead in despair. "Elizabeth didn't tell him. She confessed only to the love affair that caused her parents to throw her out. Not about her continued…fall."

Solomon said nothing.

"Oh, drat the girl," Constance whispered.

"It's an understandable silence."

"No wonder she wouldn't tell him about *me*. She would have had to explain how she knew me. There is so much *secrecy* here."

"And at Fairfield Grange. But where do we go from here?"

Constance sprang to her feet. "To find out the truth about Frances's baby."

"I really doubt Laing will tell us."

"No, but his assistant might."

DR. HAROLD MURRAY apparently lodged with his master in Dr. Laing's cottage. However, Sir Humphrey said he was frequently to be found in the late afternoon enjoying a quiet pint in the village hostelry.

"If Laing has no need of him," he added.

Since they both thought they would have more chance of learning the truth if Murray was away from Laing, Solomon and Constance repaired to the village inn.

Here, they ordered a light tea and sat in the genteel coffee room. Solomon made occasional unsuccessful forays into the taproom, in search of Dr. Murray, but when asked, the landlord said it was still a bit early for the lad—and in any case, he was normally kept pretty busy.

"Sometimes he barely has time to swallow a half-pint," the landlord said with a grin. "Hardly worth his time coming, but I think he enjoys the break."

"Dr. Laing keeps his nose to the grindstone?"

"Good for the young." The landlord chortled.

"His father will be pleased," Solomon said.

"I'll send him through to have a word with you and your lady wife if you like."

"Thank you. Please do."

No one disturbed them in the coffee room as they ate their scones and drank their tea. Constance had just ordered another pot, despite feeling awash with the stuff, when a young, brown-haired man wandered in with a mug of ale in his hand. He had a guileless, friendly face and an eager expression, a bit like a labrador retriever.

"Mr. Grey?" he said amiably. "I hear you're a friend of my father's."

"Ah. Not quite," Solomon said under Constance's amused gaze. "I think the innkeeper must have misunderstood me."

"I'm the wrong Murray? Then I'm sorry to have disturbed you."

"No, we're always glad of company," Solomon said. "Please join us. My name is Grey. This is my wife. We're guests of Lady Maule at The Willows."

A look of curiosity entered Murray's face. "You called on Dr. Laing earlier."

"We did. You'll have gathered we are trying to assist Sir Humphrey in discovering what happened to Miss Niall."

"Good," said Murray. With a bow, he sat down opposite Constance. "So you don't believe this nonsense about his wife either?"

Constance smiled at him, which had its usual effect. "A fellow champion," she said with honest delight.

Murray blushed. "Well, however grieved he is, Colonel Niall has no call throwing such accusations around."

"Do other people believe in these accusations?" she asked.

Murray took a sip of ale and shook his head to her gestured offer of tea. "Some," he said reluctantly. "It's only because she's a stranger and stepped out of her so-called place. Some country people believe everything should stay the same forever."

"You don't?" Solomon asked.

"Well, I'm a stranger too. I haven't been in the neighborhood a year, and no one here would call my father a gentleman. I still won a scholarship to university and earned my degree. In my opinion, Lady Maule is better educated, kinder, and more cultured than any of the other ladies of the county."

"She probably is," Constance agreed. "Though for what it's worth, she is also a gentleman's daughter, whatever the local rumors to the contrary. Did you know Miss Niall?"

Murray gave a crooked smile. "We were bowing acquaintances. I bowed. She tended to look through me without notice, though I did receive at least one nod of recognition."

"You didn't like her."

"I barely spoke to her."

"Then you never attended her?"

"Dr. Laing tends to see patients of Quality. They don't always want an assistant observing."

"Did she consult with him often?" Constance asked.

"Just once that I recall. A brief consultation shortly after her return. I was not present. But Laing was invited to dinner at the Grange. I'm too lowly."

He wasn't lowly in his own mind, though. Solomon, who had faced down most forms of prejudice in his own life, rather liked that in him.

"But you assisted in the autopsy?" he said.

Murray nodded. "I did."

"And that was where you discovered she had not drowned, as had seemed clear in the beginning."

"Indeed."

"Did *you* discover that, or did Dr. Laing?" Solomon asked, more as a test of his character than in any expectation of receiving a different answer to what he already knew.

Laing shifted in his chair. "We both did."

"Dr. Laing gives you the credit. He implied he was merely going through the motions and not paying attention, because the cause of her death seemed so obvious."

"It's true he was…distracted. A bit thrown. Well, she was a very tragic figure lying there, so young and lovely. *I* found it harrowing, and I didn't even like her."

"Did Dr. Laing like her?" Constance asked.

"He never said he didn't. He's very closemouthed, is Laing— which is to his credit. He takes confidentiality very seriously, only ever tells me the minimum of what I need to know about patients to treat them. A death like Miss Niall's is unusual in the extreme. And it was worse for him, knowing her and her family socially. Had done since before they went to India."

"So you noticed there was no water in her lungs. What else did you find?"

"Nothing," Murray said helplessly. "The lungs jolted Dr. Laing. He was extremely thorough after that. We even tested the contents of her stomach for all the poisons we could think of. But there was nothing there."

"Nothing unusual at all?" Solomon pushed.

"Nothing," Murray repeated, looking him in the eye.

"Then she was not with child?" Solomon said bluntly.

Murray blinked. "Good God, no!"

Constance let out an audible breath of relief. The shock in Murray's voice was plain. It was as Solomon thought—Frances had been making mischief, sowing discord. What they did not know was why.

"Did you ever hear any rumors in the neighborhood, however untrue, about Miss Niall having a…*special* admirer?" he asked.

Constance regarded him with a hint of mockery that he did not say the word *lover*. But he didn't want to be thought a gossipmonger. That would only make Murray as tight-lipped as Laing. The only reason the young doctor was speaking to them now was the injustice of the accusations against Elizabeth.

"No," Murray said. "The only rumor I heard was about Sir Humphrey, and that stems from before the Nialls went to India. Apparently there was some semblance of an engagement, or so the locals believed. They were sympathetic to Miss Niall for that reason. But so far as I know, there was never any ill feeling between the two families until after she died. But then, I'm a stranger myself, and I don't gossip either."

"No, we can tell," Constance said sincerely. "Neither do we." Another thought appeared to strike her. "Does Mrs. Phelps gossip?"

Murray's eyebrows shot up. "Sarah Phelps? I wouldn't say she gossiped so much as hurled insults."

"Did she hurl any at Miss Niall?"

"Not in my hearing. But then, she was too busy insulting me."

Solomon smiled slightly. "You don't seem to mind."

Murray grinned. "No point, is there?"

"Because she's mad?" Constance asked.

"Oh, I don't think she's mad. Just says and does exactly as she wants and doesn't care tuppence for what the quack's boot boy opines."

>>>><<<<

"SO IT WAS a lie," Constance said with some satisfaction as she and Solomon took the road out of the village toward The Willows. "She was making mischief. The same with the accusations she made about Elizabeth to Sir Humphrey. She knew nothing. She was just casting aspersions in the hope something stuck."

"Why would she do that?" Solomon wondered aloud. "Why risk her own reputation with such accusations?"

"Revenge," Constance said. "Because Sir Humphrey didn't marry her."

"Six years is a long time to wait for vengeance."

"Perhaps she still thought Humphrey would marry her when she returned from India. And was furious when she discovered he had already married someone else."

"She would have known," Solomon objected. "Maule corresponded with the colonel during those years. But I suspect you're right that she bore a grudge. However, the damage was done. If *she* had pushed *Elizabeth* into the lake, I could more easily understand it."

"So was she causing trouble to inspire him to divorce Elizabeth?" Constance said.

Solomon glanced at her. "Do you think he would do that? For anything?"

"No," she admitted. "It's too...disgraceful for a respectable man. On the other hand, Frances may not have known that."

"Either way, she was behaving badly enough for either of them to have pushed her in the lake, however sorry they might have been afterward."

"Only they didn't," Constance said. "No one did until after she was dead."

"That's the heart of the mystery," he conceded. "What made you ask about Mrs. Phelps?"

"She lives between the lake and the Grange. Frances at least set off along the right path to have passed her cottage. She wields an axe like a twenty-year-old woodsman, and she was the first person I met who did not eulogize Frances. On the other hand, I doubt there was anything Frances could have said that would annoy her enough to commit murder."

"Which might not matter if she was mad," Solomon said thoughtfully. "Only, Dr. Murray doesn't think she is. Which rules out our only other suspect."

"*Only* other?" Constance repeated. "It strikes me that someone like Frances doesn't just wake up one morning and decide she might as well be nasty, whether for pure spite or some kind of social blackmail. I don't know what she got out of it, but I very much doubt Elizabeth and Humphrey were her only victims. She must have been practicing for years."

Solomon frowned. "Do you think so? Then why does everyone speak of her as an angel? Just because she's dead?"

Constance shrugged. "Partly, yes. The convention is that one does not speak ill of the dead. But also... I think she had some kind of power over people. The sort of presence that could make people believe whatever she wished."

He must have looked skeptical at this, for she cast him a wry smile. "You have it too, you know."

He was startled. "I do?"

"You create the impression you wish to create. It's probably why no one ever hits you when you ask questions."

"I thought that was because you fluttered your eyelashes at them."

"Oh, that only works on men of a certain type," she said dismissively.

"Whatever," he said. "We're only guessing about Frances, since neither of us ever met her."

"True. But I think it's a reasonable guess. Furthermore, I think she exercised it on Sir Humphrey's children, either to hurt Elizabeth or just to make them her little minions. It probably worked on most of the village—except Mrs. Phelps—and her own household."

Solomon began to deny any proof of that, but then said instead, "I suppose it would explain why the butler did not tell her father she had gone out in the evening."

"It might. Or she might have used her alternative weapon— the kind of threats she made to Sir Humphrey and Elizabeth, the people she could not get around."

Solomon shook his head. "Even if you're right, we need proof for such a motive. And supposing we had it, we would still have no idea how or where she died. I think we need to talk to the Fairfield servants again, without the presence of the brother or father."

"I didn't get the impression John was under his sister's thumb, did you? I caught a wry, almost cynical smile on his lips when she was being discussed. I think he is merely defending the respectability of the family. I would like to talk to him again." Her eyes began to gleam as she glanced up at Solomon. "I would also like to have a good look around her private rooms. If they haven't thrown out all her things."

"I can't see Colonel Niall—or even John—giving us permission for that."

"Neither can I," Constance said with a quite dazzling smile. "I'd be surprised if the police themselves had been allowed near. So let's not ask them."

BEFORE DINNER, CONSTANCE dragged Elizabeth into her bedchamber and showed her the drawings she had made of the outside of the Grange, and the plans of the inside.

"I'd forgotten how well you remember everything you see and hear," Elizabeth said with a faint, admiring smile.

"Do you know which is the window to Frances's rooms?"

Elizabeth pulled the drawings of the back of the house and the left gable out from under the others. "Those," she said, touching the second-floor windows on the corner, one at the side of the house, and two at the back. Exactly where Constance had noticed the closed curtains as she walked around from the kitchen this morning. "She waved to us from that one when we were in the garden one afternoon."

"Ah. Then you have never been in her bedroom?"

"Actually, I have been. The rooms were redecorated for her return. She has a bedroom, a dressing room, and a sitting room. More than either John or the colonel, apparently. She was eager to show them to me, as though they were a sign of her status. And I have to admit, they are lovely rooms and very tastefully furnished."

"Excellent." Constance reached for the internal plan she had begun. "Show me here."

Elizabeth stared at her. "Constance, what are you up to?"

"Don't ask."

She did not look much comforted. "*Please* don't do anything that will reflect badly on Humph! He is a magistrate, remember."

"Of course I won't," Constance said, crossing her fingers behind her back. "Now, where exactly is her bedroom door?"

ALTHOUGH IT GOT cold in the evenings, Sarah Phelps was saving her firewood for the winter. She let her fire die back once her supper was eaten and set about bottling the last of her fruit preserves. There had been a decent harvest of gooseberries, raspberries, and apples this summer. Along with the wheat and the beans and carrots she grew on her land, and the milk, butter, and cheese from her cow, it would ensure she lasted another winter.

It wasn't much of a goal, but it was the only one she'd had since George's death. God had granted them no children, and either George or the law—it didn't much matter which—had given the smithy to his wastrel nephew. Sarah would rather have been a blacksmith than a farmer, but no one considered it right for a female. So, here she was, surviving by means of work she'd known nothing about five years ago.

It was well after dark, and she knew she should go to bed. She had to be up at dawn to milk the cow and get through all her other chores before the next night. It wasn't much of a life, not on her own. The only thing that made it interesting was observing her neighbors, who discounted her because she was mad.

Fools, she thought as she wandered outside into the darkness of her yard. Would George have married her if she'd been mad? He'd had the pick of all the village maidens, for he'd been a good man, a fine-looking man, and possessed a thriving business. But he'd chosen Sarah. Admittedly, she'd been not bad looking in those days, in a statuesque kind of way. Most of the young men had been too frightened of her, but George wasn't.

They'd had a good marriage. The villagers forgot that. And

they'd have let her starve when she lost the smithy. She should be grateful to Sir Humphrey for renting this place to her for so little—and she was, underneath her grumpiness. He wasn't a bad man, despite his temper and his ill luck with wives.

Sarah had quite liked the first Lady Maule. She wasn't so sure of the second, who'd come to The Willows as the governess. Even then, she'd had the kind of eyes that had seen too much tragedy and wouldn't let it stand in her way again. But at least she was kind enough.

Not like those stuck-up fools at the Grange. She almost laughed at Frances Niall's airs of superiority. If her neighbors had known what Frances did, they would have turned their backs on her. Her family would have thrown her out.

Usually, Sarah quite liked people who were different. Not Frances. She was all spite.

But then, Sarah herself was no angel. Even the best of her memories were tarnished now. Who was she to judge anyone?

Won't stop me...

As she leaned against the doorframe, she heard quiet footsteps in the road beyond her hedge. The faint light of a lantern glowed above, swinging slightly as its carrier walked. No, there was more than one person. Two.

They did not speak, so she couldn't tell who they were until they passed the gap in her hedge and the lantern light flickered over them. The tall, dark fellow, and his far-too-pretty wife with the veiled eyes. Eyes not unlike the new Lady Maule's, she realized now. She just hid it better. They were odd visitors for Sir Humphrey.

And what on earth were they doing creeping about the lanes at this time of night?

Like Frances had the night she'd apparently died. Sarah told the truth. She hadn't seen her come back. But she'd heard her—she recognized the girl's arrogant footsteps, she always had—and seen her lantern's glow.

But Sarah had no intention of telling.

CHAPTER EIGHT

S KULKING BEHIND THE large oak tree, whose branches spread as closely as she remembered to the first back window of Frances's rooms, Constance gazed up at the second-floor windows. Like the rest of the house, they were all in darkness. Since Solomon had doused the lantern, they were relying on the moonlight, which, fortunately, was quite bright.

The country had a different quality of silence to the city— deeper, at once eerier and less dangerous. It was only harmless animals that rustled through the undergrowth, only owls and other nightbirds breaking it with their cries, not drunks or thieves or victims.

Constance brought her lips close to Solomon's ear. "I'll climb up and let you in the back door," she breathed.

He cast her a disparaging look and at the same time swung himself up into the tree branches, deft, sure-footed, and as graceful as ever. A man of many surprises, was Solomon. But then, he'd been brought up in the country. No doubt he and his brother had run as wild as any.

Constance's climbing skills had been learned in the city and had more to do with buildings, drainpipes, and pursuit by police. At least she was used to climbing in skirts. For tonight, she wore a darker, much simpler gown that had no need of crinoline.

She waited until he had climbed up to the next branch, and then moved when he did to avoid the tree shaking constantly. It was a simple climb, almost as though the branches had been trained in the right direction. And when they came to the window, there was a simple step from the branch to the window ledge, one needing only the well-worn foothold in the wall for balance.

Given how easy it was to reach, the window was probably locked, in which case they would have to climb all the way down again and try to pick the lock to the side door. Constance had been better at picking pockets than locks, but she might manage it...

Above her, she heard the faintest rattling as Solomon drew up the sash. She smiled into the darkness and watched his shadowy figure vanish. Then, as she climbed up to the final branch and shuffled along, he reached out of the window to catch her. She wanted to fume that she was perfectly capable, but they could not afford the noise, And, in fact, stepping onto the window ledge, she didn't actually mind the extra security of his strong hands at her waist, assisting her to sit astride the sill and duck through.

He closed the window most of the way behind him and softly drew the curtains back into place.

Constance looked around her, found the shape of a large bed, and located a candle, which she lit from the flint in her pocket. It took longer than she would have liked, and the noise sounded bizarrely loud in the silent house. But eventually, by its flaring glow, she saw that the bed had been stripped of all but its curtains, the matching coverlet neatly folded on the thick feather mattress. There was nothing on the table except an oil lamp. Frustratingly, it looked as if the room had been stripped already.

Still, Constance moved toward the nightstand, which had a drawer.

It was empty. Solomon glided past her to the bare dressing table. On it stood only an almost-empty perfume bottle and silver-backed hairbrushes. He slid open the drawer and found a jewel case, and Constance brought over the candle for a closer look.

Frances had possessed a lot of jewelry—diamonds, rubies,

turquoises, and stunning lapis lazuli. Some of it was very intricate and Eastern in appearance, so it had probably been made in India. But there seemed to be no false bottom in the case, no betraying notes or accounts beneath the jewelry or in the otherwise empty drawer.

As one, they moved through to the dressing room and began a long, thorough search among the dead woman's many clothes. Constance felt behind drawers and furniture for anything a secretive woman might have hidden, but again they found nothing.

They moved through to her private sitting room, though Constance had begun to doubt the point. If she were right in her conjectures, Frances had been too wily to leave physical proof. In fact, Constance was feeling guiltily *wrong*. After all, Frances Niall was the victim of *murder*. Was it really right to blame her like this, just because of some nasty things she had said to Elizabeth and Sir Humphrey? After all, from her point of view at least, Maule had betrayed her.

At that point, Constance only kept looking because they were already here.

Like the dressing room, Frances's sitting room appeared to have been left exactly as it was before she died. The furniture had been dusted and polished, the floors kept clean, almost like a shrine. But when Constance opened the first drawer of the surprisingly substantial desk, it was stuffed with papers. As if her family could not bring themselves to go through them. To go through her private things, like giving away her clothes, would be to acknowledge that she was gone from their lives altogether.

Swallowing hard, Constance glanced over her shoulder at Solomon, who was drawing a bottle from the pretty cabinet cupboard. He unstopped it and sniffed.

"Brandy," he whispered. "Half full."

So, the woman had liked a tipple. Unladylike, but hardly a crime.

While Solomon felt beneath the chairs and squeezed the

cushions for signs of hidden items, Constance began to rummage in the drawer. There were bills for rather staggering amounts of money from dressmakers. Colonel Niall must have been both wealthy and generous. A small notebook had pages of initials and, beside each, what looked like reminder words or vague instructions.

CB – last position, law

PW – father, fear

There were pages of them, and there was no time to read them all. Would anyone notice if Constance took it with her? She set it on the desk while she rummaged beneath. The letters seemed to have been stuffed in anyhow. Some appeared to be from family and friends, with certain parts ringed or marked in some way, probably by Frances herself.

"Look," Solomon murmured.

In the bottom drawer of the desk, he had found some rather racy sketches and books. But he had drawn them out to reveal what was behind. In the candlelight, a small treasure trove sparkled. Rings and bracelets, small crystal perfume bottles, cameos, small items both valuable and otherwise.

Jewelry she did not wear? Or things she hid from her family? Did she just not like them? Or had she stolen them?

Meeting Solomon's gaze, Constance raised her brows, then returned to the letters.

One seemed out of place, on print-headed paper, such as a business would use. There was no clue as to what kind of business, no professional description such as a physician or solicitor might use, just the name—*L. Dunne*—and a London address across the top.

Holding the letter nearer the candle, she scanned it, and her stomach dropped. Something to do with tracing a child who had been adopted.

"Sol?" she said hoarsely, and he rose to read it over her shoulder. "She found Elizabeth's baby."

"She found—"

He broke off abruptly, for the door to the passage had suddenly opened and a man walked into the room.

SOLOMON SAW AT once that it was John Niall. No doubt the young man was aware only of intruders and had acted on instinct, for he dropped his candle, which immediately went out, and sprinted across the floor to attack.

Solomon threw up his fists, ready to defend himself and Constance. "Go," he growled at her, in the faint hope that she could somehow get out unrecognized, shin back down the tree, and flee to safety before John—or the crashing sounds of their inevitable fight—raised the alarm.

But he should have known better.

Before John even got close enough to take a swing, she stepped between them, holding a pretty little silver-mounted pistol in her elegant, gloved hand.

"Halt," she said quietly.

John all but skidded into stillness, his wide eyes lifting from the pistol to her face. His tight lips sagged. "Mrs. Grey?"

"Forgive me, sir," Constance said quietly, hiding the little pistol once more in whatever pocket she had taken it from. "I find it best to halt such unexpected situations before they get out of hand. I can see you are wondering what on earth we are doing in your late sister's rooms."

"I can imagine what you're doing." His gaze flickered to the window. "And how you got into the house to do it."

"You have used the route yourself, perhaps?" Solomon said smoothly, his fists back at his sides but still poised to act if necessary. He changed position so that Constance was no longer between him and John.

"Myself?" John said. "No, I never had cause, to be honest. But I know how Frances got out and in again when she was a girl. What exactly are you looking for?"

"Anything," Constance said, "that might give us a clue as to what happened to your sister."

"You could have asked," John said haughtily.

"And what would have been Colonel Niall's response?" Solomon asked. "Or yours?"

John shrugged. "The same, no doubt. I have no intention of allowing any scandal to break over my sister's head."

"It has already broken. She was murdered. People will always assume, rightly or wrongly, that she and her family are to blame for that." As Solomon and his father had been blamed in so many ways for David's disappearance...

John ran his fingers through his hair in a somewhat harassed manner. "You are right, of course. But still, I have to look after my father as best I can."

"And you think the best way to do that is to prevent him or anyone else from discovering the truth?"

"Some of it," John said steadily. Dropping his gaze from Solomon's, he regarded the open drawers of the desk. "So what have you discovered to our detriment?"

There was no sign of the letter about the baby from L. Dunne. Solomon suspected Constance had pocketed that when she took out the pistol. John's eyes were fixed on the bottom drawer and the little pile of treasures.

"Why would she keep such things there?" Constance asked.

"Who knows?"

"Then *you* don't?" Solomon said quickly. "Do you know where they came from?"

John shook his head.

"Did she steal them?" Constance asked.

The head shake was more violent this time. "I doubt it. I really don't know, but I suspect they were gifts."

"From whom?" Solomon asked. He didn't want the answer to

be *Sir Humphrey*.

"Various admirers, I imagine," John said. "She liked gifts. She used to show me things she had been given, especially when I had received nothing."

Solomon frowned. "Then these are from years ago? From before she went to India?"

"Some of them certainly are." John went back and picked up his dropped candle, putting it back in its holder before he went to the desk and lit it from theirs. Crouching down, he poked with his free hand among the hidden gifts.

He picked out a silver bracelet with a single diamond set in the middle of the band. "I don't remember this one."

"Why would she hide gifts?" Constance asked. "It makes no sense if she liked people to know about them."

John's smile was crooked and not exactly loving. "Only those who would be upset by them. Look, I can see you've guessed that Frances was not exactly what she pretended to be. It's the cross my father and I bear. Please don't make us do so in public."

"What *was* she like?" Solomon asked. "Truly?"

"Truly? She could be spiteful, manipulative, and God help you if you were her latest...target."

"Was Lady Maule her latest target?" Constance asked. "Is that why your father is so convinced she is the killer?"

John hesitated, then nodded curtly. "I think so. It crossed my mind too, and I couldn't altogether blame Lady Maule for turning on her. Only I can't see how she did it."

"I don't believe she did," Constance said. "She is too patient with people. Who else was a target of your sister's spite?"

John groaned and sat down in the nearest chair before springing back up again as he realized Constance still stood. A very polite young man, considering they had broken into his house. "I don't know. It wasn't really until that dinner at The Willows, when Frances and Lady Maule argued, that I really paid attention. Until then, I thought she—Frances—had calmed down into the person she should always have been. I thought India had been good for her."

"Why *did* your father take her off to India?" Solomon demanded. "Had he worked out that Maule would not marry her?"

"Probably," John said tiredly. "But that's something else I don't really know. I was at school and then university. I only went to visit them in India for the last couple of months and then returned home with them."

"What did you think?" Solomon asked. "At the time?"

Again, John dragged his fingers through his hair and tugged it. "I thought she had grown too wild for my father to handle here. I thought he hauled her off before she did something from which she would never recover, socially or morally. In India, she could be surrounded by strangers, servants, soldiers loyal to my father."

"Guarded?" Constance said.

"I thought maybe something like that. But when I finally went there, I saw no signs of it. Papa and Frances seemed to be getting on much better together, and I never heard a whisper of scandal. It was almost too good to be true, but I believed she had settled down after a wild girlhood."

She had been about twenty-two when she left for India. Which made her wild girlhood somewhat extended.

"Did she know Sir Humphrey was married before you returned to Fairfield?" Solomon asked.

"Yes. She didn't seem to care. She had moved on in her mind and heart, I suppose. And she no longer seemed so cruel or spiteful."

Constance pounced. "Cruel?"

Even in the dim candlelight, his flush was obvious. "Well, she could be," he said uncomfortably. "When she was young."

"Physically or emotionally?" Constance asked.

"Both. It was as if…"

"What?" Constance prompted him.

He raised his eyes to meet hers. "As though she really didn't know the difference between right and wrong. Even though she had the same upbringing as I did, such matters didn't seem to penetrate. Either that or she simply didn't care."

"What do you really think happened to her?" Solomon asked. "If you don't truly believe Lady Maule somehow murdered her."

John shrugged. "I could more easily imagine Maule himself doing it, in a fit of temper. Frances really could try the patience of a saint, and if she was up to her old tricks again... But there was no sign of anyone's temper on her. I would think it really was a freak accident, if it wasn't..."

"Wasn't what?"

He grimaced. "Do people like Frances have such accidents? Just to make life more comfortable for those she left behind?"

Solomon's skin pricked. There was a terrible admission in John's words, a guilt that wasn't necessarily over something as heinous as the murder of a sister.

"Who do you think gave her the bracelet?" Constance asked suddenly.

John blinked, turning to look at it again. "I don't know. Her latest admirer, I suppose. Though I can't imagine even the *head* groom affording that kind of trinket."

"Groom?" Solomon repeated, startled.

John gestured disparagingly with one hand. "It was a mere flirtatious glance on her part, though the man played along. I didn't mean it seriously."

"Then who *was* her latest admirer?" Constance demanded.

"I really don't know. I didn't want to." A spasm crossed his face. "Do you suppose such willful blindness led to her death?"

"I doubt it," Constance said kindly. "But we need to see the whole truth before we can tell what is relevant and what is not. We shan't divulge anything about your sister that we don't have to in order to find the culprit. May we talk to her maid again?"

"I'll send her over to The Willows in the morning." John walked across to the window and deliberately shut and locked it. "I'll show you out by the front door, shall I?"

"That would be helpful," Constance said shamelessly, bestowing upon John one of her brilliant smiles, which caused the poor young man to blink in bemusement.

"Just one more question for now," Solomon said without moving. "What brought you here to your sister's room in the middle of the night?"

John's lips twisted. "I'd finally plucked up the courage to do what you've just done. Look amongst her private things."

"Then you have no idea what is here?"

"Not beyond *those.*" He pointed at the hidden jewelry. "Which she always kept there."

"You might take a look at the notebook on top of the desk," Constance suggested. "And tell us if it means anything to you?"

John swallowed. Solomon guessed he really didn't want to look into his sister's circumstances. But he would, whether to save the task from his father, or to prevent any further visits from Solomon and Constance. Or, worse, the police.

"I'll look," he said resignedly. "Though I don't promise to understand it."

WORCESTER, COLONEL NIALL'S butler, had not slept well for months. Not since the family had come home to the Grange. Not since *she* had.

As a result, he was in the kitchen in his dressing gown, making himself a cup of hot chocolate, when he heard the unmistakable sound of the front door opening. His head jerked up. Abandoning his chocolate on the table, he flew up to the entrance hall in time to see the shadows of two people vanishing out the front door. Mr. John, fully dressed, closed it behind them with an air of relief before he began to walk toward the staircase and saw Worcester standing there.

"I heard the door, sir," Worcester said. "Is everything well?"

"I'm not very sure, to be honest. Mr. and Mrs. Grey, from The Willows, are sniffing around for my sister's secrets."

Worcester felt sick.

Perhaps Mr. John saw it, even in the dim light of two candles, for he said, "You don't know anything, do you, Worcester?"

"Such as what, sir?" Worcester managed.

"Anything that might shed some light on what happened to Miss Frances."

"Nothing like that, sir," Worcester lied. "I'm sure the inquest must have got it wrong, and the poor lady just fell into the lake."

"In her nightgown?"

"It's odd, sir," Worcester said with what dignity he could muster. "There is no denying that it is odd. But I don't believe all these questions are helping anyone."

"They're certainly not helping my father." Mr. John went on toward the staircase. "Get some sleep, Worcester. You deserve it."

Worcester did, and Mr. John was a kind young gentleman to suggest it. Unlike his sister, who, despite all the upheaval since, Worcester was glad to see in her grave. *Rot in hell, you evil witch.*

⤜⤜⤜⟪⟪⟪

"I DON'T THINK there's any malice in John Niall," Constance said as they walked back to The Willows. "And yet...I find him a more credible suspect than I did before."

"Why?" Solomon asked.

"Because he knows what his sister was—amoral, spiteful, and cruel."

"We know what he *said* she was. Perhaps he is just throwing the net wider to confuse us with suspects we might never meet."

"You still don't believe she was that bad?" Constance asked.

"We have very little proof either way. Only the word of Sir Humphrey and Lady Maule, and John, who might have his own reasons for deflecting us."

"Because he is the one who killed her?"

"He told us about a lover, and a flirtation with a groom. I don't think he likes Lady Maule being suspected, but he's quite happy to throw others into the shadow of the hangman."

"Perhaps you're right," Constance mused. "I suppose he is only helpful when we force the issue. And, when you think about it, he took our breaking and entering his family home in a very understated way. He would have been quite justified in rousing the household and throwing us out. Especially when I pointed a pistol at him."

"And yet he didn't," Solomon said. "I wonder why?"

"Protecting his father?" Constance suggested. She sighed. "Or himself. Have we actually learned anything at all?"

"We have a few more places to look," Solomon said. "Which may have been his intention in talking to us."

CHAPTER NINE

I T WAS PERHAPS fortunate that when Solomon woke the following morning, Constance was sound asleep at the opposite side of the bed.

He had dreamed she was lying cuddled into his shoulder, which had both touched and aroused him. Even asleep, he had known those were dangerous emotions around Constance Silver. And yet this morning, he did not bolt out of bed to escape temptation. He lay still beside her and found he rather liked the strange companionship.

After a long moment, he turned over to see if she was awake, propping his head on his hand.

God, she was beautiful.

In sleep, without any artifice or humor or hiding, she moved him in quite unexpected ways. But that wasn't why his heartbeat quickened. Beneath his hand, the bed was warm.

She really had been curled close against him. The memory of the dream intensified again. He wondered what it would be like to have her there every morning.

Oh yes, it was time to get up.

He turned once more and eased himself out of bed and into his trousers. As he padded toward the washstand, a soft knock sounded at the door. He opened it to discover a smiling maid with a tray of coffee.

"Good morning, sir. Coffee for Mrs. Grey, as promised, and for yourself in case you want it."

"Thank you," he said, taking the tray from her and kicking the door shut. He must look ridiculous with his nightshirt half caught up in his trousers.

When he turned back, Constance was awake and watching him with laughing eyes.

"Very fetching," she commented.

"I aim to please. Allow me to pour your coffee."

As she sat up against the pillows to receive her cup, she was damnably alluring in that ridiculous, frothy garment she called a nightgown, with her slightly tousled hair and rosy morning skin. Despite their late night, she looked well rested and eager—to proceed with their investigation. Obviously.

"Do you think John really will send the maid over this morning?" she said, and sipped her coffee with a sigh of pure bliss.

Solomon took the other cup and decided to ignore his comical appearance by lounging at the foot of the bed, his back against the bottom post. "I hope so. Otherwise we'll have to sneak into the Fairfield kitchen, and I'm not sure how that will be regarded."

"What of the letter?" she asked with obvious reluctance. "About the child and the adoption. Do you think I should show it to Elizabeth?"

"Would she want to know?"

"She didn't when she gave the baby up. She needed only to be sure he had gone to a kind and safe home, but no more. It was too painful. She was afraid of going there just to see him. She insisted a clean break was best for the child, and the only way she could go on. But things might be different now."

Solomon took a considering mouthful of coffee. "May I see the letter again?"

She opened the drawer in her bedside table and passed the folded letter to him. He read it more carefully this time.

"Who is this L. Dunne? Is he even trustworthy?" she wondered aloud.

"Yes. I have used them myself. They are a branch of a trusted firm of solicitors that specializes in investigations. What worries me about this is the fact that they are giving confidential information to someone with no right to it."

"Perhaps the Nialls are their clients. I'm sure Elizabeth is not."

"Sir Humphrey might be. No, something is wrong with this. I don't know the signature here—it clearly belongs to none of the Dunnes themselves. It must be one of their employees."

"Giving away information he shouldn't?" Constance frowned. "For money? Or favors? I suppose it fits with what we suspect of Frances—she can get around anyone, one way or another. Only...she didn't use this information, did she? She told Sir Humphrey that Elizabeth was a Covent Garden whore, and she told Elizabeth that she, Frances, was carrying Humphrey's child, a clear lie. Why did she not use the truth of the illegitimate child to cause trouble?"

"Perhaps she guessed Sir Humphrey already knew about it."

"How?" Solomon asked.

Constance sighed and drank more coffee. "I don't know."

Solomon folded the letter and tapped it thoughtfully against his thigh. "I think perhaps I should bolt up to London and see the Dunnes."

Was that a flicker of disappointment in her eyes?

"Instead of seeing the maid?"

"*After* seeing the maid. She must know more than anyone about Frances." He drained his cup and rose to his feet. "You'll forgive me if I wash and dress?"

"I rather like the nightshirt, but do what you must. I shall preserve my maidenly modestly by studiously reading this book."

SIR HUMPHREY PROVIDED Solomon with a railway timetable, and he discovered there was a train to London just before midday. He might just be in time to catch the Dunnes' office, although he would have to stay the night in Town.

Providing the maid, Bingham, didn't solve the whole mystery.

If she turned up.

But John was as good as his word, for they had just risen from breakfast when the butler informed Constance that the girl awaited her in the kitchen.

Elizabeth, who overheard, looked startled. "Do you want me to come?" she asked, looking from Constance to Solomon and back. "Use the morning room to see her if you wish."

"I'd rather talk to her where she's more comfortable," Constance said. "And no, you don't need to come. You should go and talk to your husband."

That was rather pointed. There was a definite atmosphere of tension between the Maules, relaxing only when the children were present.

Together, Solomon and Constance went down to the kitchen. Bingham, seated very straight at the kitchen table consuming a cup of tea, looked both nervous and defiant. The Willows servants were clearly curious, as though they suspected her of applying for a position with Constance.

For a moment, Constance contemplated a well-spoken, obedient maid, and realized she would miss Janey, if or when the girl ever moved on to a more respectable mistress.

"May we use your sitting room?" she asked the housekeeper pleasantly.

"Of course, madam." Mrs. Haslett even showed them inside and closed the door without as much as a sniff of criticism.

"We're sorry to drag you over here to talk," Constance began. "But we thought it might be easier without the other servants or the family at the Grange interrupting."

"That's what Mr. John said, and I don't mind. There's nothing to do back there anyway, since they won't let me box up Miss Frances's clothes and things. I'm serving out my notice doing nothing but writing to apply for new positions."

"I can imagine it must be difficult for you. Sit down. Did Mr. Niall tell you that we really need you to be honest with us? Not that I believe you have been *dis*honest previously," Constance added hastily, "but you are naturally loyal to your late mistress and her family. The trouble is, other people's lives could be ruined or even lost without the truth. And I believe I can say that we will see you lose nothing by it. If Colonel Niall denies you a character—which I doubt he will—Lady Maule will give you one instead."

"I've never worked for Lady Maule," Bingham said flatly.

"Then we shall see that you do. Should it become necessary. As things stand, it is Lady Maule who is being accused, quite unfairly, of harming your mistress."

"I know," Bingham said. "And I told you yesterday, I don't hold with that. It's the colonel's grief talking, but it still damages her ladyship."

"Exactly," Constance said. "So…we have learned some things about Miss Niall since we last spoke. Things that might mean she had made enemies."

Bingham looked down at her fingers twisting together in her lap and seemed to still them deliberately, but she said nothing. She had not, after all, been asked a question.

"I asked you yesterday, but please tell me truthfully, was Miss Niall a kind mistress?"

Bingham drew in her breath, then slowly shook her head. "She could be," she said. "When she was in a good mood, she could make me laugh and be kind as anything. Then she'd turn in an instant and slap me. Weren't a tap, neither. She knocked me down once."

"Why?" Solomon asked.

"No idea. I'd interrupted her, she *said*. If you ask me, it was never anything to do with what I did, just how she was feeling."

"And yet you stayed with her," Constance pointed out. "For how long?"

"About six months. Since she came back from India. It looks

bad if you change positions too often, and then employers won't trust you."

"Is that the only reason you stayed?" Constance asked. "Did you look for other positions?"

"No," Bingham admitted. Constance did not speak further. The maid shifted uncomfortably in the silence. "I told you why. I can't tell you more."

"Can't or won't?" Constance asked.

"Both," Bingham said, glaring at her.

"How did you obtain the position with Miss Niall?" Solomon asked. "Did you answer an advertisement?"

"No, I was with an agency in London. They put me forward. Colonel Niall interviewed me and said I would do. Miss Frances deigned to approve."

"Perhaps you would give me the name and address of that agency? Since I am going up to London today."

Bingham began to look hunted.

"Doesn't it exist?" Solomon asked.

"Of course it does!" she said indignantly. "They put me forward for the position, just like I said. They know—" She broke off, biting her lip. "It's just as I said."

Constance leaned forward. "Look, we are not interested in your past, except insofar as it touches on the death of Miss Niall. Anything else you say will be treated in confidence."

"Yes, but what if you decide it gives me a reason to have killed her?" Bingham demanded. "If they can accuse Lady Maule, they can certainly arrest *me*, however innocent I am!"

"Why?" Constance asked. "What reason did you have, except that she was capricious and occasionally unkind?"

Bingham looked from her to Solomon, then closed her eyes. "I'm damned whatever I say. Look, she *made* me stay with her. If I tried to leave, she said she'd tell everyone about the reason I left my old place. Not because she liked me—because she didn't—but because she liked the power. She liked to be in control of people."

At last. Constance cast Solomon a warning glance before she asked gently, "And what was the reason you left your last employment?"

"I lost my old place because I was accused of stealing and dismissed." Bingham glared with fresh defiance. "The old bat even admitted she was wrong, once she found the stupid ring I was meant to have stolen. Even offered me my place back, but I wouldn't go. She gave me a character instead. The agency knows all this, and Miss Niall must have got it out of them. Because if ever I displeased her, she'd point out how easy it would be to get me thrown out again without a character. And who'd believe in *two* such mistakes?"

Constance sat back in her chair, frowning. "I think...mere power might not have been Miss Niall's only motive. You knew her secrets, didn't you? How often she left the house clandestinely, what she had been up to away from home, who gave her presents. She had to keep you with her in case you ruined her reputation more effectively than she could ruin yours."

Bingham's eyes widened. "Do you think so?"

"Don't you?"

It was clear she hadn't considered matters from this angle, which at least said something for her character. "Perhaps..."

"Do you know who gave her the silver bracelet with the diamond at its center?"

Bingham frowned. "I don't think I ever saw that one."

"Did you know she had a number of such items hidden at the back of the bottom drawer in her sitting room desk?"

"Yes, but I never looked. I'd have been well slapped."

"Did she have a lover?" Constance asked.

Bingham hesitated, then nodded. "Yes, I think so."

"Who?" Solomon asked when Constance hesitated. She was too afraid, for Elizabeth's sake, of what the maid would say.

"I don't know," Bingham said. "She hinted it was Sir Humphrey Maule, which makes me think he was the one man it wasn't."

"We heard a rumor about the head groom at the Grange," Constance said.

Bingham grimaced. "Lance Godden? Could have been. He's handsome enough, and full enough of himself to risk it. She was kind of flirtatious with him. Never found any straw on her clothes, though."

"What did you find on her clothes?" Solomon interjected. "That was...unusual?"

Unexpectedly, Bingham blushed. "A funny smell sometimes. When she come home from one of her...walks."

Constance again met Solomon's gaze briefly. "When did she go for these walks? During the afternoon? Evening? Early morning."

"It varied."

"But she didn't tell you where she was going, or who she was meeting?"

"Course not. She just told me to keep quiet or say she was visiting the sick or something equally unlikely. Sometimes she took me with her and sent *me* to visit the sick on her behalf while she swanned off on her own."

Constance widened her eyes. "Like when she took you with her to see Lady Maule the night she died. And then sent you home. Do you think she went to see a lover after leaving Lady Maule?"

"I do," Bingham said with odd reluctance. "And it would explain the nightgown."

"About the nightgown," Constance said. "Did you recognize it? The one they brought her body home in?"

Bingham nodded. "I did. But I hadn't seen it for some time."

"When was the last time you saw it?"

"About two or three months ago."

"Did you ask her about it?"

Bingham regarded her with irritation. "Of course I didn't."

"So was it common for her to disappear all night on one of her—er...walks?" Solomon asked.

"It wasn't unheard of."

"Did she always head off in the same direction?"

"Not that I noticed. I didn't want to know. I wanted out of that house."

"And you were trapped," Constance said.

Solomon turned his head and looked at her thoughtfully, as if comparing her own situation to the maid's. He probably wanted to believe that Constance too was trapped in the life she led, but he knew too that she had the means to leave it. She merely lacked the desire to do so. That was what he couldn't understand.

But another thought clearly struck him, directing his attention back to Bingham. "What happened to the maid who looked after Miss Frances before she went to India? Did she go with them? Do you know?"

"Mr. Worcester says she were let go with most of the other servants when they left England."

"Did she mention a maid in India to you?"

"She made fun of the way the servant girls there talked. I don't know if she was imitating her personal maid. She mentioned an older woman, too. I didn't know if she was servant or companion. Or guard."

Constance pounced. "Why would they guard her?"

"Look, I don't want to gossip, but it strikes me that they left so suddenly before some scandal broke over her head. I think her father took her away to teach her discipline."

"But it didn't work?"

"Not once she came home again."

"Who do you *think* her lover was?" Constance asked. Then, as the maid began to look outraged, she added quickly, "I'm not looking for gossip, but we need to know, and in many ways, you knew her better than anyone else."

"Hmmm. Well, I doubt it was Lance in the stables. She might have teased him a bit, just for the fun of it, but I think she'd have gone for someone more refined. Like Sir Humphrey, if you want the truth. She wanted him before, so they say, and she was always interested in any word of him. Took special care in dressing when he was invited or when they went to The Willows."

"And if Sir Humphrey would not play?" Constance asked, hiding any dismay very creditably.

"The vicar's son's a handsome man. So's young Mr. Darby over at Shelton Hall."

Darby. The name of the Nialls' relations who had held a ball to welcome the family home from India.

"Shelton Hall? That's ten miles away, isn't it?" Solomon said.

"Not impossible for a young man."

"Did she get many letters from this Mr. Darby?"

"A few," Bingham said. "They were given to me by a message boy and I had to give them directly into her hand. Which I did."

"I don't suppose you read any of them first?" Solomon asked without obvious hope.

"God, no. Nor any of hers to him, though to be fair, I think she only wrote him the one. Unless she had poor old Mr. Worcester doing her bidding too."

"Is that likely?"

"Course it is. She had him wrapped round her little finger. He'd do anything for her."

"Had there been a recent letter from or to this Mr. Darby when she died?"

Bingham thought. "Couple of days before, maybe. She laughed when she read it."

"Did she say why it was funny?"

"No."

"But she might have gone to meet him when she left Lady Maule on the evening she died? Can you think of anywhere nearby they might have met? It would have to be somewhere discreet."

"I've no idea. I'm from London and I don't know the area."

"Fair enough," Solomon said. "Is there anything else, however insignificant it might seem, that you can tell us about Miss Niall and the night she died?"

Bingham shook her head. "Not that I can think of."

"Well, thank you for coming over here," Constance said.

"You have given us much to think about. Oh, and thank Mr. Niall for allowing you to come."

"I will. He's a decent gent. Doesn't deserve a sister like her."

"Well," Solomon murmured, as Bingham retreated to the kitchen to say farewell to the staff there, "he doesn't have her anymore."

"I THOUGHT YOU didn't like the railway," Constance said as they strolled outside to await Sir Humphrey's carriage, which had been ordered first thing to take Solomon to the railway station.

"I don't like being dependent on my hosts for transport *to* the railway while I'm trapped in their house. I never denied it was the quickest way to travel. Should you go alone to call on this Darby?"

"Elizabeth is coming with me, and he has a wife who is the Niall connection."

The plan was to take Solomon to the nearest railway station, then drive on to the Darbys' residence, Shelton Hall, where Constance would endeavor to ask questions that might reveal whether or not Mr. Darby had been Frances's lover. After that, she hoped to speak to Fairfield stable's Lothario, Lance Godden. Though how one asked a groom if he had been rolling in the hay with the daughter of the house, she hadn't quite worked out.

"How long will you be gone?" she asked.

"I should be back tomorrow. Just when tomorrow depends on whether I can see Dunne tonight or if I have to wait for the morning." He looked at her so carefully that she guessed he was hiding unease. "You will be careful? Don't go riling possible murderers."

She patted her jacket pocket. "Don't worry. I still have my own protection."

This did not appear to comfort him. "Yes, well, I don't want to have to spring you from a murder charge either."

"I wonder how I managed all these years without you."

"So do I."

Fortunately, Elizabeth emerged from the front door to join them, and the carriage and horses were rumbling around from the stables, so Constance didn't have to think of a response.

The perfect gentleman as always, Solomon handed both ladies into the carriage and joined them with his back to the horses.

"It's really very good of you to do all this running about the country on my behalf," Elizabeth said, a shade nervously. "What is it you hope to learn in London?"

"Something Frances seems to have been investigating," Solomon replied. They had agreed not to worry Elizabeth with this until they were sure of the facts. "I expect it's unimportant, but I should make sure."

"We shall miss you," Elizabeth said with a warm smile that seemed to surprise Solomon. It caused a strange, unspecific pain in Constance that he regarded his value to others only according to his usefulness. He probably had more friends than he was ever aware of.

At the railway station, he climbed down, bade them a casual good morning, and, with a tip of his hat, sauntered off to buy his ticket.

"What a very *obliging* man," Elizabeth remarked as the horses set off again. "Are you sure you are only friends?"

"Yes," Constance said. She wondered if she sounded disappointed. "My profession would always stand in the way of anything else. Supposing either of us were interested."

"But it doesn't stand in the way of friendship," Elizabeth pointed out.

Constance met her gaze. "You didn't tell Sir Humphrey about all your past, did you?"

Elizabeth's eyes fell. She shook her head. "I told him about the baby, and how you took me in. I...omitted the bit in the middle. As you say, some truths would always come between us."

Considering what Frances had told Humphrey, and the marital tensions that now existed, they had already come between them. But at least she could put Elizabeth's mind to rest on one subject.

"Frances lied. About being pregnant, at the very least."

Elizabeth caught her breath. "There was no baby?"

"No. And I'm equally sure there was no affair. Where on earth would he have found the time, apart from anything else? He loves you, Elizabeth. And I believe he is an honorable man."

Tears sprang to Elizabeth's eyes. "He deserves better than me."

"No," Constance said fiercely. "You've never changed who you are. You were always a good woman, and you still are."

Elizabeth grasped her hand and squeezed. "So are you, Constance. If only people knew…"

"Oh, I rather like being outrageous," Constance said lightly. "Though it amuses me to play the respectable lady. I'm becoming quite adept at it, don't you think?"

Elizabeth smiled. "Very adept."

"So tell me about the Darbys. Mr. Darby in particular…"

CHAPTER TEN

L EIGHTON DARBY WAS a man who had everything. Unlike most privileged people, he was well aware of his good fortune and excessively pleased by it. Born into a family of ancient lineage and considerable wealth, he had increased his personal riches considerably by his judicious marriage to the heiress, Annabelle Niall.

Annabelle was one of those glacial, very English beauties, though she doted on Darby. He rather suspected they both regarded the other as some kind of trophy to flaunt in public. Which suited him quite well, for it meant he could do more or less as he liked in private.

He was the proud possessor of several houses, though this one, Shelton Hall, had become his favorite. Handsome and gracious, it stood in a delightful park, surrounded by excellent woodland for hunting and shooting. He held excellent parties there, where his wife was the perfect hostess and he generally had the pick of his friends' wives. And daughters.

Oh yes, Darby was a happy man.

He was even happier when he was informed that Lady Maule and her friend had called on his wife, who had requested his company in the drawing room. Darby, happy to oblige—for Lady Maule was a taking little thing with a positive bear of a husband—hurried to obey his lady's summons.

No doubt there would be some lovely gossip, too, for his wife's cousin Frances Niall—*distant* cousin, as he assured his many friends—had been fished dead out of Maule's lake. Foul play was suspected. People remembered only too well that Maule had once been expected to marry poor Frances.

Even now, the memory of her made him smile.

He was still smiling when he walked into the drawing room. His gaze went straight to the delightful Lady Maule, but it was the other visitor who deprived him of breath.

She was so stunning, he didn't catch her name at first, merely prowled toward her before he managed to recall his manners and bow over her ladyship's hand. "Lady Maule, always a pleasure."

She withdrew her hand with modest decorum. "My good friend Mrs. Grey, who is staying with us at The Willows for a little."

Mrs. Grey's smile was dazzling, and her mouth... Desire tore through him. He had to have her.

Fortunately, he retained enough sense to behave with civility, although when he ferried tea from his wife to the other ladies, he made sure his fingers touched Mrs. Grey's soft, slender hand. He wanted to growl.

Apparently undisturbed, Mrs. Grey met his gaze boldly, with a murmur of thanks, and looked beyond him to continue her conversation with Annabelle.

Darby collected his own tea and sat beside his wife, from where he did his best to catch Mrs. Grey's eye.

"We came really to pay our condolences for the loss of your poor cousin," Lady Maule said. "Such a sad and shocking loss. All the more so for us, since she was found in our lake."

At last Mrs. Grey's eyes met his.

"Yes, it has been shock for all of us who knew her," Annabelle said. "Has it not, Leighton?"

"A most terrible shock," he managed, while retaining Mrs. Grey's gaze. "She was still so young and vital, a sad loss to all her family and friends. Annabelle and I are devastated."

Mrs. Grey released his gaze and turned her own upon Annabelle. "Of course, I never had the pleasure of meeting Miss Niall, but I do offer my sincere sympathies. And those of my husband. Were you and Miss Niall close friends?"

"We were most cordial," Annabelle said. "Although she was several years younger than I, so we were never terribly close. Sadly, we never will be now."

Lady Maule said, "You must take comfort in your own kindness to her and her family on their return to India. The evening of your ball was so enjoyable. Frances spoke of it often to me."

Darby almost smiled again as he remembered that night. But he had fresh fish to fry now in the delectable person of Mrs. Grey.

"Thank you," Annabelle said. "I shall remember her as she was that night."

"As shall I," Darby said piously. Mrs. Grey's eyes were upon him once more, large, mysterious eyes of alluring beauty. He would wager everything he had that she knew well how to please a man.

"It is even more shocking," she said sadly, "that detectives from London are now investigating her death as murder."

"I had heard something of the sort," Annabelle said. "In fact, they called here just the other day. Leighton sent them away very sharply, I can tell you."

"Why?" Mrs. Grey asked unexpectedly.

Annabelle blinked. "We can't have *policemen* in our house, asking impertinent questions, implying we somehow know things about poor Frances's death."

"I'm afraid you have Colonel Niall to thank for that," Mrs. Grey said. "It was on his account that Sir Humphrey asked for Scotland Yard's help. After the colonel's accusations against Elizabeth, Sir Humphrey could not be considered impartial in his investigations."

"We have to apologize for our cousin's baseless claims," Darby said quickly. "Poor old fellow is in pieces after his daughter's death. Quite knocked him for a loop, did it not, Annabelle?"

"Quite," Annabelle agreed, as she always did. "And I cannot

think much of the officers they sent. Common little men who know nothing about respectable people."

"Did they ask you if Frances had any enemies?" Mrs. Grey asked.

"They did! Leighton told them in no uncertain terms that of course she did not. They then began to imply that poor Frances was no better than she should be, going off for assignations behind her father's back! I mean, how dare they? The night she died, she went to see *you*, Lady Maule, which is hardly an assignation."

"No, but she left me and never got as far as home. Somewhere between our lake and Fairfield Grange, she died. Before someone put her body in the lake. We think," Lady Maule finished almost apologetically.

They batted the subject around a little more, but Darby barely listened. It didn't matter what Mrs. Grey said—it was the movement of her luscious mouth that held his attention.

When, after the polite half-hour of a morning call, the ladies stood to depart, Darby rose with them. So did Annabelle.

"Allow us to see to your carriage," she said, taking Lady Maule's arm, bless her. She was, he supposed, making up for her cousin the colonel's ridiculous accusations against the woman by showing her personal support.

Which worked very well for Darby himself, who had no choice but to walk with the delectable Mrs. Grey. She even took his proffered arm on the stairs. And while they waited on the front terrace for the carriage to be brought round, she displayed no objection to moving a few more steps away from his wife, who was enjoying a serious tête-à-tête with Lady Maule.

"I feel so bad for Elizabeth with such a vile accusation hanging over her," Mrs. Grey said. "Is there anything you can tell me that would help her?"

Darby tried to look sympathetic. "Such as what?"

"Oh, I don't know. How well did you know Miss Niall, sir?"

He almost laughed at his own wit as he said seriously, "As

well as any man who admires a beautiful woman."

"I see," Mrs. Grey murmured, and just for an instant he had the uneasy feeling that she did. Her eyes were damned perceptive as well as mysterious. He would have to step more carefully.

"Believe me, I am at *your* feet. Nothing compares to my first sight of you," he said. "I have never laid eyes on a woman more beautiful. Please tell me I may see you again."

God, that smile, at once enticing, knowing, and veiled...

"You know where I am. Should you have information to impart that your wife might not understand."

He wasn't quite sure what she meant by that, but it was far from a no. "What of Mr. Grey? There *is* still a Mr. Grey?"

"Very much so." She smiled dazzlingly. "He is on his way to London. I expect you danced with her at your ball."

"Who?" he asked, gazing into her eyes. "Oh, Frances? Yes, I did, of course."

She gave a teasing slap to his wrist. "Did you flirt with her, Mr. Darby?"

"Of course I did. Frances loved to flirt."

"Did you perhaps give her a secret gift? A bracelet?" she asked.

"Never," he said, amused, wondering if she was jealous or merely grasping for gifts of her own. "Actually, I think India changed her."

"What gives you that impression?"

"Well, she flirted at the ball, probably for old times' sake, but never after that. Or, at least, not with me."

"Are we still talking about mere flirting, sir?"

He allowed her to see the strength of his desire. "I am a man of deep passions, madam. Yet neither Frances nor anyone else has ever affected me as you do." The horses were trotting briskly onto the terrace. He had only a moment more. "We will meet again, very soon. I have to believe you feel something too, even if only a pale reflection of my own—"

"Goodbye, Mr. Darby," she interrupted with a smile and a

curtsey. Just as well, for Annabelle and Lady Maule were almost upon them. "It was a pleasure to meet you. And you, Mrs. Darby. Thank you for your kind hospitality."

Darby made a fuss about handing both ladies into their carriage and closed the door. Standing back beside Annabelle, he watched them drive away, fresh fire in his belly.

⇉⇉✖⇇⇇

"WHAT A REVOLTING man," Constance said.

"Mr. Darby?" Elizabeth said in surprise. "Well, he is very flirtatious, certainly, but quite open and charming about it."

Constance raised an eyebrow. "Because he behaves so in front of his wife? Do *you* find him charming?"

"No," Elizabeth admitted, "but I have Humph. And you know, you did flirt back just a little. *You* can't help it either."

For some reason, this observation annoyed Constance. "It is the only way a man like that will speak to women. Please don't tell me how alike we are, or I shall be sick. He more or less admitted to having been more intimate with Frances than he should, but then implied this had ended when she came back from India, apart from one encounter at the Shelton Hall ball."

Elizabeth's mouth fell open. "You got him to tell you that in so short a time?"

"He wanted me to know how in demand he is, such a very dashing man about town." Something had begun to curl and cringe inside Constance. Was that how she appeared to Solomon? A female equivalent of Darby? Only more disgusting because she took money for it? She liked to think she was honest, but to a decent man was she simply repellant? Why in God's name was he friends with her?

Focus, idiot. "Tell me about the ball. Darby said he danced with Frances. How did she behave that night?"

"She was lively and fun, as I recall. Very popular with both the gentlemen and the ladies. But then, she and her family were the guests of honor. She never overstepped the mark, if that's what you mean." Elizabeth frowned. "At least, not in public."

"Go on."

"She did vanish for a little while, for I remember John looking for her. Then she reappeared with some tale of a torn hem and an emergency repair. Something that could easily happen."

"Did Darby—er...vanish at about the same time?"

Elizabeth thought about it. "I...don't know. He might have. He was a very genial host, flitting from group to group, playing cards, smoking cigars on the terrace, and dancing, of course. He danced with me, too, and was perfectly well behaved. Oh, Constance, are you saying you think the baby was Darby's?"

"There *was* no baby, Elizabeth. The doctors would have found it during the autopsy."

"Perhaps they decided not to tell. To save Colonel Niall worse distress."

"It's possible," Constance admitted. "But I saw Dr. Murray's face when the subject came up. He was shocked."

"It's a very odd thing to lie about."

"Not if your aim is to wreck a marriage."

"But Humphrey would *never* have married Frances. Not even if he divorced me. Not even if I died."

"I suspect she would have found a way to force him, if that were what she truly wanted. But she might have been merely punishing him. I think she had another interest, one she was actually able to indulge in the present. Another lover she met in secret." Who probably gave her a silver bracelet with a diamond at its center.

"Darby?"

"I doubt it. I have the feeling whatever their relationship in the past, it was over for Frances. Though perhaps Darby did not take his congé well. Or she threatened to tell his wife about their past affair. From what she said to you and Humphrey, this would be quite in character for her."

Just for a moment, Constance had forgotten she was not talking to Solomon.

Elizabeth was staring at her. "What did she say to Humphrey?"

Damnation. "Oh, vague slanders against you that he didn't believe for a moment."

"Constance!"

Constance sighed and gave in. "That in London, before you came to The Willows as governess, you were a street whore."

"Oh, dear God." She buried her face in her hands. "Constance, how could she know? How could she have found out?"

"She didn't," Constance said, grasping both her hands. "She was spreading lies, like the nonsense about her own child. There is no way she could ever have found out about your past. She was in India."

Although, would this firm of L. Dunne, who had told Frances about the baby, have told her other things, too? Could *they* have found out? If Frances had judged it more damaging than the baby story, it could explain why she hadn't used that to upset Humphrey.

What other terrible information would John Niall find among his sister's documents? Constance wished she'd taken them all last night.

"No wonder he is so cold to me," Elizabeth whispered.

"Is he?" Constance asked, her heart aching for her friend.

"He tries not to be. And I have not helped, afraid Frances told the truth about carrying his child."

"Maybe you should tell him the whole truth."

"And bear his contempt, his disgust? I would rather die."

"Oh, Elizabeth," Constance said helplessly.

Frances was dead, but her damage lived on. Who else was suffering from it? And would the truth of her death change that?

LEAVING ELIZABETH PLAYING with the children at The Willows, Constance walked up to the Grange and followed the path to the stables.

Although Colonel Niall seemed to have locked himself up in the house with his grief, his stables appeared to be run still with military efficiency. He had a number of handsome, well-cared-for horses, one of which was being groomed in the yard. The others poked their heads over the stable doors, no doubt hopeful of a gallop with whoever approached.

"What a lovely animal," said Constance, who knew very little about horses, pausing to stroke the nose of the horse being groomed.

"That he is, ma'am," the groom agreed, regarding her with curiosity. "Can I help you?"

"Mr. Niall said I might come and see the horses," Constance lied, "since I miss my own so much. I should speak to the head groom, should I not? Godden, is it?"

"Lance!" the groom called, and a tall, handsome fellow in an unexpectedly white shirt and leather waistcoat swaggered out from the stable building.

Constance felt a ripple of excitement—not because of the man's undeniable physical attractions, but because she recognized that he might well have appealed to the dead woman she was beginning to understand. He was strong and dark and confident in his body. And he was undoubtedly forbidden fruit in a way even a married man of her own class was not.

Constance went to meet him. "You are Godden, the head groom?" she said. "I'm Mrs. Grey, a guest of Lady Maule over at The Willows. Mr. Niall says you would tell me about the horses here and which might make a suitable lady's mount."

"Did he?" Godden looked amused, his roving eye definitely roving. "He never mentioned any such thing to me."

"I expect he forgot," Constance said.

"I expect he did." The man's eyes were positively gleaming now with the knowledge that Constance had sought him out with such a feeble excuse. He probably imagined she had glimpsed him from a distance and fallen into instant lust. Time to disabuse him of that notion.

"He has a lot on his mind just now, poor man," she said. "Which is the real reason I wish to speak to you. Walk with me."

His expression changed as he recognized her tone of authority. Obediently, he walked beside her back toward the stable doors. Listening, Constance could hear no signs of activity within, except the horses themselves shifting on their feet. At the far end, from where Godden had emerged, she could hear voices—the other grooms enjoying a well-deserved break from their duties. Good. She would not be overheard.

She paused to pet the nose of the first horse.

"Careful," Godden said. "She'll nudge you so hard for apples that she'll knock you over."

Constance, who had come prepared, drew a quarter of an apple from her pocket and let the mare take it from her palm while she kept her gaze on the head groom. "Tell me about Miss Frances."

"Nothing to tell," Godden said stolidly. "Which I already told the police."

"What did they ask you?"

"If I ever accompanied her when she rode out."

"Did you?"

"Once or twice. I told them that too."

"Where did she go?"

Godden shrugged. "Different places. She wasn't much interested in scenery or in horses, truth to tell. Just liked the fresh air."

"Did she ever meet anyone when she was out?"

Godden sighed. "Perhaps I can save you some time, ma'am. She never went on any assignations, never rode to The Willows, or met Sir Humphrey nor anyone else outside. At least, not while I was with her."

"Is that what the police inspector asked you?"

"And what I told him. Which is the truth."

"I'm very glad to hear it," Constance said honestly. With luck, it had deflected the detectives away from suspicion of Elizabeth. She moved on to the next horse, offering another piece of apple. "And when you rode out with her, did she always behave as a lady ought?"

"Of course."

Constance blinked as though surprised. "You mean she never flirted? Not even with a handsome fellow like yourself?"

His smile was a little crooked. "Well, if she did, she did no more."

"Should I believe you?" Constance asked.

"Yes, for I won't deny I was disappointed. I only applied for the job because Josh Rennie—who used to be head groom here before the family went to India—told me I'd be in luck with her. But I never was. Her eyes promised, but she never gave an inch. And if you repeat a word of that, I'll deny I spoke to you about anything save horses. Not that Mr. John will ask, will he? Because he never sent you down here in the first place."

"No, that is true. But I needed the answers to a few questions, and I believe you just gave me them. Thank you." She turned away, then back again. "Oh, one more thing. I don't suppose you ever gave her a present? Perhaps in the hope of favor?"

Godden stared at her. "What could I give someone like her? Beyond the obvious," he added crudely.

"The night she died," Constance said, changing tack, "did you see her return from The Willows? Did she come by the stables?"

"No. The police inspector asked me that, too."

"And you didn't happen to see her going anywhere else?"

"No," Godden said with exaggerated patience.

He answered immediately, with no pause for over-careful thought. It sounded like the truth. She was about to give up when another thought struck her.

"Why did Rennie leave his post as head groom?"

Godden shrugged. "They were all let go when the colonel went to India. Only a steward for the land, old Worcester, and a maid were left behind to keep the house. The horses went to India, too."

"Yes, but why didn't Rennie reapply? If he found his position so...rewarding?"

"Got a better place, I reckon."

"Do you know where?"

Godden stared at her. "No."

"Never mind. I'll ask Worcester. Thank you, Godden." She swept regally away as though she had every right to be there.

CHAPTER ELEVEN

S OLOMON ARRIVED IN London feeling as if every bone in his body had been well rattled. Still, he rather enjoyed the exhilaration of speed and found himself unwilling to face the frustration of a hackney inching its way through the traffic between London Bridge Station and Dunne's offices in the city. He walked.

Dunne and Sons was a respected firm of solicitors, with a special department for private inquiries, which was managed by the eldest son of the founder. Another son was a senior partner in the firm, yet another a barrister. But it was the eldest son Solomon asked for, and within ten minutes he found himself in that gentleman's private office, drinking a very decent cup of tea and munching on a spicy biscuit.

"So, what can I do for you today?" Mr. Dunne inquired.

Solomon swallowed the last of his biscuit and fished out the purloined letter signed by Dunne's underling.

The lawyer read it, his eyebrows flying up. "Might I ask how this came into your possession?"

"It was discovered among the effects of a lady recently deceased."

"Miss Niall, in effect," Dunne guessed. His eyes were still not friendly, although he remained polite. "May I know what your interest in the matter is?"

"I am trying to help a friend who has been accused of involvement in Miss Niall's death. What I would like to know is why one of your employees is sending private information to Miss Niall."

A hint of confusion flickered in Dunne's eyes and was veiled. "Because she asked for it, of course."

"For such specific and delicate information concerning someone else?" Solomon retorted, not troubling to hide his disappointment.

Dunne frowned. "I'm afraid I don't understand you."

The truth dawned on Solomon. "She pretended the child you traced was hers!"

"Mr. Grey, though it is no business of yours, and I tell you only to preserve the integrity of my firm, the child *was* hers. There is no doubt about that."

RELUCTANT TO FACE either Colonel Niall or his son, Constance took the easier route and knocked on the kitchen door.

"Bless you, ma'am, what you coming in this way for?" demanded the flustered kitchen maid, opening the door wide to let her in.

"Oh, I didn't want to disturb the family," Constance said. "Would you please ask Mr. Worcester if he could spare me a few minutes of his time?"

While the girl scuttled off, Constance caught the resentful stares of the other servants. They didn't like their own space being invaded, especially with no notice, and not even by family, but by a friend of a friend of the family. If the Maules were still accounted friends. Had Frances really wanted to cause this much damage? Or had she just not cared very much?

The maid came back and took Constance to the butler's pantry.

Constance waited until the door closed and the girl's footsteps faded back across the kitchen floor. The butler stood impassively before her, waiting to learn her business.

"I'm sorry to disturb you again, Worcester, but I'm afraid I have to. And I have to speak of things that I'm sure will cause you pain."

"*You* may have to, ma'am," he said firmly. "*I* do not."

Uh-oh. "Then I hope you will choose to," she said steadily. "Because the more I learn of Miss Frances, the more I think she was not only a dangerous person, but putting herself in danger, too. She found unique ways of manipulating people, did she not? Of getting them to do her bidding."

He inclined his head but said nothing. Nor did he invite her to sit, and somehow, in his private space, she didn't quite like to without invitation.

"May I know," she said as delicately as she could, "what hold she had over you?"

"What makes you think she had any?"

"The fact that she no longer troubled to sneak out of the house. She knew you would see her. I daresay you opened the front door for her on many occasions. And yet you never told the colonel."

"I couldn't. It would have broken his heart all over again."

"He might have stopped her." She didn't want to say the rest. *She might not have died.*

But it seemed he had already thought of that, for he closed his eyes in clear pain. "Don't, ma'am. I know what I've done, and I doubt the colonel can bear much more."

"Did she threaten you with some discredit?"

"Not me so much as my father. He got into trouble once, when he was young. He's been a good man ever since, but she threatened to have him arrested again, and I don't doubt she would and could have done so."

"If you hadn't kept quiet about her little expeditions?"

He nodded miserably.

"Worcester, this is the heart of the matter. To discover who hurt her, I need to know where she went, whom she was seeing."

"She never told me that," he said. "It would have given me something to hold over her and get myself free."

Damn her, Frances had been good at the dreadful games she played. "Then you have no idea? Not even a guess by how long she was gone at a time?"

"Sometimes she went out in the afternoon and didn't come home until morning. Other times, she was gone a bare half-hour. There was no consistency in her movements."

"Did you see what direction she took?" Constance asked without much hope.

"Different directions."

"But she didn't ride, did she?"

"No, she usually walked."

"I don't suppose you ever intercepted notes addressed to her? Or from her to someone else?"

"No." He didn't say that Bingham had been responsible for ferrying them, though he probably knew. In his own way, he was trying to protect the girl. It seemed they all needed protecting in this house. Even Frances, who must have gone too far in the end for someone…

"*All over again,*" Constance said suddenly, staring at the butler.

"I beg your pardon, madam?"

"You said, *It would have broken his heart all over again.* When was the colonel's heart broken by her the first time?"

"When she died, of course."

"Oh no," Constance insisted. "You were talking about before she died. Worcester, we need the truth before we can end all of this."

Without permission, Worcester sank onto the chair by his desk, as if his legs would no longer bear his weight.

"It's not my place to say. Family secrets should remain in the family."

"Not if an innocent woman is hanged to keep them. Not even if only her reputation is spoiled, which would be to the severe detriment of herself, her husband, and her children."

The poor man looked even more miserable. Constance felt unspeakably sorry for him. After all, he was still trying to do the right thing. Frances had left him very little room to do so.

Something seemed to shift in her head, and a piece of the puzzle fell into place.

She could have saved Solomon a journey if only her brain moved faster.

"I believe I can guess," she said slowly. "All you need to do is nod. I should have suspected from the suddenness of the colonel's decision to whisk everyone off to India. Only, it wasn't everyone, was it? John was sent to school in England. His father and sister didn't go directly to India either, did they? They stopped off somewhere no one knew them while Frances gave birth to her illegitimate child."

There was a pause. Very slowly, he nodded.

Frances had not been looking for scandal in Elizabeth's past. She had been looking for her own baby, no doubt taken from her and put up for adoption, as Elizabeth's had been. And like Elizabeth, she had hurt for the loss. Was that the source of the change several people had noted since her return from India?

A resurgence of pity filled Constance. Despite the fact that the girl had still behaved unforgivably to Elizabeth and Humphrey after that.

"Who was the baby's father?" she asked quietly.

"I don't know."

She held Worcester's gaze. "Mr. Darby?"

He gazed back.

"Rennie, the old head groom?"

Still he said nothing.

"Worcester, this man might have *killed* her. However badly she behaved, no one had the right to do that to her. To her family. You have to tell me. Or the police will have to be involved." They might well have to be anyway, but she didn't want to think about that just yet.

"It could have been either of them," Worcester said hoarsely.

"She was running wild, driving her father demented. Rennie took liberties, but she also rode over to Shelton Hall a good deal more often than Mrs. Darby knew. It was Miss Frances's maid at the time who told me her mistress was with child. I had to tell the colonel, and arrangements were made at speed. All the servants were let go, so that any nasty rumors they spread would be taken as sour grapes and disbelieved. But in reality, the only people who knew—me and the maid—never said a word."

"Where is that maid now?"

"With a new mistress in London. She was given a glowing character. I believe she just wants to forget her time at the Grange. It wasn't happy for her."

"Did the father know about her pregnancy?" Constance asked urgently.

"I have no idea. But I doubt it."

Unless Frances cast it up when she came home again—another threat to hold over someone, whether for a practical reason or just to feel important. It could have been her death warrant.

Rennie had gone, but Darby was still here, and still married to a wife who thought he only flirted with other women.

More to the point, Sir Humphrey was still here, too. And he would not want his beloved Elizabeth to know he had fathered a child with Frances. Was that what Frances had meant when she'd told Elizabeth she was carrying Humphrey's baby? That she *had* carried it five years ago?

And found it again...

Constance drew a breath and rubbed her forehead. "Thank you, Worcester. I think."

CONSTANCE WISHED SOLOMON were here. As she walked back to The Willows, her brain seemed to be reeling with the huge discovery that Frances had given birth to a child five years ago, probably en route to India. Surely this information changed everything, and yet she wasn't sure how.

Who had known about the baby at the time? Colonel Niall, Worcester, the lady's maid who had left... Had Frances been examined by a doctor? Did Dr. Laing know? Constance rather doubted it. His view of Frances still seemed to be rose-tinted, and she doubted Colonel Niall would have let any local physician near his daughter after the maid's discovery.

But a subtly different version of Frances was emerging in Constance's mind. A curious, undisciplined girl, running wild and discovering forbidden pleasures—and, like many a curious girl before her, paying the price. Or at least some of it. She had probably imagined, in her naughty escapades, that she was taking control of her own life, doing exactly as she chose without interference. But pregnancy had ended that.

At last, Frances's father had stepped in and acted decisively. Unlike Elizabeth's parents, he had not thrown his daughter to the wolves. He had looked after her, overseen her confinement well away from prying eyes, and arranged for the adoption of the child.

Still, just like Elizabeth, Frances had lost her baby in the end. Elizabeth had chosen this path, for the good of the child, but had Frances? Weak, probably frightened, and with all a new mother's turbulent emotions, was she given any choice? Had that loss of control then contributed to the behavior of the woman who returned from India? Seeking power over everyone, not necessarily for any reason other than that she needed it?

It made a sort of tragic sense to Constance. Even the woman's deliberate nastiness to both Elizabeth and Humphrey was understandable if he were the father of her child, and he had paid no price at all, but gone on with his life and married someone else. To Frances, ironically, Elizabeth must have seemed a goody two-shoes, a perfectly behaved wife and stepmother. She had had no way of knowing that Elizabeth's past was even more shocking than her own, whatever tale she had chosen to tell Sir Humphrey.

Humphrey... Constance had to speak to him alone. How was that to be contrived without Elizabeth knowing and asking questions? Constance had advised her friend to tell her husband the whole truth. Maybe Humphrey needed to do the same.

Just past Mrs. Phelps's cottage, Constance became aware of Mrs. Phelps herself walking rapidly from the direction of the village, a basket over her arm.

"Good day, Mrs. Phelps."

The woman grunted. "Not looking for me, are you?"

"I wasn't, but I am happy to see you."

"Why?" Mrs. Phelps asked. "Been listening to rumors, have you?"

"Sometimes there's a trace of truth in rumors."

"Not in this one. I didn't poison the silly girl."

Constance blinked. "Frances Niall?"

"Who else is dead?" The old woman stumped on, though not before Constance had seen that her basket was full of herbs.

"Wait," she exclaimed, turning and catching up with the woman. "Who said Frances was poisoned, and why pick on you?"

Mrs. Phelps smiled sourly. "I'm the witch of the village now. And no one knows how she died. Blame me. What's more, I taught myself about herbs—cheaper than yon quack up the road—and there's some that leave no trace behind."

She marched on, leaving Constance staring after her. Eventually, she turned back toward The Willows.

She and Solomon had been getting bogged down in Frances's somewhat colorful life, looking for motive and forgetting about means. Everyone seemed to have reason to want rid of Frances, but how had she died? The doctors had found no trace of poison, but as Mrs. Phelps—and indeed the villagers, by the sound of things—were pointing out, not all poisons left a measurable trace.

She almost swung back yet again to seek out Dr. Laing or Dr. Murray, but she needed to straighten her thoughts first. She was still reeling from the discovery that Frances had borne a child that she was seeking—why was she doing that?—and now, poisons were filling her mind.

How on earth could Frances have been secretly poisoned without the rest of her household getting ill too?

Bingham...lacing her hot chocolate with venom? *Worcester*...contaminating her plate or her wine at dinner?

If Constance went down that road, then Elizabeth was again a possibility. They had drunk tea together, or something else before their walk beside the lake. She still didn't believe Elizabeth capable of such a thing, and certainly not before Frances had told her about carrying Humphrey's child. So thankfully, that theory made little sense.

Constance stopped in her tracks once more as another idea struck her.

Would Francis have poisoned *herself?* Overcome by the awfulness she had made of her life, alienating everyone who loved her, and having assured herself of her child's safety, had she decided to end it all?

Then the only crime was Frances's, and her family had a different cross to bear. As did, perhaps, the father of her child.

Impatiently, Constance marched on. This was all mere speculation. As far as fact was concerned, she had the lowering feeling that she knew as little as she had when she first received Elizabeth's plea for help.

"Where are you, Solomon?" she muttered aloud. "I need to talk to you *now*."

CONSTANCE CHANGED EARLY for dinner and went down to the drawing room immediately, in the hope of finding Sir Humphrey alone. Instead, she found Elizabeth, sitting tensely upright on the sofa, twisting her hands together in her lap.

Refusing to waste time, Constance sat down beside her and

said at once, "The night Frances died, did you and she drink tea or wine together?"

"We had a glass of wine. It made her company easier for me."

"Did you both drink it all?"

"I didn't," Elizabeth said, frowning. "I only had a few sips before she suggested we walk. I think she drank all of hers, though."

"Who poured the wine?"

"I did."

"From a fresh bottle?"

"No, it was one Humph and I had drunk from at dinner. It was in the decanter. Does it matter?"

"I doubt it. Did she seem ill, that she wanted fresh air? Did you see any sign of illness or distress of any kind as you walked?"

"None. In fact, she set off pretty briskly when we parted."

Constance was blundering in the dark here. She had no idea about poisonous herbs, or how long it took them to work, or what the symptoms might be. In any case, she was merely trying to prove, for the benefit of others, that Elizabeth could not have done it. And she was achieving nothing.

She sighed. "Elizabeth, do you think Frances was the kind of person who would ever take their own life?"

Elizabeth's jaw dropped. "No," she said emphatically.

"But she was not a happy person, was she? To behave as she did, say the things she did, she must have been terribly *un*happy."

"Perhaps." Elizabeth did not look convinced. "And I hardly think Colonel Niall would thank us for suggesting such a thing."

"No, you're probably right... Do you know anything about herbs?"

"For cooking?" Elizabeth asked, baffled by the change of subject.

"More for medicinal purposes."

"Not really. My mother preferred modern physicians to wise women where health was concerned. Although I have heard it said that wise women are less likely to kill you!"

Constance, who had witnessed the sickening results of so-called wise women's work in the back streets of London, did not believe that either.

"Do you think Frances had such knowledge?"

"If she did, she never spoke to me about it."

Constance hadn't truly expected such inquiries to bear much fruit. She was really just avoiding the other things she had to ask. There was a short silence, tense now on Constance's part, and then Sir Humphrey walked into the room, and she was unspeakably relieved that she had not asked. It was best—probably—that she approach the man himself.

Her moment did not come until after dinner, when Elizabeth had gone upstairs to see to the children. Sir Humphrey had chosen not to linger alone with his port, but had brought it with him to the drawing room to be sociable. In fact, it was he who brought up the subject that Constance had been studiously avoiding over dinner.

"How goes your investigation, Mrs. Grey? What is it your husband hopes to learn in London? Or has he truly gone there on business purposes?"

"No, he went on *your* business, following a letter we found among Frances's things. I suspect now he could have found the truth without going there, but at least it will be proof. May I ask you a private question, Sir Humphrey?"

A wary look entered his eyes. "If you must."

"I really think I must. When you were courting Frances five years ago—"

"*Thinking* of courting Frances," he corrected her.

"I beg your pardon. Whatever your thoughts, I need to ask you exactly how intimate you were with her at that time."

Color stained his cheeks. He tried to look haughty, but it was anger that chiefly showed. "Physically? You are asking if I took my neighbor's gently born, unmarried daughter to bed?"

"Or anywhere else," Constance said brazenly. "Were you physically intimate with her?"

"I most assuredly was not!" he exploded. "I am horrified that you need to ask. You may not think much of me, Mrs. Grey, but I am a man of honor, and had I overstepped the bounds of propriety in any way with Miss Niall, I should not have let her go to India but married her immediately. It would have been a terrible marriage, for both of us, but right is right!"

Constance sat back in her chair, metaphorically mopping her brow. *Thank God.* "I hoped you would say that. I apologize for asking. I'm afraid I have to further ignore good taste and ask if you ever heard rumors, either before or after the family went to India, about indiscretions on Miss Niall's part?"

"None," he said frigidly.

"Truly?"

He blinked. "I do not listen to gossip, Mrs. Grey. I advise you not to either."

"Often, it is the only way to learn anything. Take heart, Sir Humphrey—I rarely pass it on. Do you have any idea what the police are looking into?"

"Everything and nothing," he said, his scowl deepening. "They seem to have left off persecuting Elizabeth and are now annoying the villagers about anything and everything."

"Ah. That might explain an odd encounter I had with Mrs. Phelps this afternoon. She seemed to think the villagers were accusing *her*."

"It's always the way of it. In a crisis, a woman alone is an easy target. One of the viler aspects of human nature."

"But a perceptive one," Constance said, covering her surprise.

"To be honest, I think the police investigation is doomed. There is nothing to show how poor Frances died, or even if anyone is to blame. I suspect we will never know the truth."

"Does that bother you?"

"It bothers me that people might still look askance at Elizabeth. Even decent people like Colonel Niall."

"Why *does* he believe so fervently in Elizabeth's guilt? No one else seems to."

He was silent for a moment, sipping his port. "I suspect...because Frances did not like her. He feels he is his daughter's sole defender because, I suspect, by the time of her death, despite all her advantages of beauty and charm, no one else loved her. And that is sad."

In fact, it was so sad, it made Constance want to cry.

She swallowed hard. "Did you notice a difference in her after her return from India?"

"What sort of difference?"

"Anything, really. I suppose she was a little older, a little wiser. Was she calmer? More unhappy? Less flirtatious or lively?"

"Yes, I think she *was* outwardly calmer. I suppose she had grown up. Certainly, she was a little more circumspect in her behavior, but then, she was beyond the age when flirtatiousness can be put down to innocence. I thought she had grown kinder...until she said what she did about Elizabeth."

"You don't believe her," Constance said carefully. "And yet I think things are not quite right between you and Elizabeth."

He smiled with more than a hint of bitterness. "Ironic, is it not? That in death she finally comes between us."

"Only if you let her," Constance said, and smiled brightly toward the door as she heard Elizabeth's footsteps approaching across the hall.

FOR TWO NIGHTS Solomon had lain beside her, without touching her except by accident. She had imagined she could never sleep in such a situation, but to her astonishment, she had found only a unique comfort in his nearness. So much so that she had once wakened cuddled into his shoulder. She had taken her time to roll away from him, telling herself she didn't want to wake him with sudden movement.

This night, lying alone and staring into the darkness, she

missed him.

Not just that peculiar comfort, or the way they could discuss the mystery before them. But *him*. His very presence.

Constance wanted to explore that, for she was curious by nature. It was part of friendship and trust, of course, to sleep in someone else's presence. She had experienced that, but it had never been with a man before.

Am I falling seriously in love with Solomon?

She hoped not. It would be disastrous and could easily end the fragile friendship between them. The best she could hope for was that he missed her too.

Meanwhile, she tried to think of her next path of inquiry. She should talk to one of the doctors about poisons. She also still needed to find out who had been Frances's lover. Her last lover.

As she began to drift off to sleep, she jolted awake again. What if Frances had returned to the father of her child? Had he given her the silver bracelet? If so, he must be relatively well off, no servant or farm laborer. A well-to-do tenant farmer, perhaps. Or the vicar's son. She had not spoken to him yet...

Her dreams were troubled, full of threat and insult, but she woke more determined than ever to find out what had truly happened to Frances. This was no longer just for Elizabeth's sake. It was for Frances herself.

CHAPTER TWELVE

D ETERMINED TO FIND out something concrete before
Solomon returned, Constance took an early breakfast and
set off to call on Dr. Laing.

"Dr. Laing's at his breakfast, ma'am," the doctors' housekeeper told her at the door, "and Dr. Murray's out on calls. Beg
your pardon, but are you sick?"

"No, you might call it more of a social call," Constance said.

"One moment," the housekeeper said with a sniff of disap-
proval. She vanished into a room opposite the consulting room
where Constance had met Dr. Laing before, and a moment later
returned and asked her to follow.

Constance was shown into a tiny dining room, where Dr.
Laing rose from his chair and invited her to sit and have a cup of
tea.

"I have a few minutes before my next appointment. Murray's
doing the visits today, since I was up most of the night with a
difficult birth."

"I hope the outcome was happy for all concerned."

"Mother and child doing well so far," he said, resuming his
seat after she took her own. The housekeeper put another cup
and saucer on the table, and he poured Constance some tea while
the housekeeper sniffed again and departed. "Toast?"

"No, thank you. I breakfasted before I left The Willows."

"What can I do for you this morning?" he asked civilly.

"I am still inquiring into the matter of Miss Niall's death."

A frown flickered on his brow. "Really, I can't help thinking you should leave such matters to the policemen. Or even to your husband, who is, I understand, up in London."

"He should be back today. But two brains are better than one, doctor, and three better yet. Which is why I want you to tell me about poisons."

"Poisons?" he said, startled. "We found no trace of poison in Miss Niall's stomach."

"But they don't all leave a trace, do they? I'm thinking particularly of plants like foxglove or monkshood."

"There is no point in speculating, Mrs. Grey," he said impatiently. "We will never know, never have proof if they leave no trace—and the poor lady is already buried, in any case. And then there is the matter of how she could possibly have swallowed such poison. Arsenic tastes of nothing, but we tested for that. Most plant poisons taste bitter, and she would certainly have noticed it in her food or drink. Then again, no one in her household was taken ill either."

Constance placed her cup carefully back in its saucer. "In your opinion, doctor, is there any chance she might have taken it herself?"

His eyes widened. "Deliberately?" For a moment, she could see him thinking about it, considering it, and then discarding it. "I would not go down that road, Mrs. Grey. Her family has suffered enough."

"I would never bring it up," Constance assured him, "unless it was a genuine possibility and they were about to hang an innocent woman. Look, doctor, I never knew Miss Niall, but I have spoken now to many people who did, and it seems to me she was a troubled soul, constantly looking for something she never found. In your opinion, was it possible she killed herself? Was she that unhappy?"

Dr. Laing pushed his plate aside and grasped his teacup with both hands. "You are right, I think, that she was a troubled lady, in search of something. But that something was not death. Miss

Niall was a lady of great spirit, a fighter. She would never give in to such despair. She would find another way."

"Then we are left with sudden heart failure for no obvious reason—unless you can think of another way someone might have killed her without leaving any sign?"

"I can't, or I would have said so at the inquest."

He was very downright, but then, she was questioning his professional judgment.

"Of course you would," she murmured.

Perhaps he heard the sigh in her voice, for he said more gently, "Take heart, Mrs. Grey. The truth may be obscure, but there is assuredly no evidence against Lady Maule. I believe even the Scotland Yard detectives are about to give up and return to London."

"Leaving Colonel Niall free to say whatever he likes."

"Give him time, ma'am. It is not yet a fortnight since he lost his daughter." He reached for the last piece of toast, almost apologetically.

"Just to change the subject," she said as he took a bite, "where do lovers meet in this neighborhood?"

He stilled for an instant, either in surprise or distaste or both. "You are asking the wrong man. I may be a bachelor, but I have no time for dalliance. Neither has Dr. Murray. A young doctor in his position has to be very careful of his reputation."

"And in these parts, I expect everyone is your patient. At least potentially."

"That is the way I regard it, and I have advised Murray accordingly."

"I'm sure the advice is sound, and I wasn't really expecting you to answer from experience, just from hearsay. Every neighborhood has its lovers' lane or trysting oak."

"There, you have the advantage of me. There is an old oak where couples carve their initials, but it is rather public for trysts!"

"Oh well, I shall ask around." She took a last sip of tea and rose to her feet. He stood at once too. "I'm sorry to have disturbed your valuable free time, and thank you for your help."

In fact, she realized as she took her leave, her last question had been foolish. Frances would not have trysted where other couples might have seen her. But Constance could hardly have blatantly asked about disused cottages with closed shutters or abandoned shepherd's huts far from prying eyes. She had already outraged the poor doctor enough for one day.

It was at Laing's garden gate she suddenly remembered Worcester's words about Frances's assignations.

"Sometimes she went out in the afternoon and didn't come home until morning. Other times, she was gone a bare half-hour…"

Which surely meant at least some of her trysts were a less-than-fifteen-minute walk from the Grange. Allowing for no more than a quick kiss and perhaps an exchange of love letters, none of which Constance and Solomon had found in her rooms. Perhaps John had had better luck.

She turned right along the road leading to Fairfield Grange.

Frances had been pulled out of the lake wearing a nightgown her maid recognized but had not seen for some weeks, so her trysting place was somewhere she could keep such personal items, somewhere undercover where she and her lover could spend hours alone together.

On impulse, instead of going up to the gates of the Grange, Constance took a less-trodden path on the left that led between fields and toward a wooded area. She had not gone far, however, before a horseman skirted the woods and trotted along the path in her direction. He raised his hand in greeting, and she saw that it was John Niall.

She found she was relieved. She did not really want to go up to the house, which felt so unhappy and tense. Nor did she wish to run into Colonel Niall, whom she remembered as all grief and spite. Compared to those, John was a breath of fresh air.

"Good morning, Mr. Niall," she said cheerfully as he trotted up to her, removing his hat. "I hope you don't mind my trespassing."

"Not in the slightest. In fact, I was on my way to The Willows, now that I've stretched old General's legs a bit." He replaced his hat and patted his horse's neck. "Shall we walk down?"

"Why not?" It would be quicker to ask John than blunder about without knowing where she was going.

He dismounted and walked beside her, leading his willing horse by the reins.

Constance cast around in her mind for a way to ask what she needed to know without insulting his late sister.

Eventually, she said bluntly, "I'm looking for a love nest."

Inevitably he looked startled and then alarmed, with just a hint of hope. "You are?" he said, and sat just a little straighter in the saddle.

"Following a certain path of inquiry," she said. Was that disappointment in his eyes? *Oh dear...* "I have reason to believe certain local lovers met in some otherwise unused building, probably on your land. A semiderelict place, perhaps, an old barn, or shepherd's hut, or woodsman's cottage? My hope is these lovers might have seen something that would help us, only I need to find where they met to be sure."

It was a thin story, and she was fairly sure he would see through it. He rubbed his gloved hand over his chin, perhaps trying to give himself time for thought. "I can't really help you there. All our buildings are in use. Apart from an abandoned shepherd's hut over the hill there." He pointed with his whip into the distance.

"How long would it take you to walk to this hut?"

"Oh, at least two hours, unless the ground was muddy, in which case it would be three. Listen, I had a look through Frances's notebook, and the other things in her desk."

"Did you find anything interesting?" Disappointed at the apparent lack of love nests, she allowed herself to be distracted.

"The notebook initials could conform to the names of friends, neighbors, and servants," he said uncomfortably. "And beside them, I think, were reminders of what she either had discovered about them or suspected. In order to pressure them into obedience if she needed to."

"Like Bingham. And Worcester."

"Precisely. The thing is...I don't think they're important."

She stared at him, wondering if he had become as morally bankrupt as his troubled sister. "You don't?"

"No." He sighed. "My sister remembered the truly important things. The notebook was probably merely future planning for unforeseen eventualities."

"She'd used some of them already."

He said nothing, though she could almost feel his misery.

"Did you uncover anything else that might help us?" she asked.

"Not really. I found no love letters, nothing mentioning the gift of the bracelet you were interested in. But as I say, Frances kept the truly important things to herself."

"Why?" Constance asked. "Did her servants—or even your father—keep close watch on her?"

"I suspect they might have when she was younger," he said, twitching his shoulder. "When she came home, my father appeared to trust her more. But old habits die hard."

And Frances's habits, it seemed, had merely been driven under cover.

"Did you ever fear your sister was suicidal?"

"Good Lord, no."

"Not even over, for example, Sir Humphrey's marriage to someone else?"

"Frances wasn't the type to give up. On anything."

Did that include Sir Humphrey?

John drew in his breath. "Everyone else seems to be ignoring the fact that my sister was found dead in her nightgown. You don't believe she came home at all that night, do you? Despite finding that she could get in and out of the house without being seen. Despite the fact that anyone else could, including yourself and your husband. And you don't believe she sleepwalked. That is why you are looking for this *love nest*."

"Could anyone sleepwalk out of a window? Besides, her maid had not seen that particular nightgown in weeks. Your sister could have hidden it with the other things in that bottom drawer. I just can't think why she would."

"Neither can I," John admitted. "But there is another possibility. Whoever killed her dressed her in the nightgown just to tarnish her reputation."

"We thought of that. But if that was the purpose, why not leave her naked?"

John's mouth twisted. "Decency seems a ridiculous answer."

"It does," she agreed, a nagging thought resolving in her mind, "but it might well be right." In fact, she wished Solomon was back so that she could discuss it with him. She needed to know what he had discovered in London.

"Well, I suppose I have no need to go on to The Willows now," John said. "I seem to have told you everything I meant to."

Though not necessarily everything he knew? "I'm sure Sir Humphrey and Lady Maule would be glad to see you," she said.

His expression was uncertain, making him look even younger than his years. "Do you think so? I wondered if I would be unwelcome, considering my father's accusations…"

"Sir Humphrey called on you," she reminded him. "And frankly, a friendly call from you might well mitigate the nastier rumors."

He seemed much struck by this and said little more until they reached the house. A stable lad ambled down to take John's horse.

"You go in," Constance said. "I have something else I want to do first."

She felt his gaze on her back as she strode off toward the lake path. It was several seconds before she heard the crunch of his feet in the gravel as he headed to the front door. Constance hurried on.

She had a sudden urge to see the lake again, to approach it as Frances's killer must have done.

A strong man could have carried her body from the house. But the wheelbarrow tracks had come from the other path, the one that led to the road connecting the village to The Willows and to Fairfield Grange. She prowled several yards along each path before returning to the lake, until she could almost imagine herself inert in the wobbling, bumping barrow, or clutched in a man's arms, her nightgown trailing in the mud.

She stopped at the place Frances had probably gone into the water, imagined herself sinking beneath the lilies. Had the murderer stayed to watch, or just bolted as quickly as he could? Had he loved her as well as hated her enough to kill? She had been the kind of woman who could arouse all sorts of powerful and contradictory emotions—even in Constance, who had never met her.

"Where did you die?" she murmured.

Wherever, she had been brought here, to this spot, and tipped from the wheelbarrow into the lake...

Behind her, in the trees, leaves rustled, a twig cracked, and she shivered, feeling the hairs on her neck prickle. It suddenly felt as if Frances were with her, as though the dead woman's spirit sensed she sought the truth.

Her family didn't. They wanted it covered up even if it meant blaming an innocent person. No one had understood her in life, and they refused to look too closely at her death. Even the police were obstructed by everyone's misguided pride or loyalty.

"A clue, Frances," Constance whispered. "Whom did you really love?"

Humphrey...

It was all that made sense. Frances had been good in India, remaining true to him, and yet he had married another. Surely only hurt would have made her behave as she did to Elizabeth, seeking out her secrets, and to Humphrey, who had betrayed her. And she never gave up.

Constance stared into the lake at her own reflection, unwilling to think of him as the killer. Had they trysted here at the house? Beneath Elizabeth's nose?

She could not imagine it. But someone had tipped Frances's dead body in here...

Slowly, she bent, picked up a loose stone, and dropped it into the water with a splash—a tiny splash, surely, compared that made by a body. The ripples from the stone disturbed the water, distorting her reflection—until, with a sudden lurch of her stomach, she saw another figure reflected behind her.

She tried to spin around, but her foot slipped and hands pushed her hard. She skidded down the bank, grasping desperately for the dry earth that crumbled in her fingers. Water tugged at her skirts, soaked her feet, but it wasn't the lake she feared. It was whoever had pushed her.

Floundering, she finally found a hold on the tree root poking above the ground and hauled herself back up the bank. She even rolled, as if that could have saved her from continued attack, and opened her mouth to scream for help.

But there was no one there.

Stumbling to her feet, she turned quickly, searching all around her. Trees rustled as a breeze blew through the leaves.

Someone is in there. The killer just tried to kill me, and I could not even see his face.

Her heart thundered, spreading chilled blood through her veins. Frustration warred with utter fear. She been so close to the killer. She had seen his face in the water, maddeningly distorted in the ripples, but it *was* a man, for he'd worn a tall hat...

He was still there, hidden among the trees and bushes. And she was still in danger.

Yet she had to know.

She took a step toward the place she had last seen him. A footstep sounded behind her, and she whirled around to face a man strolling out from the trees nearest the house.

DR. MURRAY'S FINAL call of the morning was on old Sarah Phelps. Not that she had summoned him, but he had heard her coughing rather worryingly in her yard yesterday evening and thought he should look in on her. Without charge, of course, for he doubted she could pay. He wouldn't tell Laing, unless the cough was serious, for the senior doctor had already dismissed his concern.

"Sarah Phelps is as tough as old boots, and whenever she *is* ill, she sends for me."

Of course, Laing had the odd mean streak, especially if he was not the one being noble about it.

People around here liked Laing, though, even if Murray thought *he* was the better doctor.

Walking up from the village past The Willows, he thought of Frances Niall with an intense blend of longing and regret. Wild and beautiful and inclined to spite, she had been like no one else he had ever met. He had yearned for her, but she had never looked at him, damn her, only at…

On impulse, he turned onto the path that led to the lake. He hadn't gone far before he realized he was not the only person on those grounds. Curious, he stepped off the path and made his way through the trees instead, until he saw her.

Mrs. Grey stood very still, gazing into the lake as though it could offer up some precious treasure. Like the truth. Another beautiful, over-curious woman. For an instant, with the sunshine glinting off her golden-and-strawberry-blonde hair, she dazzled him. He suspected she dazzled most men.

If I were her husband, I would not leave her behind when I went to the city… A woman like that could make or break the career of an ambitious man. He wondered, vaguely, how ambitious Grey was, then hastily stepped back in case she looked up and saw him.

Impulse overcame him again, and he moved carefully closer.

〉〉〉〉〉〈〈〈〈〈

I<small>T TOOK</small> C<small>ONSTANCE</small> an instant to see through her own startled terror and recognize the man she had seen only yesterday.

"Mr. Darby," she said faintly. Relief overcame fear, if only for an instant, for if Darby had pushed her, if Darby was the murderer, then Sir Humphrey could not be guilty. "What on earth are you doing here?"

Should she scream for help anyway? Should she bolt for the house?

"We have an assignation," Darby drawled, all but swaggering toward her. His gaze, amused and lustful, was all over her. "Though it looks as if you have not waited. Mrs. Grey, have you been rolling in the hay—or indeed the earth—without me?"

"I beg your pardon?" she said frostily, while her brain tried to adjust. He was implying his pursuit was merely amorous, and now that she could think again, she was sure someone else was moving among the trees close by. Reluctant to take her eyes off Darby for long, she cast a hasty glance toward the sound, but saw no one.

"My dear Mrs. Grey, you are wet and filthy, and your hat is almost off your head. Allow me to—"

As he reached for her, she stepped smartly aside and straightened her own hat.

"I slipped into the water and had to pull myself out."

"How awful! I wish I had been here earlier."

"Weren't you?" she said, holding his gaze.

His eyes widened with an expression of confusion. It looked genuine. "What do you mean?"

"Did you really not…see me falling in?"

"Of course I did not," he said, sounding shocked. "Else I should have pulled you out. You must have got a terrible fright."

Dare she believe in his sincerity? "At least you are in time to escort me to the house," she said, setting off with rapid steps.

"Wait!" He caught her arm, forcing her to halt, for his grip was strong if not overtly threatening. "I like an eager woman, but are you sure the house is currently unoccupied?"

She blinked. "Of course it is occupied. By our host and hostess and at least one other caller, to say nothing of the servants."

"Then let us stay here. The day is not cold and I find the risk of discovery, even by the odd yokel, adds a delicious fillip to such encounters."

"I need to change my dress," she said, pretending to misunderstand him. Most of her attention was still on the trees nearby. Was somebody else still there? Or had it only ever been Darby? She met his gaze once more.

Either he was very good at pretending lust or he had *not* just tried to push her in the lake. She suspected he was a little perverse in his tastes, but surely trying to drown someone was not much of a seduction technique?

But she had looked at him too intensely and too long, and inevitably he drew the wrong conclusion.

"There's a little boathouse at the end of the lake," he said huskily, running his fingers down her arm to close them around her hand. "Let me take you there. Any distress to your raiment is then easily explained by your almost falling in the water..."

She jerked her hand free. "Mr. Darby, you clearly have the wrong idea! I am a respectable, married lady and my husband is expected back imminently." How many lies were there in that claim?

His arms closed around her. "You would be surprised how many respectable ladies are eager to enjoy me. I promise you delight, my lovely one."

Constance stamped mercilessly on his instep. "And I promise you pain."

He emitted a muffled howl, surprised into releasing her, but even as she spun away, he grabbed her once more, and now his expression was ugly and his grasp designed to hurt.

"There is a word for women like you. You can't entice me all the way over here and give me nothing in return. To the boathouse with you. I'll have what I came for one way or another."

It was a long time since she had allowed a man like him so close. The inevitable panic swamped her, but even so, the instincts that had preserved her more than once already had her twisting and lifting her knee. Before it could connect, another voice spoke, cracking through the tense air like a whip.

"And what exactly did you come for?"

Solomon.

CHAPTER THIRTEEN

C ONSTANCE'S KNEES WENT weak with relief, and she almost staggered when Darby released her as suddenly as if she really had assaulted him. *How's that for the fillip of discovery?*

But Darby was an old hand. He chose the attitude of haughty entitlement, looking Solomon over with contempt. "Who the devil are you?"

It was a mistake. She could see the realization dawning on Darby as Solomon strolled toward them. He ignored Darby, his hard gaze on Constance, assessing her. Many people misjudged Solomon for many different reasons, but one glance assured her that Darby would not make the same mistake twice.

Solomon loomed, lithe, dangerous, just waiting for the slightest reason...

"My husband, Mr. Grey," she said mildly. "Solomon, this is Mr. Darby of Shelton Hall."

"And you came here for...?" Obviously, Solomon was not about to let the question go in favor of polite introductions, and Darby hastily changed tack.

"To call on my old friend Maule, of course. As you see, I was just in time to prevent your wife from falling completely into the lake. She had a fright. But I require no thanks."

"Then I shall merely escort you both to the house." Taking Constance's numb hand, Solomon threaded it through the crook of his arm, and she clung to his warmth, inhaling his scent for strength.

Quite suddenly, she was safe again.

"When did you get back?" she asked as they walked around the line of trees and down the path toward the front of the house.

"Just a few minutes ago. The servants told me you'd gone toward the lake, so I followed."

She was glad he had, even though he would no doubt think the worst of her for encouraging the likes of Darby.

"Then you don't know if Maule is at home?" Darby asked, as though looking for an excuse to leave as quickly as possible.

"I believe he just arrived and is with Lady Maule and Mr. Niall from Fairfield Grange."

"Excellent," she said, nodding to the footman who opened the front door. "Then I shall go and change my dress."

Leaving Darby to the footman who clearly knew him, she forced herself not to dash to the staircase. Even so, it was some moments before she realized Solomon was climbing steadily beside her. He said nothing until he closed the bedchamber door beside them.

"What happened? Did that lecher assault you?"

He wasn't blaming her.

The knowledge stunned her. Even so, she managed to say lightly, "Not quite, though I very nearly assaulted him. You rather saved his—"

"What was the 'falling in the lake' story?" he interrupted her before she could be indelicate. "You certainly look as if you fell into something, and your skirts are wet."

She shivered and fumbled with the fastenings of her cloak. He walked over, brushing her hands aside and removing the cloak for her. He untied her hat too and cast them both on the bed without looking at them. His gaze remained fixed on her face.

She swallowed. "Someone pushed me."

"Darby?"

"I don't know. I don't think so, but it could have been. I was sure there was someone creeping among the trees while I was walking around the lake. Then I stopped where we think Frances went in. I was deep in thought and forgot to pay attention. I even dropped a stone into the water, trying to feel what could have happened. I saw a reflection behind me, just in time to twist away, but I couldn't make out his features for the ripples. He was wearing a top hat."

"Like Darby's?"

"Yes, I suppose so. My foot slipped further down the bank—that's why my skirts are wet—and I managed to pull myself back up the bank by that tree root. But whoever pushed me had vanished. I'm sure I heard him moving away from the lake before Darby appeared from the other direction. But I could be wrong. He seemed more bent on lustful pursuits than murder, though he was quite eager to get me to the boathouse."

He released her gaze at last. "I'll go and take a look around. There may be footprints."

"Wait," she said, unreasonably annoyed—she wanted to look around too, but if it wasn't Darby, whoever had pushed her was long gone, and she had more urgent questions. "What did you learn in London?"

"Ah." His face cleared, and he sat down on the bed. "Quite a lot. Frances was not looking for Elizabeth's child. She was looking for her own."

"Like any other mother forced to abandon her baby," she said. "So when she told Humphrey about Elizabeth's past, she was just stabbing in the dark. It makes a horrible sense, Solomon. It must always have been Humphrey she loved, Humphrey she waited for and probably even trysted with after she came home from India. I don't want to believe that."

"Neither do I," Solomon said. There was a rueful twist to his mouth. "But that isn't everything. Tracing her child was not the first task Dunne had performed for Frances. She also wanted information about the death of Humphrey's first wife."

Constance stared at him. "Oh no. Was there something suspicious about how she died?"

"She contracted fever after the birth—which is not unusual.

But it was comparatively mild, and she appeared to recover. And then suddenly, she sickened once more and died. There seemed to be no other reason. A recurrence of the fever was assumed, and no further action was taken. There was no autopsy. Dr. Laing signed the death certificate."

Constance lowered herself to the chaise longue. "Does that sound terribly familiar to you?"

"I'm afraid it does."

"Humphrey just *kills* women who are inconvenient to him?" she said with horror. "He killed his first wife to be with Frances? Only then he changed his mind, or perhaps just forgot about her when her father took her to India, and then he met Elizabeth. So when Frances came home, threatening his peace and his happy marriage, he killed her too. It fits horribly."

"Except we don't know how he did it, or even *if* he did."

"But he seems so…"

"People are rarely the same beneath the face they show the world."

"You don't have to tell me that."

They sat in silence for several moments, both deep in thought, before Solomon rose. "You need to change your dress. I'll leave you in peace."

She blinked up at him as he brushed past her. "You really don't blame me?"

He paused, frowning down at her. "For what?"

"For misleading Darby."

"Did you?" He actually sounded surprised, which felt like a healing balm.

"I encouraged him to come and speak to us without his wife, to give us details of his affair with Frances."

Solomon's lip curled. "A man like that only ever sees women in one light. The problem is his, not yours."

He had said something similar once before. It was a rare man who did not blame a woman for such misunderstandings. Especially a woman like her.

"Thank you," she said hoarsely.

His brow twitched. "How much danger were you in?"

"None I could not have dealt with—somewhat less discreetly than you managed. And yet he doesn't know me. To him, I am a respectable lady, and yet still fair game."

"No one is fair game," he snapped. "The man is a menace."

Constance had spent years protecting women whom no one else believed were not "fair game" in one way or another. His words enchanted and distracted her.

"He is a menace," she said slowly, "and I think Frances found him so in the end. Is he not a far more likely murderer than Sir Humphrey? Who is faithful to his wife and a basically kind man?"

"You want it to be Darby because you don't like him."

"Frances rejected him."

"So he rode ten miles, poisoned her or whatever, dressed her in a nightgown, and dumped her in his neighbor's lake? I won't say it's impossible, but it is unlikely."

"And we have no evidence," she admitted, jumping restlessly to her feet. "There must *be* some. We need to look for the place she met her lover, whoever that was. It must be within fifteen minutes' walk from Fairfield Grange."

Quickly, she told him about her conversation with Worcester, and then with Godden. He listened carefully, his eyes never leaving hers, which made her suddenly self-conscious. She stopped speaking. It came to her, with a strange little tingle in her stomach, that the light in his dark eyes was almost...admiration.

He raised his hand and touched her cheek, butterfly light. Then he strode to the door. "We'll begin exploring this afternoon."

THE DISCOVERY OF Darby's assault—and it was already assault, however Constance chose to interpret it—unsettled Solomon profoundly. Not just in the general sense of anger against a bully and the need to protect the weak. This was something much more personal to Constance, connected to the dangers of the profession she would not leave. Such encounters upset her, and yet she never let them hold her back. He admired that spirit, that courage, even while it made him ever more anxious.

If she—to Darby's knowledge, a respectable married lady—could face such insult here, what dangers did she face as the courtesan she was? Some men felt entitled to any woman, let alone one they considered bought and paid for.

He hated that she could be bought. He hated that she could be hurt and afraid. Somehow she had overturned all his preconceived ideas about her, personally. He should not allow his feelings to soften, and yet he did. There was danger in this fascination, and he was well aware of it. He always had been.

He should not have touched her. Even as a friend. And yet it was human nature, human comfort, and she did not object. Why would she? She was too used to the touch of men—men who did not assault her.

He strode along the passage from their room to the staircase, trying to calm the turbulence of his feelings so that he was fit for Lady Maule's drawing room. And to deal properly with the various matters he had to.

He found both the Maules entertaining the unspeakable Darby—and John Niall, who stood to shake his hand.

"Welcome back," Maule said affably. "How was your journey?"

"Quick and surprisingly smooth." Deliberately, Solomon chose the chair next to Darby, who shifted away from him almost unconsciously. He was probably marshaling his defense in the event of any accusations Solomon might make. But then, they both knew the futility of any such accusations, which would only hurt the woman in question, not the man who assaulted her.

For the moment, Solomon contented himself with making Darby feel uncomfortable, and conversed with the company about the railway and London and the latest news.

Only when John rose to take his leave did Solomon grasp the opportunity for a private word with Darby.

Keeping the smile on his lips but nowhere near his eyes, he held Darby's oddly defiant gaze. "Did you offer Frances Niall such violence, and did she threaten to tell your wife?" *Is that why you killed her?*

"I am not a violent man," Darby said haughtily. He genuinely seemed to believe it. "It may be a fault that I love the ladies a little too much—I am a man of passion, after—"

"Then you did," Solomon interrupted.

Darby blinked rapidly. "Did what?" His eyes widened in clear alarm. "Dear God, of course I did not kill her! She changed her mind, grew hysterical, and made threats, but they were no danger to me."

"Why not?"

"My wife would not have believed them," he said with rather monstrous complacency.

Solomon stretched his lips once more. "Oh, I think Frances would have found a way to convince her. It was what she did best. However, from your reaction, I doubt she got the chance. She had bigger fish to fry. However," he added as Darby opened his mouth once more, "there are dangers in what you do. Dangers to you—I mean, since it's clear you don't pay attention to anyone else. If you ever come near my wife again, I will show you exactly what those are. In fact, if I hear of your going near *any* woman who is not your wife, I will have you so tangled up in court cases that your life will not be worth living. I expect your wife will divorce you."

Darby's facial expressions were almost ludicrous. His mouth worked without any sound coming out. Finally, after glancing around to assure himself that his hosts were temporarily absent, he exploded into bluster.

"How dare you address me in such a manner? How dare you threaten me? Who do you think you are, you—"

"I am Solomon Grey, and I am the man who will kill you if you ever lay a finger—or a whisper of scandal—on my wife again. Is that clear?"

"You jumped-up... Your wife—"

"*Is that clear?*"

Humphrey's voice drifted in from the hall, growing closer. Darby closed his mouth and swallowed. "Quite clear."

"All of it?" Solomon said softly.

"All of it," Darby said between his teeth.

It was the best Solomon could do without beating the man to a pulp. The strength of the itch in his fists to do just that surprised him. It was almost as if Constance really were his wife.

"I don't think he killed Frances, though," he said reluctantly to her after luncheon, when they went upstairs to fetch coats and hats for their walk.

"Don't you think he's just the sort of man to dump her in someone else's lake once she's no more use to him?"

"No, I think he's the sort of man to simply walk away if he killed her, and that would only have been an accident. He doesn't *care* enough to kill."

"He cares for himself enough," Constance said contemptuously. "If Frances threatened him, as she was prone to do..."

"He genuinely thinks his wife could believe no ill of him. He would just find another woman to bother. Like you. And by the way, I doubt he will trouble you again."

She searched his face, a faint smile lurking on her lips. "Did you threaten him, Solomon?"

He grimaced. "I think I promised him. We are none of us so different, are we?"

She took his arm. "Oh, I think we are."

And just like that, his spirits lifted. She knew he was her champion, and she liked it. So did he.

Almost embarrassed, he seized his hat. "I'll have a quick word with Sir Humphrey and then meet you in the front hall."

He found Maule in his study poring over estate ledgers,

which he shoved aside with clear relief when Solomon entered. He was obviously a conscientious man, but the business side of things did not come easily to him.

"I'm sorry to disturb you," Solomon said, "but I need your help on a delicate matter. The more we discover about Frances Niall, the more questions it throws up. We know she lied for malicious reasons when she felt the urge, but she also sought the truth. Did you know she had inquired into the death of your first wife?"

Maule's bushy eyebrows flew up. "Gillian? Why?"

"I don't know. She may just have been shaking the tree to see what fell out, but—forgive me—was there any reason to imagine your wife died from any cause but the one given by Dr. Laing?"

"None that I know of." He looked genuinely bewildered. An old pain drifted back into his eyes.

"Was she taking any medicine at the time?"

"Not then, no. Her fever had abated several days before, and her appetite was returning. She really seemed to be on the mend."

"Did Frances ever imply to you that she was suspicious of your wife's death in any way?"

"Never. But maybe there was talk in the village. It wouldn't necessarily reach my ears."

He spoke bitterly, and Solomon was not surprised. After all, the man was dealing with gossip against his second wife.

"People do talk," Solomon said with vague sympathy. "It isn't always malicious. Again, I apologize, but I'm going to ask you something else indelicate. The trouble is, to get at the truth that will exonerate Elizabeth, I need to know exactly what that is. Did you ever meet Frances clandestinely, either before she went to India or after she came home?"

"Never," Maule said stiffly.

"Then it was truly impossible that she could ever have carried your child?"

Maule looked ready to explode, which was answer enough in

itself. The trouble was, could he believe that answer?

"Did she ever inveigle—or try to inveigle—you into an assignation?"

"Only to go for walks. I told you, she would follow me sometimes. Before India."

"And were you never tempted to—"

"No." Maule's glower was thunderous. "What in the world are you getting at, Grey? Do you suspect me of killing her? How am I supposed to have done it?"

As it happened, Solomon had an idea about that. It had come to him when he thought of the first Lady Maule in her sickbed, recovering from fever. Frances Niall, in her nightgown, had probably also been in bed. Someone's bed. *A* bed.

He sighed. It was a pity to end a burgeoning friendship. He rather liked Maule. And his wife. But he had to know.

"Would Elizabeth kill to protect you?"

Maule stared at him, apparently deprived of words. Solomon didn't speak either, though he began to suspect he should have mentioned this idea to Constance first.

"From what?" Maule demanded. "From accusations of killing my first wife? You think Frances put the idea in her head, so she killed Frances?"

"It crossed my mind. Women can be unexpectedly fierce when protecting those they love."

"So can I," Maule growled.

"For the record," Solomon said, standing up, "I don't really believe it. Constance certainly doesn't. These things have to be eliminated, preferably by proof of some kind. In its absence, I'm merely looking for opinions. And I think you have doubts of your own concerning your wife."

"Not about murder!" Maule exclaimed. "And they're not doubts, just things I can't get out of my head."

"What Frances said about her."

He nodded curtly. "Doubt is worse than anger sometimes. Wouldn't it bother you, Grey? If such things were said about *your* wife?"

Solomon almost laughed, although it wasn't really funny. "Trust what you know," he said with a quick, lopsided smile, and walked out in search of Constance.

She was in the hall, in low-voiced conversation with Elizabeth, although both smiled brightly at him as he approached.

"Have a pleasant walk," Elizabeth said lightly.

BY THE TIME he had told Constance about his conversation with Sir Humphrey, they were almost at Sarah Phelps's cottage. Her lips tightened when he talked of Elizabeth killing to protect her husband, but she did him the courtesy of considering the theory.

"Do you believe him?" she asked.

"Yes, I think I do. But..."

Mrs. Phelps was glaring at them from the opening into her yard. Without warning, Constance veered across the road to speak to her. Solomon trailed after.

"Good day, Mrs. Phelps," Constance said cheerfully. "How are you?"

The old woman grunted in a discouraging kind of way, which Constance ignored.

"You make up herbal remedies for people in the village, don't you?" Constance said.

"Makes me a penny or two."

"Did you ever make any for the first Lady Maule?"

Mrs. Phelps curled her lip. Her eyes were watery today, but still fierce. "Don't be daft. The likes of her don't trust anything not prescribed by physicians at vast expense."

"Did Frances Niall ever ask you for any herbal remedies?"

"No, and I wouldn't have given her any if she had," Mrs. Phelps said rudely, and stomped off, coughing rather horribly into her shawl as she went, then vanishing through a gate in the back of her yard.

"I think she was smothered with a pillow," Solomon blurted.

Constance stared at him as he began to walk on up the road, though she caught up with him quickly. "Why?"

He shrugged. "It would leave no marks of a struggle. She was wearing her nightgown. There probably are medical signs of smothering, but no one would have looked for them when they thought she had drowned."

"We could call on Dr. Laing, but I think I might have annoyed him enough for one day."

"Let's keep to our original plan for now," Solomon said. "If we can discover where Frances met her lover, it might tell us all we need to know."

It proved to be a long and frustrating afternoon in many ways. Having walked a brisk fifteen minutes beyond the Grange gates, they turned onto narrower tracks, examining every cottage, farmhouse, barn, and hut they saw. With the aid of the map Constance had consulted at The Willows, they cut across country where necessary, keeping to around the same distance around the Grange estate.

"It seems John Niall told me the truth," Constance said. "There don't seem to be any unoccupied buildings remotely suitable for a lovers' tryst. Perhaps the short meetings were merely to pass notes or plans to meet elsewhere at a greater distance."

"Perhaps, though I doubt her body could have been easily carried from a much greater distance," Solomon argued. "Besides...was she that giddy a girl? She liked excitement, liked to break the rules. But if you are right, she was not devoted to this lover but to Humphrey. Unless her lover *was* Humphrey."

Constance sighed, pausing to glance around at the drainage ditch below them and the open fields beyond, then back up to the woodland behind that they had just passed through. "I don't believe it was him. Certainly, he is away from Elizabeth a good deal during the day, about estate business and so on, but he never leaves her alone at night."

Solomon glanced at her in surprise. "You asked her?"

"How else were we to know?"

"How do you know she told you the truth? We have already agreed she is protective of him. The truth is, we don't want to believe it."

"Elizabeth asked for my help. *She* doesn't believe it. Solomon—"

But Solomon was distracted by the distant sound of hoof-beats. They came from the bridle path that formed the boundary between Fairfield Grange and The Willows land. Solomon did not particularly want to be discovered on the wrong side of it by anyone more influential than the tenant farmers and servants they had encountered already. A horseman surely meant Colonel Niall or his son. Still, it was more curiosity than embarrassment that caused him to throw his arm around Constance's waist, sweep her forward, and jump into the ditch.

CHAPTER FOURTEEN

Dropping to a crouch as he landed, Solomon dragged Constance down with him and whipped off both their hats with his free hand in case they poked up out of the ditch. Fortunately, the weather had been fine for some time, and the ditch was dry.

Which didn't stop Constance's glaring at him. She opened her mouth, no doubt to give him the verbal blistering he deserved, so he hastily dropped the hats and put one finger to her lips.

He was not wearing gloves, and the touch was unimaginably intimate. He held her crouching body close against his to prevent her keeling over. She was curved and fragile and he could smell her skin, and the floral perfume in her hair that was uniquely Constance. Her parted lips were so soft under his fingertip that he knew a powerful urge to trace their shape in a slow, sensual caress.

The rhythm of her breath quickened as she stared at him, her expression changing from stunned curiosity to…what? Something gentler. She had the most beautiful eyes of anyone he had ever seen, layers of sorrow and sweetness and joy, a profound compassion that had always drawn him, and, surely, a mysterious, enticing passion.

It was she who freed her gaze first, releasing him to concentrate on the beating hooves that had led him to this moment of confusion. He let his finger fall from her mouth as she turned her head away. He knew he should release her completely, but he didn't want her to lose her footing. Really.

He had never forgotten the feel of her in his arms the first time they met on a foggy night in London, when he had whisked her out of the path of a falling body. That purely instinctive response had got lost somewhere in the fascinating contradictions that were Constance Silver. And they had to be lost again now as the single horseman rode around the bridle track toward the wood.

Very carefully, he released her and raised his head above the parapet, as it were. The rider was not John Niall. He was older, straighter, grayer.

"Colonel Niall," he murmured.

Constance shuddered, causing him to glance at her in sudden anxiety. Did she regard him like Darby? She wasn't looking at him but continued to shake. Hastily, he shifted position and found her whole face brimming with hilarity. She was laughing, silently and uncontrollably.

Perhaps it was relief, but suddenly his own lips twitched as mirth surged up. He knew without words they were both imagining being caught in this ridiculous position.

"Perhaps we should just have wished him good afternoon," she said unsteadily.

"We can run after him if you like." As Colonel Niall vanished into the trees, Solomon picked up the hats, plonked them on their respective heads, and climbed out of the ditch before reaching down to help Constance.

This time, he kept his hold impersonal and brief. Stupidly, he felt too shaken to do anything else. Though he thanked God for the gift of laughter.

Constance pointed with the hand he had just released. "There's a building of some sort down there. It looks like a barn."

"It's on Maule's land," Solomon said, "but it must be within our fifteen minutes' walk from the Nialls' house. We can probably guess what's in it, but for the sake of thoroughness, let's look."

It was only as they crossed the bridle path and got a closer view that he realized where they were.

"This is Sarah Phelps's farm. That must be her barn."

Mrs. Phelps did not take kindly to people on her property, so they approached with some caution. Constance touched his arm, a welcome contact that brought relief as well as foolish pleasure. He followed her gaze and saw Mrs. Phelps in the distance. A deep, racking cough reached Solomon, though it didn't seem to slow the woman down. Her back to them, she appeared to be digging up vegetables near her cottage. Behind a dry stone wall near her, a few goats and sheep were grazing a patch of scrubby land. At the other side, a cow raised her head and regarded Solomon and Constance with interest.

The barn was enclosed on all sides, although the half-open door at the side was hidden from Mrs. Phelps's view. Solomon slipped around the barn and inside, Constance at his heels.

The barn was surprisingly neat. A penned area for animals in the winter, stacks of hay and winter feed against the walls. Boxes of layered apples, some vegetables, and drying herbs hung up. Solomon moved toward the latter, while Constance went toward the haystacks.

Rosemary, sage, feverfew—nothing dangerous like foxglove or monkshood.

"Solomon."

He turned toward Constance's voice and found her gazing between two large haystacks. On a thick pile of clean straw was piled two folded blankets and two pillows. And poking out between the pillows, the thin sleeve of a nightgown.

IT WAS THE first day since the death of his daughter that Colonel Niall had ridden around his land. He knew John had kept his eye on things, but that wasn't really good enough. The land needed its lord.

As he let his horse walk the last of the way back to the house, he realized he felt almost…good. He had been so anxious for so long, so worried what Frances would say or do next that he had been living on his nerves for years. He still cringed at the many narrow escapes, at the shameful, illegitimate birth of his grandson among strangers.

In retrospect, India had been the best of times. She had behaved better there, subdued by the trials of birth and loss—and, he had hoped, brought back to the sense of duty and propriety he had tried so hard and so fruitlessly to instill.

Coming home had been the mistake. He had thought they were safe with Maule remarried. Frances had told him Maule was not the father of her child, though she had refused to say who was. Even when he lost his temper and whipped her, she had kept silent on that score. In fact, she laughed, which had fed his deeper fear that she was truly mad.

Now he wondered if mad was better than bad. Certainly, she had seemed determined to bring shame after shame upon them all.

He dismounted and gave his horse over to the care of the groom, uttering a grunt of acknowledgment.

He realized with surprise that he was moving easily as he strode almost jauntily toward the house. What *was* this feeling? This surge of energy, of well-being? He entered the house, nodding to old Worcester, who loyally kept so many family secrets, and felt whatever it was intensify. It was…

As recognition dawned, he stopped with one foot on the first step. The feeling was the *absence of Frances*. It was relief.

"HOW UTTERLY BIZARRE," Solomon said. "I would not have thought Frances the type to enjoy such rustic trysting among the old smell of animals. Besides, it makes no sense. Surely Sarah would have noticed. Why would she keep silent?"

"Blackmail, I suppose." Constance frowned and reached out to touch the drooping sleeve of the nightgown. "Only… I don't think this belongs to Frances. It's too old, too rough."

His breath caught. "It's *Sarah's*? She sleeps here? Why?"

Constance shrugged. "With sick animals, perhaps? Everything's neatly folded and prepared. I doubt she does it every night. Damnation, Solomon, I thought we had actually *found* something at last."

"Well, let's go before *she* finds *us*. I've never cared for old women's curses."

He meant it as a throwaway remark, but her eyes suddenly sharpened. "Who dared curse you, Solomon Grey?"

"A mad old woman in Jamaica. She cursed my brother David and me when we were children, for dragging down her clean washing twice in as many days, even though we hadn't meant it." And for years he had been afraid that her curse had come true. He still wasn't sure it hadn't, for he and David had been separated only months later, and the loneliness still corroded his heart, never mind whatever it did to David.

"Old women's curses are just temper tantrums," Constance said firmly. "They mean nothing and influence nothing."

They stepped out into the daylight, which, along with Constance's words, felt like relief. It wasn't, of course. They mystery of Frances's death remained. As did the loss of his brother.

CONSTANCE WASN'T SURE what to make of Solomon's mood. There had been a moment—several moments—in the ditch when his gaze had seemed to melt her bones. Breathing had been unaccountably difficult. The laughter had helped, releasing the tension, and then he had been back to aloofness, and now this vulnerability over the past and his lost twin brother. She suspected it never really left him. But the self-blame she would not allow, not if she could help it.

"It's probably about the right time to catch Dr. Murray at the inn," he said as they turned onto the familiar road that led past The Willows to the village. "If you think Laing's patience might have run out."

Constance was tired and her feet were sore. She really didn't want to walk to the village and back. She wanted a comfortable seat and a cup of tea as soon as possible. She seemed to have spent most of the day walking and achieving nothing, and right now, she wasn't convinced they could learn any more from Dr. Murray.

However, she rarely gave in to weakness.

"Why not?" she said, and turned to see a pony and trap rumbling down the road toward them. One of the Fairfield Grange stable lads drove the shaggy pony, and sitting on the trap with her disdainful nose in the air was Bingham, Frances Niall's personal maid.

The lad holding the reins touched his cap to them and slowed. "Drop you at The Willows if you like," he said cheerfully.

"I don't suppose you're going as far as the village?" Constance asked hopefully.

"Hop on. Taking Miss Bingham to catch the stagecoach to London."

Only then did Constance realize the maid had a large bag with her. She seemed stunned when Constance condescended to climb up onto so rustic a vehicle, with Solomon's polite aid. He climbed after her, and all three of them jolted their way down the road.

"So you're off to London?" Constance said. "Do you have a new post already?"

"I'm to interview for one, but the agency says if I don't get it, there are plenty of others to be had."

"I hope you have somewhere to stay," Constance said uneasily, for London offered a horde of dangers to a girl not up to snuff. Bingham said she had come from there in the first place, but she was also naïve enough to have got into trouble.

"No," she said, "but I'm told it's easy enough."

Constance delved into her reticule and found a pencil and someone else's calling card, which she scribbled out. On the back of it, she wrote an address. "Go here, if you need to. It's respectable, cheap, and safe."

"Thank you, ma'am," Bingham said in clear surprise. "Everyone is being so kind. The colonel and Mrs. Haslett both gave me lovely references. And now you give me this. I feel guilty for being so glad to leave."

"I think your position has been difficult," Constance said tactfully.

"You're telling me. Everyone swore Miss Frances was an angel—which she weren't, not by a long chalk—and then it got even worse when she died. The funny thing is, I'm almost sorry for her now."

"Why is that?" asked Constance, who shared that inexplicable pity.

Bingham shrugged helplessly. "I don't know. I just find that house oppressive." She lowered her voice so the lad wouldn't hear. "The colonel's so strict, and I gather the late mistress was so sour faced she'd curdle the milk. Maybe if I was able, I'd have rebelled, too, and taken my temper out on other people."

"Is that what Miss Frances did?"

"I think so, yes. I told you she weren't happy."

"Why was that, do you think?" Constance asked as they passed the turning up to The Willows.

"Crossed in love, I expect. Always trying to make him jealous, if you ask me, only he never was."

Constance felt a jolt of excitement. Deliberately, she did not look at Solomon. "Who?"

Bingham leaned closer. "Sir Humphrey. I told you before, I reckon it were always him she had a thing for. Not saying he returned her affection, mind. No secret notes ever came from The Willows. But I'm sure that's why the colonel's so convinced Lady Maule is the culprit." Bingham smiled suddenly. "Don't look so worried, ma'am. I won't talk about it in London. No one wants a lady's maid who can't keep her mouth shut."

»»×«««

"IT ALWAYS COMES back to Humphrey," Constance said discontentedly over her tea and toast at the inn.

"If you believe her," Solomon said. "She didn't give him that kind of importance the last time we spoke to her, did she?"

"No, but she's out of the house now. I got the impression she was being more open and honest." Constant sighed and picked up her teacup. "Though not necessarily right."

"It's possible Frances remained obsessed with him," Solomon said thoughtfully. "Perhaps because he was the one man she could not manipulate. That doesn't make him her murderer."

"But she *could* manipulate him. She told him Elizabeth was a whore, and he doesn't quite disbelieve it, does he?" Constance drank her tea and helped herself to another dainty piece of buttered toast. "There's something we're not seeing."

"Something we're not meant to see. I can't even see Dr. Murray."

"Shall we give up looking and start thinking?"

"We can't do any worse that we have so far."

»»×«««

DINNER AT THE Willows was another slightly tense affair, so Constance decided to ask questions.

She addressed Sir Humphrey. "I don't suppose you know if Sarah Phelps happens to have had any sick animals recently?"

He let out a crack of laughter. "I shouldn't think they'd dare.

174

Certainly, I've never known any to die, not even her chickens."

"She cares for them religiously," Elizabeth put in.

"Then why do you suppose she sleeps in her barn?" Constance asked.

"Carrying eccentricity too far," Humphrey said. He scowled. "No wonder she's got a bad chest. Dr. Murray went up to see her today, said she was wheezing like a...whatever it is that wheezes badly."

"Did she let him treat her?" Elizabeth asked in surprise.

"Lord, no, sent him away with a flea in his ear. She only ever tolerates Laing, so I don't know why Murray even bothered. But with luck she'll stop sleeping in the barn!"

"Why would she sleep there, anyway?" Elizabeth asked. "It's only a step to her cozy little cottage, and it must be chilly in the barn by this time of year."

It was another nagging, annoying little mystery, but Constance couldn't see how it affected the main issue of who had killed Frances and put her body in the lake. She meant to spend the evening writing down everything they knew and trying to make sense of it. At first, she had been too eager to absolve Elizabeth, and then she had become too absorbed in the cruelty and tragedy that was Frances's life to see what must surely be under her nose.

However, the evening turned out quite differently. She and Elizabeth withdrew as usual, leaving the gentlemen to their port. But before she could excuse herself—she was itching now to begin—sounds of disturbance issued from the hall.

"What now?" Elizabeth groaned.

The butler appeared, stiff with outrage. "My lady, the policemen are here again. They seem to imagine you will see them at this time of the evening."

"Oh dear," Elizabeth said, panic flitting across her face. "I suppose you had better show them in."

"In *here*, my lady?" He seemed even more scandalized by this sacrilege.

"The sooner they're dealt with, the sooner we may be rid of them," Elizabeth said, straightening her shoulder. "Show them in, Manson."

"Perhaps," Constance intervened, "he should also inform Sir Humphrey?"

A flash of fear crowded into Elizabeth's eyes, as though she didn't really want him there, but some instinct told Constance they might need his forceful presence.

"Yes," Elizabeth said huskily, "do that too, Manson."

"Very good, my lady." The butler bowed and departed.

Hastily, Constance moved to sit beside Elizabeth on the sofa, giving her hand a quick squeeze for strength.

"The police, my lady," Manson announced with clear distaste, not even troubling with their names.

Inspector Omand eased into the room almost apologetically. But Constable Napier, hard on his heels, positively strode in, passing his superior and issuing a curt bow that was more of a disdainful nod.

"Inspector," Elizabeth said graciously, wisely ignoring the underling.

"Forgive the intrusion, Lady Maule," Omand said, bowing with more respect than grace. The constable cast him a glance of contempt. "But new information has come to light, and we are obliged to ask you a few more questions."

"Please, sit," Elizabeth said distantly, indicating the solitary chair opposite the sofa.

It was a clever move, establishing her superiority and excluding the mere constable from their circle simply by the placement of chairs. But as Inspector Omand sat, Constable Napier picked up an upright chair and carried it across the room to sit beside his superior.

Elizabeth continued to ignore him. "What can I tell you now, inspector?"

"You understand it is expected of us to confirm all the information we are given concerning our case."

"Of course."

"We have just come from London," Omand said, holding her gaze. "Perhaps there is something else you would like to tell us about your life before your marriage?"

Elizabeth paled. Constance had to concentrate on keeping still so that she didn't grasp her friend's hand. Omand's eyes, outwardly benign, missed nothing. Napier's were avid—he was eager for the lady's fall, or perhaps just to prove his own cleverness.

A low growl issued from the door.

"No there isn't, you insolent jackanapes," Sir Humphrey barked. "For one thing, it's not remotely relevant to your investigation, and for another, it's none of your dashed business. You may leave!"

As Maule strode into the room, Constance quietly vacated her place beside Elizabeth, to let him sit there instead. She chose a more distant chair, from where she could still hear and see everyone present.

Maule's face was an impressive, angry glower, his bushy eyebrows almost hiding his eyes and meeting across the bridge of his nose. It should have terrified the policemen, but Omand, although he looked meek, remained clear eyed. Young Napier was almost triumphant.

"Sadly, sir, I may not leave just yet," Omand said. "My duty requires me to investigate, and I'm sure the matter is easily solved. Perhaps, however, her ladyship would prefer to answer in private?"

"Her ladyship would not," snarled Sir Humphrey. "Say what you came to and be damn—"

"Humphrey," Elizabeth said quietly, and he subsided, merely taking her hand in a show of support that at least relieved Constance of one worry. Until she glanced at Napier and saw the gleam of victory in his eyes brighten. He was sure that support was about to be broken.

"Very well," Omand said in a resigned tone. "You previously

stated, my lady, that you are the daughter of Mr. and Mrs. George Lorimer, who reside at Cedar Grove, Kensington, and that you came from there to The Willows to take up employment as governess to Sir Humphrey's children."

"I did," Elizabeth said. Her shoulders remained tense. She knew what was coming.

Napier leaned forward. "Would it surprise you to know that Mr. and Mrs. Lorimer denied they had a daughter?"

Elizabeth lifted her chin. "No, it wouldn't surprise me at all. They disowned me."

"So we established," Omand said with a glance of annoyance at Napier.

"Then what the devil is your business here?" Humphrey demanded. "Family quarrels are scarcely your concern."

"They are when they reflect on the character of a murder suspect," Napier said.

Sir Humphrey shot to his feet in fury, his fists clenched, while Napier gazed back at him with undisguised insolence.

Inspector Omand rose also. "Perhaps you'd be better employed taking notes, Napier," he said acidly. "Too many speakers drag the matter out unnecessarily. Forgive my constable, Sir Humphrey. He is young and overeager."

Sir Humphrey allowed himself to be mollified, and resumed his seat with dignity, although his scowl remained firmly in place.

"Mr. Lorimer informed us," Omand said, also sitting down again, "that he cut all ties with your ladyship when... Are you sure, my lady, that you would not rather have this conversation in private?"

"Quite sure," Elizabeth said with dignity. "Although your tact does you credit, both my husband and Mrs. S—*Grey* are aware that my parents disowned me for bearing a child out of wedlock. I still fail to see that it is a matter for the law."

Napier leaned forward once more, apparently unable to contain himself, until Omand snapped his fingers without looking at him and pointed to the notebook on the constable's knee.

"It is not, of course," Omand agreed. "But the trouble is, this leaves a certain part of your life unaccounted for."

How much did they know? Hiding her dread, Constance glanced from the inspector to Napier.

"How on earth is that relevant?" Humphrey exploded. "We were married months before the Nialls returned from India! And Lady Maule lived here for almost a year before that."

"You must have a very forgiving nature, sir, to employ a governess with such a past," Napier said. "And then to marry her."

Sir Humphrey's fists clenched again, his face a mask of anger. Before he could rise, Omand said between his teeth, "Wait in the hall."

"With all respect—" Napier began, although he clearly had none.

"*Now*," Omand snapped. "Close the door on your way out."

For an instant, Napier looked as if he would disobey even this direct order, though in the end, he rose with ill grace and walked very slowly to the door, so focused on his own outrage that he brushed against Constance's skirts without noticing.

Omand did not wait for his departure. "I apologize once more for my constable's insulting words. He seems to forget you are a justice of the peace. And then, he still sees life in black and white like a child, with no understanding of the complications faced by responsible adults. I hope he will learn before it is too late for his career. And his character."

The door closed with a decided *click*.

Elizabeth's shoulders relaxed slightly. Constance did not. Of the two policemen, she had always known Omand was the wiliest and most dangerous, because he troubled to understand people.

"My wife was the victim of an unscrupulous, evil man," Humphrey said stiffly. "There has never been a question of forgiving her. She remains what she has always been, a good and proper lady."

Elizabeth blinked rapidly, as though trying to be rid of sudden tears.

"And such sentiments do you both credit, sir," Omand said. "The world can be a dangerous and censorious place, and ladies often have little power in it."

"That is very perceptive of you, inspector," Humphrey said.

"Which is why Miss Niall was so unusual," Omand continued. "Having spoken to several of the servants at Fairfield Grange, I am led to believe she seized her own power through—er...knowledge she acquired about various people. Loath as I am to think it, Lady Maule, did Miss Niall ever imply she knew anything to your discredit? Such as, perhaps, your illegitimate child?"

Elizabeth swallowed convulsively. "No," she said. "She never implied she knew anything about my child. He was adopted, if you are wondering."

"That must have been difficult for you," Omand said, his eyes kind—too kind. "We made inquiries at all the usual hospitals and such like, and none of them know of you. My lady, where did you have the baby?"

Elizabeth twitched her brow. It was not the question she had been expecting, and she did not see the trap. Constance did.

"Where?" Elizabeth said a little wildly. "At the home of my friend, Mrs. Grey."

Omand spared Constance a glance. She offered a faint smile and prayed he hadn't also inquired into who *she* was. "And where do you reside, Mrs. Grey?"

"Just off Grosvenor Square," she said steadily.

"In a quiet cul-de-sac," he murmured. "A discreet establishment."

Damn and damn and damn... "No more than any with such an address."

Sir Humphrey was looking puzzled, Elizabeth anxious.

"And when exactly did Lady Maule—Miss Lorimer, as she was then—join your household?"

"She came as my guest," Constance said. "And I cannot quite

recall the precise date."

"I can," Elizabeth said disastrously.

It was all Constance could do not to glare at her. *Be silent, for your own sake. Or at least lie...*

She didn't. "It was Monday the eleventh of March, 1850. I will always remember the date for Mrs. Grey's kindness."

"As no doubt," Omand said, "you remember the date of your parents' *un*kindness."

"What?" Elizabeth said, bewildered.

"Your father states he told you to leave on the morning of the eighteenth of February, 1850. Exactly where did you go before you found refuge with Mrs. Grey?"

The wretched man knew perfectly well that Constance wasn't Mrs. Grey.

But it was Elizabeth who really concerned her. Tears of shame and confusion filled her eyes. And Sir Humphrey was staring at her as if he had never seen her before.

"I don't know," she whispered. "It was such a terrible time for me. I was so afraid."

"Of course you were," Omand said soothingly. "Quite understandable. My trouble is, Lady Maule, that this gives you a motive. I think Frances Niall found out about this lost time and tried to blackmail you with it. Whether for money, or to quit the field of competition for your husband's affections."

His words seemed to slam into Elizabeth, devastating her, and yet Humphrey made no move to comfort her or counter the inspector's conclusion.

"But she never did," Elizabeth protested.

"Would it surprise you to know she had made inquiries with a solicitor in London? And if *we* could find your missing three weeks, so could the solicitor. Lady Maule, with regret, I have to arrest you on suspicion of the murder of Frances Niall."

CHAPTER FIFTEEN

Below stairs, in her sitting room, Mrs. Haslett sat fuming. She was barely able to contain herself, and in fact, the furious words had already erupted, though thankfully only to Manson, with whom she had been enjoying a cup of tea when the policemen were admitted to the kitchen.

"Never in my life have I had to tolerate officers of the law in this house!" she had burst out. "Not until *she* came!"

Manson, of course, had looked all quelling and disapproving. Worse, he had actually taken the policemen upstairs. Which made her very uneasy. Were they informing the master that they meant to arrest one of the staff? Who at The Willows could possibly be responsible for poor Miss Niall's death?

No one, of course. The fools would be making a mistake, but that wouldn't necessarily stop them, and another life would be destroyed...

Manson's stately step sounded on the stairs. Mrs. Haslett jumped to her feet and opened her door. All the servants were staring toward the butler in dread.

"Don't gawp," he commanded. "Finish your work."

He turned toward Mrs. Haslett, who stood aside to let him return to her sitting room, and closed the door on the whispers outside.

"Well," Manson said heavily, "you finally have your wish to be rid of her ladyship. They've arrested her."

The blood drained from her face so quickly she had to sit

down. "Arrested Lady Maule? But that's ridiculous!"

"It is."

"Sir Humphrey won't stand for it," Mrs. Haslett declared.

"I don't see what he can do," Manson said.

"But...but that poor girl... He can't just leave her to the wolves!"

Manson, who had been staring at the wall, turned his curious gaze upon her. "I thought you would be pleased. You've had it in for her from the moment Sir Humphrey told us he was going to marry her."

A twinge of shame shook Mrs. Haslett, but most of what she felt was anger. Martial anger. Very different from her previous *whining*. She sprang to her feet, all but tearing off her apron and throwing it onto the chair.

"That may be. But I will not sit back and let those presumptuous fools take our mistress away! Stand aside, Mr. Manson, or at least bolt the back door. They're taking her nowhere, and so I shall tell them!"

With that, she marched out of the room and up the stairs, ready for battle.

SIR HUMPHREY MAULE felt his world crumble about his ears. This was his worst nightmare. It all made a horrible kind of sense. Frances's accusations against Elizabeth, Elizabeth's own reticence, Colonel Niall's apparently not-so-bizarre accusations... Even the presence of the Greys in support of Elizabeth.

He wasn't quite sure what Omand had implied in that passage with Constance, but the inspector clearly knew something about her, and it was not to her credit. No wonder she had thought nothing of helping an unwed mother, had known so much about how to arrange a respectable adoption...

And none of that mattered before the blinding truth that

Elizabeth had *lied* to him, and repeatedly. The lost weeks that Omand spoke of seemed to burn into his soul, bringing vile, terrible visions that horrified him. Of his wife, whom he loved to distraction. Who was about to be exposed, arrested as a murderess. He would lose her. His children would lose her.

She was already lost...

He tugged at his collar, finding it hard to breathe. He could not bear the sympathy of the policeman, the agony of his wife, the *lies*...

"Arrest?" Constance said with surprising mildness. "Is that not somewhat hasty when this is based on mere speculation on your part?"

"I know Miss Niall was in correspondence with Mr. Dunne of—"

"But not why," Constance interrupted. "You should have spoken to Mr. Dunne himself, but there, I expect that inpatient young man you sent outside was nagging at you to act. He, poor idiot, probably thinks that arresting the wife of a baronet and magistrate will be a feather in his cap."

A spasm crossed Omand's face. He was clearly well aware of the dangers of such an arrest and such an enemy. Maule began to pin his hopes—*hopes for what, dear God?*—on Constance Grey, or whoever she was.

"So, you did not speak to Mr. Dunne," Constance said, locking eyes with the inspector. "Mr. Grey did. And he learned that Frances Niall was not inquiring about Lady Maule but about the adoption of her own illegitimate child. In short, Frances knew nothing to Lady Maule's discredit. Which deprives your theory of any motive."

It seemed Maule was right to rely on her. But it was up to him to play his part now, though he had no idea what he would do after that.

He stood. "I should take that scandal-loving constable of yours away before he manages to get you both dismissed for incompetence. Good evening, inspector."

Omand was already on his feet and managed a jerky bow. "Good evening, sir, my lady. And my apologies for disturbing you, although the matter really did require our attention."

Maule did not trouble to answer. He merely waited in silence until the door closed behind Omand, and then he regarded the stranger who was his wife.

The world was in chaos around him and he wished more than anything to display only dignity and distance. Like Grey. But it was not in his nature. Not when the fear in Elizabeth's eyes maddened him.

"Well?" he exploded. "Who is she?" He jerked his head toward Constance with unforgivable rudeness.

Constance rose. "My name is Constance Silver. And I stand your wife's friend. Yours, too, did you but know it."

The name was vaguely familiar, though he could not place it. His brain was full of Elizabeth and unspeakable ugliness.

"You are my guest under false pretenses," he snapped.

"They are *my* false pretenses," Elizabeth said hoarsely. "I would not let Constance use her own name because I knew you would disapprove."

His lips twisted in more pain than anger. "Did you? Perhaps you should go to bed, Elizabeth."

For a moment, she looked as if she would defy him. Then she bowed her head in misery and left the room.

Sir Humphrey glowered at Constance Silver, who, however, did not look remotely intimidated. Once, Elizabeth had stood up to him too. It was what he had first liked about her.

"I think you had better leave my house, don't you?" he said abruptly. "You and Mr. Grey, or whatever *his* name is."

"We will if you wish, of course, but I should warn you, I will go only as far as the village inn, which might cause the kind of talk you would rather avoid. Not to spite you," she added, raising one hand before he could accuse her of it, "but because I promised to help Elizabeth."

He glared at her, mostly from habit, not because he was

angry. In fact, he didn't seem to be angry at all, though he wanted to be. He didn't know what this feeling was. It might have been at least partly shame because Constance was determined to stand by his wife and he was considering…what? Abandoning her?

He rushed into speech, running from his unbearable thoughts. "Why do I know your name?"

"Perhaps because Elizabeth mentioned me—perhaps because we have mutual friends."

"In Grosvenor Square," he said slowly as bits of chatter in gentlemen's clubs began to come back to him. "In the discreet establishment Omand spoke of. Dear God, did my wife *work* for you?"

"Of course she did not," Constance snapped. For the first time since he had met her, she looked angry. "She was almost five months with child and in no condition to work for anyone."

Inside, he cringed with shame and pity. He didn't want to know, and yet he had to. "Then what was she doing in your…house?"

"Getting well and having her baby. In my house, she was safe."

Safe? Dear God! "And where she came from was not," he murmured, mostly to himself.

"Did her self-righteous father neglect to tell you that he sent her away with nothing but the clothes on her back? You are a large, fit man, used to taking care of yourself. Would *you* like to be alone, friendless, and penniless on the streets of London? She, a gently bred, sheltered young girl, had nowhere to go, nothing to eat, no roof over her head, no protection."

He felt the blood drain from his face. He could not bear much more. And yet what had Elizabeth borne?

Why had she lied?

He stared blindly out of the window. "Where did you meet her?"

"I can't tell you that."

"Why not?"

"Because I promised her my discretion."

"That does not comfort me."

"It wasn't meant to."

He caught his breath and met her gaze once more. "There were three weeks between her leaving her parents' house and entering yours. Where was she?"

"I don't know. Staying alive. Keeping her baby alive."

He closed his eyes. *Why did she keep this from me?*

He knew the answer, of course. Because she thought he could not bear it. And it seemed he couldn't. Or not yet.

He was walking blindly toward the door. "You had better not go immediately. Not until I can work out whether or not I should truly thank you."

He went out of the room without closing the door. Manson and Mrs. Haslett seemed to be arguing by the baize door to the servants' quarters. Ignoring them, he strode straight to his study, where he could be sure of being left alone.

⇥⟫⟫✕⟨⟨⇤

ELIZABETH DID NOT go straight to bed. She went blindly across the hall and almost bumped into Mrs. Haslett, whose eyes glittered with fury.

Go on, then, give notice, say what you like. I don't care. In fact she had no intention of listening.

But the housekeeper's voice was gentle enough to halt her with astonishment. "They didn't do it. Thank God. We won't let them, you know. Will I bring you a calming posset to your bedchamber?"

The unprecedented kindness almost undid Elizabeth. Later, perhaps, she would feel the warmth of it and be grateful. Right now, she could not bear it.

"Thank you, no," she managed. "I am not yet ready to retire. Goodnight, Mrs. Haslett."

She marched away to the dining room, where she found Solomon Grey sitting alone and brooding, twisting his empty wine glass in his fingers. But he glanced up as she entered and rose quickly to his feet.

"Trouble?"

"They tried to arrest me for Frances's murder, but Constance saw them off."

A smile flickered across his full lips. It struck her, irrelevantly, that he should smile more often.

"She is rather wonderful, isn't she?" Elizabeth said shakily. "The trouble is, I'm not sure Humphrey will see it that way. Not once he knows who she is. I think the police know already. I thought I should warn you."

He shrugged very slightly. "I believe the police have an understanding of some kind with Constance."

"Humphrey doesn't." She sat down suddenly in the chair at the head of the table, the one Humphrey must have vacated in such a hurry less than half an hour ago. His half-empty glass stood in front of her. "What should I do?"

"Tell him the truth. He already knows the worst of it."

"No, he doesn't!" Elizabeth replied with more than a hint of desperation. "He might suspect, but he does not *know*."

"Don't you think suspicion is worse than knowledge? For both of you?"

"No," Elizabeth said flatly. "Knowledge would require him to *do* something. I am his *wife*."

"Exactly," Solomon said. "And he is a good man who has already shown himself capable of understanding and kindness. Why should you believe his affection is so limited?"

A frown quirked her brow. "Why? Isn't yours?"

He looked startled. "Mine?"

"For Constance. The kindest of gentlemen might forgive a single fall from grace, an advantage taken by the worst kind of man for purely selfish reasons of his own. But more than one man? For money? Isn't that why you are not married to Constance? Because you can't forgive her for all the men that came before you?"

A mask came down over his face like a shutter. "Constance and I are friends," he said coldly. "There is no question of marriage between us."

Elizabeth laughed, with more anger than mirth. The stupidity of men appalled her. "Oh, *please*. I've seen the way you look at her when you think no one is watching. She is beautiful, intelligent, fun, kind to a fault, devoted to you. And all you see is a *courtesan*." She picked up Humph's brandy glass and took a healthy swallow. "What if I were to tell you I have never seen her with a man? That no clients at her establishment *ever* have appointments with her? Not in the months I was there, not in the years some of the other girls have been with her. No one works there in that way if they don't want to, and that includes Constance. Now do you look at her differently?"

His eyes were impossibly icy. "No."

Her smile was twisted. "Because you don't believe me."

"Actually, I do believe you. It is you who doesn't believe me when I tell you Constance and I are friends. But we are not the issue here. If you wish to keep your husband with any hope of happiness, tell him the truth."

She pushed the glass away from her. "I can't," she whispered. "I love him and he's all I have. He and the children. I would rather have doubt than outright contempt."

"Would you?" Solomon rose to his feet. "Think about it," he said gently, the compassion back in his melting, dark eyes. He walked behind her and on toward the door, where he paused and glanced back at her. "Why does she keep doing it? Why does she not walk away?"

"Because she is needed. And she makes a difference. I am far from the only one."

His lips quirked. It might have been a smile, but she still could not read his eyes. He turned and quietly left the room.

Further along the hall, a door closed. Humphrey, seeking

solitude in his study. He had sent her to bed like a naughty schoolgirl because he could not bear the sight of her. Solomon's footsteps moved steadily on to the drawing room.

Tomorrow, probably, she would be ashamed of throwing Constance in his face. In fact, their relationship baffled her, though it was none of her business and she should not have interfered. But she was tired of women being blamed for men's failings, of being reviled for doing their best, for falling and failing... Whatever Constance's past—and Elizabeth knew very little about it—Solomon should understand that she was the best person Elizabeth knew.

Apart from Humph.

Tears prickled. Would she be proving her innocence of murder at the expense of her marriage, her happiness with the funny, kind, grumpy bear of a man who was her husband? She put her head in her hands and closed her eyes, squeezing them tight.

Then, slowly, she opened them again, let her hands fall, and rose to her feet. She left the dining room and walked down the hall to Humph's study, a silent, wordless prayer in her head.

She opened the door and went in. He too was sitting with his head in his hands, although he raised it at once, looking more disoriented than irritated.

"Humph," she said, "will you hear the truth and still believe I love you?"

He was unusually pale, even in the dim candlelight, and almost haggard. The pain in his eyes devastated her, drowning her last hope in despair.

"I don't know," he whispered. Then, blindly, he took her hand and drew her on to his lap. Burying his face in her neck, he said in muffled tones, "Tell me it all this time. If you can bear it, so can I."

"IT'S NOT HUMPHREY," Constance said as soon as Solomon entered the drawing room. She was pacing the floor like a caged if graceful animal, not even pausing as she flung the words at him over her shoulder. Her wide skirts rustled expensively. The glow of the candles caught glints of red and gold in her hair, enhancing the flawless beauty of her skin.

It hurt to look at Constance sometimes. He had assumed that was because she could never be his. But now, suddenly, it was as if some glass wall between them had shattered. Only illusion, misunderstanding, had kept him from acknowledging his attraction to her.

Even *attraction* was a poor, weak word for intense feelings that rocked him in utter confusion.

Just because Constance did not lie with men for money? Was Elizabeth right about that?

Partly. A man wanted to be the only one...or this man did. But there was more. In some ways, Constance's profession had been a crutch to him, preventing him from falling, and he had grasped it like a weapon. Because he was afraid of the depths.

Solomon had known women before. Charming, witty, soft, sweet or fierce, each had fascinated and soothed him for a while. But he had always been in control. With Constance...

He reminded himself sharply that he was not *with* Constance. What the devil had she just said to him?

"It's not Humphrey."

"Why?" he managed. "What did you learn from him? Or from the police?"

She shook her head impatiently, whirling to face him. "Nothing we did not already know. But he is too honest, Solomon, too hurt and *soft* inside. He loves Elizabeth, but he could no more kill another woman who threatened her than she could. Nor could he conduct an affair behind her back, on his own doorstep, not from lust and not from blackmail."

"And his first wife? Could he have killed her?"

She gazed at him. "Do you think he could have?"

"We have no evidence either way. But...no, I don't see it."

"We have no physical evidence at all," Constance said. "And if there is none to be had, then we have only what we do know or feel to solve the puzzle." She swung abruptly toward the door. "Let's go up to our room."

Cynically, Solomon supposed there were any number of men who would have given their right arms to hear such an invitation from Constance Silver. If only for the bragging opportunities. *Unforgivable...*

He followed her out of the drawing room. At the top of the stairs, he heard Elizabeth cross the hall below and enter the study. Metaphorically, he crossed his fingers for them.

The maids had not yet lit the bedroom lamps, so he and Constance did, before she grasped all the letter paper from their desk and a sharpened pencil from the drawer, then sank to the floor in a flurry of skirts that folded around her like a pretty, silken nest.

"We know character," she said. "So we know neither Elizabeth nor Humphrey are guilty."

"Very well."

"They both saw Frances walking away from the lake by the path that leads to the road, just after ten o'clock the night she died." She seemed to merely scribble on the paper, and yet what appeared was the small, neat lettering he had seen before.

"Where did you learn to read and write?" he asked, because he had wondered for months. "At school?"

"My mother taught me." She paused, casting him a quick glance as though, belatedly, she wondered if she had given away too much.

He kept his gaze bland. "Who was your mother?"

"Who *is* my mother," she corrected him. "Pray you never find out. We don't think Frances went home. If she did, she entered the house secretly, probably by the window as we did. If she didn't, where did she go?"

Solomon sat astride the desk chair, resting his arms along its back so that he could see what she was writing. "Somewhere she kept the nightgown she was found in, which her maid had not seen for months. Presumably the place she met her lover. Though would you need a nightgown for such a tryst?"

To his surprise, color seeped along the delicate lines of her cheekbones. "Perhaps it depends on the nightgown. Or how warm the trysting place. Which we believe to be no more than fifteen minutes' walk from Fairfield Grange."

"And we found no such likely place. No abandoned cottages or even derelict huts or hidden caves or empty potting sheds. Apart from Sarah Phelps's barn. If Frances ran, she could probably have got to the lake boathouse in fifteen minutes, but there's hardly room to swing a cat in there, let alone lie down in acute discomfort."

"Then we're left with occupied houses," Constance said thoughtfully. She sighed. "Which is hardly feasible. No such affair could have been conducted in secret. But for the sake of it, which occupied houses could she have reached? The Fairfield gardener's cottage, Waterside Farmhouse..."

"The cow byre at Waterside, which is hardly salubrious," Solomon added. "And the large barn at the Grange, which is constantly busy and has nowhere to hide. The same with the stables and the carriage house, both of which have servants living above them."

Constance wrote it all down, adding quick notes. "Where else? Dr. Laing's cottage, which is constantly full of people, and his shed is full of pots and herbs."

"Sarah Phelps's house, and The Willows," Solomon finished. "Also constantly full of people—or person—in their own ways, with nowhere to hide. Even if her lover were a servant—and we think she had grown out of that particular taste—how could they have met at The Willows with no one knowing?"

Constance met his gaze. "Someone *could* know. She could have blackmailed them to silence. We know she used such tricks to get her own way. What if it were Darby? He could run rings around his wife, ride over here whenever he chose."

"Hiding his horse where?" Solomon asked. "Making love to her where? Even supposing Frances could have found a secret way into The Willows—and I admit I wouldn't put it past her, not least to punish Humphrey and Elizabeth—surely any of the staff here could and should have seen the signs. Mrs. Haslett might not like Elizabeth, but she would never keep such an outrage from Maule."

Constance threw down her pencil with frustration. "It's the secrecy that is so impossible! She could never have rushed down here so often without someone noticing! She might have forced poor Worcester to silence, but think of everyone who must have seen her rushing—and she would need to have rushed to get here within fifteen minutes—and for what? A quick kiss before she turned and ran back? It makes no sense."

"You're right," Solomon said slowly. "It has to be the Grange. With someone who had every right to be there."

Her breath caught. Incest was not as unheard of as decent people thought, even among the most vocally righteous. And Frances had been undeniably troubled... But John had been a child when they left for India, and the colonel had had her watched in the subcontinent if not at home. Surely he would not have done so with such a gross secret to hide. But still, the Grange was a distinct possibility for other assignations.

"Locked doors," she said. "Attics. Frances ruled the roost at Fairfield. She could keep the servants away from wherever she chose. She might even have pretended to go out, to stop people looking for her, when in reality she crept straight back in again. Oh, the devil, Sol, we have to go back to that house!"

CHAPTER SIXTEEN

S INCE JOHN HAD locked the window to Frances's bedroom, they had decided Constance should pick the lock on the kitchen door, a feat she wasn't quite sure she could accomplish, though locked doors on the inside should give her less trouble.

Most of the house was already in darkness, but a light still came from the servants' hall, so Constance and Solomon waited with what patience they could muster behind the herb garden wall. The kitchen door looked bright and jaunty to Constance, a lantern of a particularly fat, bulbous shape unlit beside it. She recalled seeing several that shape during her previous visits.

Despite her doubts about being able to pick the lock of the kitchen door—and the fact that even if she could, the large old bolts she remembered could be shot too—Constance felt good about the evening's chances. She didn't know why, but a sense of lighthearted excitement had seeped through her during their walk from The Willows. Although she didn't like the Grange, there was nowhere she would rather be than here in the silent company of Solomon Grey.

She liked his silence. She liked it more when his eyes spoke, and for a while tonight, they had. He had come from his talk with Elizabeth looking slightly dazed, almost bewildered, and yet he had focused on her with a glow in his eyes that made her heart beat and caused everything to seem worthwhile. Like the morning he had kissed her goodbye in Norfolk and she had known she would see him again. Tonight seemed to hold some equal significance, and the knowledge made her recklessly happy.

Crouching close to her, not quite touching, Solomon remained still and watchful. Sometimes, she was sure he was watching her, and then that he was merely listening for movement. She wanted to lean against him and make him fall over, just to laugh. Just for the excuse to put her arms around him...

The opening of the kitchen door took her by surprise. Peering over the wall, she saw Worcester step outside and gaze up at the sky. He was quite alone. After a few moments, he strolled up the path that led through the herb garden, parallel to the wall and several yards away from it. He seemed to need only the light spilling from the kitchen through the open door, for he left the unlit lantern where it was.

Constance caught her breath. This was their chance. Rising, she pulled herself up and over the wall. She thought Solomon might have grabbed at her skirt, but he was too late. She ran swiftly and silently to the kitchen door and bolted inside, narrowly avoiding kicking the lantern on her way.

The rest of the kitchen, and the servants' hall beyond, seemed to be deserted. Fortunately so, for when Solomon skidded inside and hid behind the door, he crashed into her and she let out a breathless giggle.

He glared at her. She patted his arm. He didn't move away, but she supposed he couldn't for fear Worcester would come back in and see them. His lips twitched and she smiled at him.

An instant later, Worcester stepped back inside and pulled the covering door away from them. Constance forgot to breathe while the butler closed and locked the door—he *did* bolt it, too—and walked away without seeing them. He didn't look back.

He lit a candle from the branch on the kitchen table, then blew the others out and carried his solitary light up toward the baize door.

Constance could not believe their luck. Neither, she suspected, could Solomon, who gazed at her with a sardonic twist of his lips. They waited in silence. Constance didn't mind. She was quite warm now, and Solomon's arm was pressed to her shoulder, his leg against hers. They had no need to stand so close anymore, but for a long time, neither of them moved.

At last, when she could discern no movement in the house, Solomon stepped away from her. Well, it was why they had come.

With her old drawings and Elizabeth's description of the house still in her head, Constance led the way. But they could not blunder silently about a strange house with no light whatsoever. Solomon lit a candle and followed her, shading the light with his hand.

As they crept along the main hallway, she saw the lantern by the side door, and another by the front door. She felt sure Frances had placed them there, inside and out, to ease her clandestine departures and arrivals. Or to make people think that was what they were for, when in reality she was in some secret room in the house.

The main public rooms would have been too difficult to use. Likewise the bedrooms on the second floor, which her family could have entered at any time, however she ordered the servants.

Creeping up the stairs, Constance heard what sounded like an animal snarling, and almost grasped Solomon's hand in terror. Then she realized it was snoring and had to swallow down another surge of laughter. The room it came from was the first they passed, probably Colonel Niall's.

No light shone under the door of the room she knew to be Frances's. Nor the one next to it, which must have been John's, for it had been open when he showed them out. At least he did not appear to be up and about tonight. He could be asleep, or out at the inn, perhaps, if the innkeeper had not thrown him out at this time of night.

There was another door opposite. She tried to peer through the keyhole, and when Solomon lowered the candle, she saw that it was a linen cupboard with no space for trysts. Moving forward to the last door, she realized it was slightly ajar. Solomon pushed it open, and she tensed in case the hinges squeaked.

They didn't. It was a guest bedchamber, which had possibilities, for the bed was fully made up. They crept inside, closing the door again. Constance sniffed. She could smell the faintest scent of lavender, but it was slightly musty, as though it had been there a long time, as if the room had not been aired out for months.

Would Frances tolerate that? Or the very real risk of discovery that had seemed to so excite Darby? It would have been very different for her in her own home. Why would she do it? It wasn't even love.

Without exchanging so much as a whisper, she and Solomon moved around the room, opening drawers and cupboards as silently as they could. All were empty, apart from one or two old lace lavender sachets. Constance felt beneath the pillows on the bed, ran her hands over the sheet. Clean.

She looked up and met Solomon's gaze. She shook her head, and they moved toward the door. While Solomon closed it, placing it in exactly the same position as before, Constance ignored the way to the back stairs used by the servants—they would have little or no cause to be in their attic rooms during the day, but several of Frances's apparent assignations had been at night, when the servants might well have heard her in their territory. She was looking for a part of the attic more accessible to the family, like a storage area.

Her heart was beating fast. This was surely the likeliest of areas for a love nest. They were about to discover something of massive importance, something that would solve the mystery, clear Elizabeth's name, and identify the true culprit...

It was certainly a storage area. Moonlight gleamed through two skylights, bathing the large, crowded room in an eerie silver glow. Furniture smothered in Holland covers, piles of ancient boxes, dust dancing before her eyes. Her blood chilled and she realized she had unconsciously moved closer to Solomon.

He walked away at once, quite rightly, for there was no point in them both searching the same area. But Constance, sensitive to atmosphere, liked this place even less than the rest of the house. Generations of Nialls had abandoned their possessions here. It felt as if some part of those long-dead people clung to their things, to this place. The kind and the angry and the malicious... Even Frances herself.

She shivered as she crept reluctantly to the far side of the attic. Her lightheartedness had long since vanished into discomfort, a nameless dread of the *presence*...

Some movement caught the corner of her eye, and she swung toward it, gasping. Her heart lurched and froze at sight of the ghostly figure before her—an insubstantial being, tall and thin yet gauzy and transparent like a spider's web, only moving, fluttering toward her.

She could not move, though some strange, inarticulate sound spilled from her lips.

"What is it?" Solomon closed his fingers around her wrist before she dropped the candle.

And immediately she saw the ghost for what it was—a very thin bedsheet with moth holes, draped over a tall, Grecian-style lamp as a makeshift dust sheet.

"Nothing," she said shakily. At least she could keep her voice as low as his.

"Nothing over there either." He moved on, keeping with her now, as though he sensed her reasonless dread.

Or perhaps he felt it too. Would one ever know with Solomon?

Steadied, she realized now that every surface was covered with the dust of years. They were probably leaving footprints on the floor. Nothing seemed to have been moved or added since before the family went to India. And there was certainly no comfortable, cozy love nest like the one they had found in Greenforth Manor this summer.

"Nothing," she murmured. "Why is there nothing? Are we wrong?"

"Wrong about the Grange, I think. Unless you want to search the coal cellar."

"The wine cellar is a possibility. Darby would like that."

"But would Frances have liked Darby?"

"I don't think she liked any of them. Except perhaps Humphrey. She was lost."

He nodded as though he understood, which he probably did. In his own way, he had been lost too since his twin brother vanished.

She shuddered. "Let's get out of here."

Obediently, he led the way back to the staircase. As soon as she closed the door on the attic, a weight seemed to fall from her shoulders. Even the small click of the latch only made her smile. They had been lucky this far. Why should that change?

From John's bedchamber came the sound of movement, perhaps of him turning over in bed. Hopefully. How embarrassing to be caught by him for the second time, creeping uninvited about his home.

Perhaps that should have made her feel guilty. She was too eager to get out and move on. Though to where?

It came to her quite suddenly.

Sarah Phelps.

If her animals were not sick or giving birth, why would she sleep in the cold barn?

Without meaning to, Constance increased her pace, hurrying on to the main staircase and all but running down.

Above, a bedchamber door opened, and she glanced back instinctively. She missed her footing on the next step, coming down too heavily and going over on her ankle. Pain shot through her, and she bit her lip in an effort to muffle her involuntary gasp.

"Papa?" came John's voice from above. "Is that you?"

Solomon swept an arm around her waist, lifting her entirely off the ground. She felt herself fly through the air, heard rather than felt the thud of his landing. Apparently they were favoring speed over silence now.

She felt like a sack of potatoes under his arm, and it made her want to laugh, even past the pain that screamed through her ankle. Solomon bolted across the hall, through the baize door to the kitchen, almost in a blur. He had to let her go to pull back the bolts and unlock the door at the same time.

She hobbled after him in agony, but this time, as soon as the door was closed behind them, he picked her up like a baby in both arms and ran. He jumped the herb garden wall like a horse, and she reached down and grabbed the unlit lantern they had left there.

His breath of laughter vibrated through her, and she couldn't prevent her own responsive giggle. Hastily, she muffled it in his shoulder. He ran until they reached the cover of the trees, then paused to glance back at the house.

No lights were obvious. She hoped they had not been seen, although surely John would realize there had been an intruder. Even if he assumed it was his father and went back to bed, the servants would see in the morning that the back door was unlocked and unbolted.

"Oh well," she murmured philosophically. "You can put me down now, though I might have to hop."

"Wait." He carried her farther through the trees, probably until he could be sure there was no pursuit. His arms felt too good around her, strong and firm, though his grip was unexpectedly gentle. She hated feeling helpless as a rule, but she didn't hate this at all. She inhaled his familiar, distinctive scent of spice and sandalwood, soaked up his warmth, his nearness, his sheer masculinity.

You poor, silly fool of a woman. Pull yourself together.

He halted and bent, depositing her gently on the ground. Her breath caught and she grasped her bottom lip between her teeth.

Without a word, he took the lantern from her and set about lighting it from the flint and tinder box in his coat pocket. "We'll have to take the boot off before your foot swells—if it hasn't done so already. I'll cut it off if necessary."

She tensed and had to concentrate on not yelping, which at least distracted her from the shock of his quick, deft fingers untying the laces of her boot, holding her calf just above the ankle while he eased off the boot.

Well, it might have been easy for him. It wasn't for her. He touched the hem of her gown with clear intent. She hoped he didn't feel her jump. Hastily and discreetly, she reached under her own skirts and pulled down her stocking. He brushed her fingers aside, rolling the stocking gently off her foot, which he inspected closely.

"Can you move it?" he asked.

She did so, side to side, and arched her foot. "It isn't broken. I think I've sprained it."

"I think you have. We should get one of the doctors to look at it. Either that or borrow Sarah Phelps's wheelbarrow."

"Bad taste, Solomon. But about Sarah, we need to go and see her." She met his frowning gaze with a resurgence of excitement. "Sol, if she slept in the barn, *who slept in her house?*"

SOLOMON STARED AT her, almost forgetting her injury and the inappropriately tempting feel of her slender foot in his hand. "Of course... Frances had an arrangement with her. Most likely a forced one of blackmail. What on earth could she have known that Sarah would care about?"

"I don't know, and I'm not sure it matters." Constance snatched her stocking from his fingers, shook it out, and, gritting her teeth, pulled it over her foot. She left it folded around her ankle and tried to rise.

At once, he helped her up to her one good foot and reached around her back.

"I can walk," she said quickly. "If you just let me lean on your arm."

"Just let me help you." He spoke more curtly than he'd intended, probably because her desire for distance hurt him in some way he wasn't ready to examine. Elizabeth's revelations about Constance, leading to his own about himself, were still too new and confusing.

Without waiting for permission, he picked her up again, one arm at her back, the other beneath her knees as though she were a small child. If only he could think of her that way. She was light enough, but her curves and her scent were all woman, all Constance.

He marched along in silence, which she did not break either. Turning onto the road, he changed his grip slightly. She was no longer laughing into his coat, but nor was she rigid with outrage.

"It needs a bandage," he said abruptly, "at the very least."

"I can see to that myself at The Willows. I expect it will be fine in the morning."

He found himself smiling because she was always so positive.

"I thought we would solve it all tonight," she said with a sigh. "That was overoptimistic."

"If you're right about Sarah, then we are very close."

"If we can persuade her to tell us who Frances met there."

"If she knows. Unless… Frances was petty enough to exert her power just because she could. Would she have thrown Sarah out of her own house, for no real reason but punishment for some slight? Would she substitute her home comforts for Sarah's hovel for no real gain?"

"You think Sarah did it after all?" Constance said, raising her head to peer into his face. She brought the lantern up for a closer look. "Because she'd had enough of the blackmail?"

His lips twitched. "She has a wheelbarrow."

"But would she have dumped the body in Sir Humphrey's lake? He seems to be one of the few people she tolerates."

"He is. Elizabeth isn't."

She fell back into silence.

Disappointingly, Dr. Laing's cottage appeared to be in darkness.

"We shouldn't disturb them," she said, "not for something so trivial."

Reluctantly, Solomon walked on past the gate. Which was when he caught a glimmer of light at the side of the house. It seemed to be coming from the back, probably the kitchen. On impulse, he swung back, changing his grip of her to one arm so that he could open the gate, then walked up the path that led around the house to the back garden.

The kitchen curtains were not closed, and a lamp burned within.

"It's probably the housekeeper," Constance hissed.

"Perhaps. Knock on the door."

She scowled, and for a moment he thought she would refuse. Instead, she wriggled against him to draw her squashed arm free, while he endured the exquisite torture. Reaching beyond him, she scratched quietly at the door. He opened his mouth to demand greater effort, but already, he heard the scraping of a chair on the floor. The door opened and Dr. Murray was revealed in his shirt sleeves, his throat bare and his waistcoat unfastened.

His eyebrows flew up and he threw the door wide. "Good grief, what has happened? Bring her inside."

"I'm fine," Constance said crossly. "We shouldn't be disturbing you for something so trivial. I'm afraid I went over on my ankle, but I'm sure it will be fine in the morning."

"You had better let me judge," Murray said. "Since you are here."

Solomon lowered her to one of the four kitchen chairs at the well-scrubbed table. Murray went to the sink and washed his hands with soap. After drying his hands on a clean towel he took from a drawer, he dropped to his knees before Constance and gently placed her foot on his lap. Without fuss, he removed the stocking.

Her ankle was more swollen now, and a dark bruise was forming there and along the roots of her toes. He passed the towel to Solomon. "Soak that for me, would you? And wring it out."

While Solomon obeyed, Murray felt around the ankle and foot. Constance gritted her teeth but didn't otherwise complain, even when the doctor manipulated her foot, then, with a grunt of satisfaction, wrapped the cloth around it. Dragging forward another chair, he placed her foot upon it.

"A sprain, as you thought," he pronounced. "It will be painful for several days and will require rest. Let me fetch a bandage."

As he stood and went to the cupboard at the other side of the room, Solomon examined her face. Her pain made him anxious, uncomfortable in ways he was not used to. But her gaze was beyond him, fixed on the little table by the back door, where he had dumped their lantern. Beside it sat a flint and tinder box, a tiny candle, and another fat, bulbous lantern of the type he had seen...where?

Fairfield Grange.

Constance lifted her gaze to Solomon's face. A blaze of triumph lit her eyes as she glanced quickly, significantly, at Murray.

Murray!

CHAPTER SEVENTEEN

S OLOMON'S HEAD REELED all over again, and yet lots of mental gears were slipping into place.

They had never truly considered Dr. Murray because he was the one who had drawn attention to Frances's lungs, pointing out that she had not drowned as was originally assumed, and setting off the whole murder inquiry.

But if Murray was the dead woman's lover... Surely, it made sense? She'd wanted to be a physician once, had studied books on anatomy that appalled her parents. She must have been drawn to a doctor who was young, personable, a gentleman by education if nothing else. No doubt he had been flattered and easy to manipulate—until he had had enough. Perhaps she had betrayed him, taunted him as she had done Elizabeth and Maule, because he had only ever been a substitute for Sir Humphrey. From a lover, such cruelty must have been unendurable...

If Murray had been with Frances in Sarah Phelps's cottage, then it would have been easy to smother her with Sarah's pillow, or poison her or whatever was done to her, then put her in the wheelbarrow in the dead of night to dump her in The Willows lake—taking with him the lantern Frances herself was carrying when she'd left Elizabeth and gone to meet her lover.

Oh, yes, Murray...

The young doctor placed a bandage on the table and poured two cups of tea from the pot beside it. He put sugar in one without asking and pushed it toward Constance, along with a jug of milk. The other cup, he gave to Solomon.

"Thank you," Constance said meekly, although she did not take sugar in her tea.

Murray picked up his own half-full cup and finished it before reaching for the bandage. Solomon waited for fear and anger to slice through him. But they were unaccountably slow to form, even though a murderer should not be touching Constance.

Nor should he be such an instinctively kind man, a healer. Murray had not even asked where she had fallen or why they were out walking so late. Healing was his first priority. Had he not pointed out that Frances had not drowned, everyone would have gone on assuming she had.

"I do like that shape of lantern," Constance said idly, as though making mere small talk while the doctor bandaged her foot and ankle.

"Hmm?" Murray spared it a quick glance. "Oh yes. It's not ours. It comes from the Grange. Laing keeps forgetting to take it back."

Because not Laing but Murray had brought it to the house? Then again, only Laing attended the Nialls, so how had Murray met Frances? By chance?

Sarah insisted on seeing Laing too. Solomon took a breath. Where was Murray's excuse for going to Sarah's house so often? Maule had given the impression that earlier today had been the first time. Sarah, like the Nialls, only consulted Laing.

Solomon wanted to bang his head on the table for his own stupidity.

"Does Dr. Laing get called often to the Nialls?" he asked casually.

Murray grimaced. "All the time. They must be a household of hypochondriacs. Poor old Laing barely gets a night's decent sleep."

"Even now?" Solomon said. "Since Miss Niall's death?"

Constance was staring at him over Murray's head. The doctor's fingers paused in the act of tying off the bandage. "Actually, not so much. She must have been the worst offender. Or should I say the sickest."

Constance's eyes widened. Was she following Solomon's groping for the truth? This *was* the truth. It slotted everything into place.

Laing had either deliberately ignored the state of Frances's lungs at the autopsy or been too upset by his lover's death, or by his own act of violence, to realize that Murray would see the evidence better than he.

"What are the visible signs of asphyxiation?" Constance asked.

Murray rose and stared at her. "If you are talking about Miss Niall, there were none." He frowned. "Except perhaps those tiny brown spots on her eyelids, but Laing's opinion was that they were not distinct enough to—"

"Why did you attend Sarah Phelps?" Solomon interrupted, for his mind was racing. Laing *had* interfered with the autopsy report, just enough to prevent any certainty. Murray was observant and smart, but Laing was the man of experience and decision. "I thought she insisted on Dr. Laing."

"Laing was too busy, but I was worried about her and went myself. She didn't summon either of us." Murray looked bewildered, turning back and forth between Solomon and Constance. "Why are you...?"

Laing had not been too busy to see Sarah. He had been afraid to go near her because she knew... The same reason she had not asked for him.

A footfall sounded beyond the door to the hallway. Everyone looked toward it, and Solomon forgot to breathe. He should have got Constance out of there as soon as the truth hit him. She was in no condition to face a murderer, to run... Their only hope was that Laing did not suspect they knew.

In the sudden tension, he risked a glance at Constance, willing her to understand. *Not Murray. Laing.* Their eyes met for barely an instant of silent communication, but he saw that she was already with him. She knew.

The door was pushed open with a creak of unoiled hinges, and Dr. Laing stepped into the kitchen. No monster of murder and lies, just an overworked medical man with rumpled hair and shadows beneath his eyes, still fully dressed as though he had been working.

He smiled amiably. "What a lot of chatter for the small hours. It's after midnight, you know. Are we having a feast?"

"Cup of tea?" Murray offered. "Mrs. Grey sprained her ankle."

The two doctors were on good terms, Solomon saw. Did that matter? Was Murray an ally, deliberately covering for Laing? Did he know what Laing had done? The cottage was not large. They could not help but be aware when each other went out, when someone visited...

Focus.

"Bad luck, ma'am," Laing was saying, concern on his face that was surely genuine. "But you should have sent a servant for one of us to come to you. I'm sorry, I didn't even hear your conveyance arrive."

"Oh, we don't have one," Constance said. "We were out walking when I foolishly turned my ankle."

"Walking in the dark is unwise, even in the country. Rabbit holes, poacher traps, and all sorts of obstacles that you can't see or would even think about coming from the city. You must have fallen close by."

"Up toward Fairfield Grange," she said with a lightness Solomon knew was forced, though he doubted the doctors would notice. "My husband carried me here, though I told him not to disturb you."

"Mr. Grey was quite right," Laing said, taking the last available chair at the table. "To walk on it without support would have been much more damaging. As it is, you should rest it as much as possible for the next few days. You should not, for example, walk home. Murray, if you harness old Betsy to the gig, I shall drive Mrs. Grey back to The Willows."

Oh no, you won't. Solomon summoned a smile, the kind of meaningless yet implacable expression he normally reserved for business meetings. "I confess the use of your gig would be welcome, but there is no need to disturb either of you. I can harness it myself and have one of Maule's people return it immediately."

"First light will do, won't it?" Murray said with a quick glance at Laing. "That way, you and I can get a tad more well-earned rest."

"Well, I'm glad you are awake enough to think more sensibly than I," Laing said with a tired smile.

Murray reached for an old coat hanging from a hook on the back door, struggled into it, and lit a spill from the lamp before choosing the shabbier lantern beneath the table, the one that had not come from the Grange.

"You must remember to take *that* one back to the Nialls," he said, tapping the bulbous lamp.

"I doubt they'll miss it," Constance said. "They have lots of them."

It was a mistake.

Solomon knew she spoke to ease the curious tension in the room, which she was extremely good at. But the words drew Laing's attention. Just for an instant, and his expression was unreadable. More sorrow than panic or anger. As if the lantern was the last memento he had of his lover? Or was he just reluctant to return it now, while the police were still poking around and one of the mysteries surrounding the death was what had happened to Frances's lantern?

"They have lots of everything," Laing said lightly. "But you are right. I will take it back tomorrow." As Murray left by the back door with his lantern, Laing turned his gaze back to Constance. "How does your ankle feel? Are you still in much pain?"

"It feels much better with the bandage," she replied.

Laing glanced from her to Solomon. "I suppose you are still

investigating Miss Niall's death for Lady Maule? Is that why you were up at the Grange?"

Damn... Solomon shrugged. "Yes, though it was a waste of time. We didn't find anything."

"Except a rabbit hole," said Constance, "or whatever it was. Those policemen actually came up to The Willows this evening, intending to arrest poor Lady Maule."

Laing's idly drumming fingers on the table stilled. "You mean they didn't?"

"Thankfully, no. Their information was incorrect."

"Well, that is a relief. They were here this afternoon, asking questions about her, about her past. Obviously, I could tell them nothing except she had come initially as the governess and I knew nothing against her. I have always found her a most pleasant lady. I am glad she is still free, though one can't help wondering what on earth they thought they had against her."

"Lies, I daresay," Constance said amiably. "There are many lies and deceptions surrounding Miss Niall's life and death. If only they were not so wretchedly impenetrable."

Good girl. Solomon breathed again.

"Then your investigations do not prosper?" Laing asked sympathetically.

"Quite the opposite," Solomon said, flicking one hand toward Constance's ankle, still propped up on the kitchen chair.

"Ah, let me fetch you a cushion for your ankle, ma'am. And perhaps a blanket?"

"No, no," Constance said. "It will be too short a drive to get cold."

"Although the cushion will be welcome," Solomon said.

At once, Laing rose and left the kitchen, leaving the door ajar.

Solomon looked at Constance, who gazed back, eyebrows arched. They did not speak, in case Laing overheard them. And yet to say nothing must surely seem unnatural... Not that it would matter once they had left the cottage. Solomon had every intention of driving straight down to the village and rousing

Inspector Omand from his no-doubt-uneasy slumber.

On its own, perhaps the Fairfield lantern was not enough evidence against a trusted man, but among Laing's private things, Solomon was sure they would find proof of the liaison. If they did not give him time to destroy them.

And with all of that, Sarah Phelps would surely break her silence.

"You know, it really does feel much better," Constance said in light, admiring tones, even though he could feel her rigidity next to him. He covered her hand in her lap for an instant, giving it an understanding squeeze.

"All the same, I think you'll be glad of the cushion—and I will be glad of the gig."

"Are you calling me fat, husband?"

"I would not dare, wife of my heart." The bantering words came easily, almost as if he meant them.

Laing returned to the kitchen, clutching a plump cushion, which Solomon rose to take from him with thanks. From outside came the clop of hooves, the rumble of wheels coming along the lane and onto the road.

"Your carriage awaits," Laing said with a smile. "Don't forget your lantern."

Solomon lit it with a spill, as Murray had the other one. Behind him, he heard the change in Constance's breathing and whipped around to see that Laing had lifted her from her chair. She did not cringe, and surely her odd stiffness would seem natural in a lady being handled by a man not her husband?

Solomon, who was not her husband either, was conscious of much more powerful emotions. He wanted to snatch her from Laing's hold and knock him down for daring to touch her. Only fear for her held him back. The man held her, could hurt her, throw her... The blood rang in his ears and his stomach twisted into knots.

Somehow, he managed to move forward, to open the kitchen door for Laing to pass through with his burden.

"You see?" Constance said cheekily. "Dr. Laing carries me easily. He does not find me fat."

Her performance enabled him to breathe, to keep up with her. "He is clearly far fitter than I," he said mildly, following closely on the doctor's heels and watching closely for any attack from Murray, who waited at the horse's head. Solomon hadn't yet decided if Murray was the dupe or the active ally. After all, he had allowed himself to be overruled at the autopsy, if not on the lungs then on the spots on the eyelids.

"You go up first," Laing instructed Solomon. "And I shall pass her to you."

Solomon hesitated. He would be in the gig, with Murray in control of the horse, and Constance in Laing's hands. He didn't like it. He didn't like it all.

But Constance was already in Laing's hold. Solomon could not challenge him.

"Of course," he murmured, hooking the lantern to the side of the vehicle and then climbing in. His heart in his mouth, he reached for Constance as though he had no doubts whatsoever of Laing's next move.

Laing surrendered her with no reluctance at all, and helped settle her comfortably on the bench. Solomon placed her sprained foot on the cushion, and Murray darted inside briefly to retrieve her forgotten boot.

"Thank you both so much," Solomon said, shortening the reins. "We are in your debt. I'll be sure to see horse and gig returned to you at dawn. Goodnight."

He flicked the reins, and the old horse ambled off.

"Goodnight." The voices of Constance and the doctors mingled with the sounds of horse and gig. Solomon was afraid to breathe until he heard the distant closing of the cottage door.

Constance sagged beside him. "Oh, thank God. Does he know we know? Is Murray covering for him?"

"I think he knows," Solomon said grimly, trying to shake the old horse into an increase of pace. "Shall I drop you at The

Willows before I go on to the village?"

"Absolutely not!" she exclaimed, making him smile in spite of everything. "Speed is of the essence now."

As though she agreed, the old mare finally broke into a reluctant trot.

Which was when a light suddenly flew over their heads and dropped beneath the traces in a tinkling of glass. An instant later a sharp crack rent the air and Betsy screamed, trying to rear up, while flames licked up over the front of the gig.

Solomon dropped the reins and dived into Constance, hurling her with him into the road, just as another shot rang out.

SARAH HAD FALLEN asleep in her chair by the stove. She woke with a start to a loud bang. Disoriented, she didn't know if it was a clap of thunder, a firework, or a gunshot. She had no idea of the time, but alarm set her struggling out of her chair.

The candle had burned down an inch or two—which was a waste, since she should have gone to bed and blown it out—but it couldn't have been so very late. She just felt so very tired and groggy with this damned cough.

As another bang sounded, she staggered across to the cottage door. Definitely not thunder. Opening the door, she saw the flaring glow at once. It was further up the hill, on the road where nothing should have been able to burn. No one but poachers hunted in the middle of the night, and surely they would not risk shooting or burning...

But someone *was* risking it. With a spurt of angry shame, she knew she had stayed silent too long. The girl had been vile in many ways, but she hadn't deserved to die. Killing was wrong, but once committed... Well, one might as well be hanged for a sheep as a lamb. She couldn't change that murder. And she was probably too late to stop this one, but she would try.

She didn't even bother with a coat as she stormed across her little yard, seized the wheelbarrow, and put the shovel into it. Then, as fast as her stiff legs would carry her, she ran out into the road and charged up the hill.

MAULE FELT SICK. That such things could happen in the world, that a woman was so reduced... And yet he was no blind, sheltered fool. He had always known. But these were things that happened to other females, not to women he knew, let alone to his wife.

And yet the world would blame her. In his heart, he knew it would take time before he did not. A single fall from grace, he could understand and forgive, although if he ever met the man who had so cynically seduced Elizabeth and left her to bear her shame and her child alone, he would probably beat him to a pulp.

That was different. Different from the three weeks when she had been unable to find shelter or to eat, and had finally sold her body on the streets for pennies.

Elizabeth's words tore at him, and yet he still clutched her close, keeping his face hidden from her lest she should see his disgust, even while they talked and talked. He understood she had been left no other choice. There had been more than her own life at stake. There was her child, whom she had both hated and loved in those weeks, and yet whom she had fought so fiercely to preserve through her own degradation.

His whole being twisted with pity and anger for her pain, her fear, the awfulness of that time. So did hers. But she said, "I'm not the only one. Women are used and blamed and face impossible choices all the time. I could feel it killing me. I was ill and I thought I would die with my baby, despite everything I had done. If it had not been for Constance... She found me and took me to her house. Whatever it was, I thought it had to be better than the sick vileness my life had become."

"Was it?" he whispered into her hair. His eyes were tight shut. He felt her nod.

"I didn't quite believe it at first. She said a friend had told her about me. She gave me a comfortable bed, a room of my own, even though some of the girls shared. You know about her establishment—it is a very exclusive, extremely expensive brothel. The men she employs to protect the household are large, fierce, and decent. But not all the women are whores. Only those who choose to be. She trains others to be servants or teachers, or finds them employment in shops and the more decent factories. There is even a female accountant... And as the women move on, others come in. All the women on the street, even some of the reformers, know about her. Some of them try to shut her down, but her connections are too powerful."

It sounded like a bizarre mixture of decadence and philanthropy that he could not quite appreciate.

"From the day I first entered her house, there were no more men. I was well fed and got well. When I had my baby, Constance helped me find good people to adopt him. The rest you know. I worked at various rag schools and church schools, where I was given character references that enabled me to apply for the post with you. And that is everything, Humphrey. This time, it is everything."

He wanted to shout at her for not telling him at the beginning. And yet if she had, would he not have sent her away? He would never have married her.

Resentment and anger mingled with his pity. It all *hurt*.

"Is it over?" she whispered. "Should I go?"

Something jolted through him. He actually lifted his head to look at her in alarm. "Go where?"

She shrugged hopelessly. "To Constance, I suppose. Begin again. But you must make the children understand I still love them. And make up some story for the neighbors—tell them I am traveling or something..."

"No," he said, unreasonably revolted. "How can I condemn your lies and tell more of my own?"

Alarm crossed her face. "It would not be kind to the children to tell everyone the truth about me."

"Damn it, that is no one's business but yours and mine." He searched her eyes, wondering if he looked as frightened as he felt. "Do you want to leave? Have you had enough of my temper and bluster?"

Wordlessly, she shook her head.

"Then it wasn't lies?" he blurted.

Her eyes narrowed with incomprehension, then widened impossibly. Tears gathered in the corners and his own throat closed up. "That I love you? Oh, Humph, how could I lie about that? How could I bear...?" She threw her head back with a gasp. "You think because I endured other men for money, I did the same with you? Oh God, I *do* have to go..."

She jerked away, and perversely, he tightened his arms around her. "No! I need time, Elizabeth, to be comfortable again, but I...I couldn't bear you to go. The children love you."

He could not say aloud that he did too. Not yet. He didn't know if the words were true. He didn't even know if her revelations had changed his feelings, though it seemed he didn't want them to.

Abruptly, a sharp crack sounded, like a firework, or a gun in the distance. He greeted it with relief, an excuse to rise, to walk away from her to the window and gather himself away from his need to touch her.

"What the devil was that?" He pulled back the curtain. His study window at the side of the house looked up the hill toward the Grange. Another bang sounded, but what really scared him was the glow in the sky. "Fire! Dear God, it must be Sarah's cottage!"

Seizing his coat on the way, he strode from the room. "Rouse the men to help!" he threw over his shoulder at Elizabeth.

From the front door, he began to run, taking the quick path

to the road before he recognized that if he arrived exhausted, he would be unfit to help Sarah. So he forced himself to slow to a brisk walk.

He had a soft spot for grumpy old Sarah. She reminded him of himself, and he had always thought her heart was good. She had been devastated when her husband died. As Maule would be devastated without Elizabeth.

Abruptly, his throat closed up again. And as if he had conjured her from his thoughts, her hand slipped into his. He blinked down at her.

"We can help together," she said breathlessly. "I've wakened the grooms, and they'll rouse the others. They won't be far behind us."

Thank you. He found he couldn't speak, but he curled his fingers around her hand in gratitude. Gratitude and love.

"I love you," he whispered. "I always will."

Her head pushed against his arm. She emitted something like a sob and then straightened with a jerk. "It isn't Sarah's house that's burning!"

CHAPTER EIGHTEEN

A s Constance landed on the ground, agony shot through her ankle. She couldn't even breathe to cry out, for the force of the fall had winded her. And yet she was aware that despite the speed and violence with which Solomon had pushed her, he had done his best to save her from the worst of the fall, twisting so that at least he did not land on top of her.

Stupefied, it took her an instant to realize what she had seen and heard. A glass lantern, fat and bulbous, flying through the air and breaking amongst the traces, the lick of fire. The scream of poor Betsy with a chunk out of her ear, the crack of gunshots.

Laing had followed them, moving quickly behind the hedges, thrown the lantern to stop them and no doubt destroy the evidence, and shot at them. Who had he hit, apart from the horse?

Solomon rolled away from her, bounding to his feet, so surely he was unharmed. He had a pocketknife in his hand with which he cut the screaming horse free of her harness and the burning gig. Old Betsy clattered away, and yet she didn't get far before she stopped and whinnied piteously.

Ignoring the pain, Constance sat up to see Solomon running back toward her. A figure hurtled past her from the hedge, all but jumping over her before he crashed into Solomon and brought him to the ground.

Laing.

He no longer carried the gun. Unless Murray had done the

shooting and still held it? In fresh fear, Constance doubled over, trying to crawl instinctively toward Solomon. But how could she help him? She had no weapon.

The men wrestling on the ground did. A steel blade glinted in the light of the fire. Solomon's pocketknife? Or Laing's? It didn't matter. Solomon was in possession, but Laing, on top of him, was trying to force the blade toward Solomon's throat.

Laing's head snapped back in response to Solomon's punch, and they rolled again. This time, Solomon reared up astride the doctor, hurling the knife away to the far side of the road. Laing lashed out with his fist, but Solomon dodged it, keeping his balance and grasping the fist, bearing it down to the road with one hand while the other sought Laing's free hand.

He was too late. The doctor grasped Solomon by the throat and squeezed.

Dear God. Constance staggered to her feet and hirpled across the road at speed, though every step was agony. The merrily burning gig lit up Solomon's knife quite clearly. She grasped it with a sob, then nearly jumped out of her skin as Besty whickered into her ear.

As she advanced on the struggling men, she saw Laing now had both hands around Solomon's throat. Solomon struck him in the face and then hard in the side. One of Laing's hands loosened, and Solomon grasped it, slamming it back into the road.

Constance raised the knife, wondering wildly how she was meant to use it. Would she just get in Solomon's way? Their movements were so quick, she could easily stab the wrong man. And even if she could reach the right one, could she really risk killing him?

In a flash, she knew she could, to save Solomon. She thought his gaze flickered up to her, but he was already winning the fight, clinging on to both Laing's hands now while the doctor bucked furiously beneath him.

Then, quite suddenly, their positions changed. She could have sworn that Solomon initiated the roll, but with a cry of triumph,

Laing emerged on top, with one of his hands free.

Now, Constance told herself. *Stab him in the arm and he is ours and he won't die...* With a gasp, she raised the knife and swung it downward—and was shoved roughly out of the way.

Sarah Phelps held a shovel in both hands and brought it down hard on Laing's head.

Constance let her arm fall. Solomon hadn't been presenting her but Sarah with the target. He had seen her coming.

Laing collapsed onto him. Solomon threw him off and leapt to his feet.

"Thank you," he said politely to Sarah, as though she had given him a cup of tea, but his eyes sought out Constance as he closed the distance between them and swept his arm around her, holding her up as though he knew her ankle was screaming in pain.

It was, and she didn't care. She didn't care about anything except his safety, his hold. For an instant, she let her forehead drop against his heaving chest.

"He won't stay like that forever," Sarah said crossly. "I can tie him with something, but you'll have to put him in the barrow."

Constance began to laugh.

CONSTANCE COULD DO little but supervise as Solomon and Sarah tied the unconscious Laing's wrists with bootlaces and his ankles with Solomon's necktie. Solomon was heaving him into the wheelbarrow when Murray appeared, his hair wild, his eyes large and frightened.

"What the devil has been going on?" he demanded. "Did you hear shots? Dear God, was that our gig? Where is Betsy?" His jaw dropped as Solomon straightened, revealing the contents of the barrow. "Dr. Laing!"

"Wheel the barrow," Solomon commanded, returning to

support Constance. "May we use your house, Mrs. Phelps?"

"Why not?" The old woman coughed. "Everyone else has." She put her hand on Betsy's neck, and both elderly females began to walk. Murray followed, wheeling the barrow with some difficulty, while Solomon and Constance brought up the rear.

It seemed somehow inevitable that they run into Humphrey and Elizabeth at Sarah's gap in the hedge. More surprising, and filling Constance with hope, was the fact that they were hand in hand.

"Someone should fetch Inspector Omand from the inn," Solomon said.

"Oh, I think he'll be here," Humphrey said. "There's a whole gaggle trailing up from the village, and from The Willows. If nothing else, they can clear up the mess. Er...what was the fire? And why is Dr. Laing in a wheelbarrow?"

Solomon said calmly, "The fire was the doctors' gig, in which I was bringing Constance home. She has sprained her ankle. Laing is in the wheelbarrow because Mrs. Phelps hit him with a shovel."

"How does a gig go on fire?" Elizabeth wondered aloud, while Humphrey's jaw dropped.

"With the aid of a burning lantern thrown beneath it," Solomon said.

"By Dr. Laing, if you're wondering," Constance added. It was beginning to be fun again, watching all the expressions from the shelter of Solomon's arm.

"Let's go inside," he suggested. "Maule, will you help Constance? She can't walk on that foot, and you may have noticed she has no shoe. I'll help Dr. Murray with Laing."

Constance would have preferred to keep Solomon with her, though she could hardly complain. Gratefully, she accepted the help of Humphrey and Elizabeth, and fell with some relief into the upholstered chair they put her in.

Without a word, Sarah filled her kettle and set in on the stove.

Laing was groaning as Solomon and Murray half carried him inside and dropped him onto a hard chair.

"There's a halter rope in the corner," Sarah said.

"There's no need," Laing said dully. But Solomon bound him to the chair anyway.

"Who doesn't want tea?" Sarah asked. "There's only three cups."

Solomon produced a flask from his coat pocket and saluted her with it. "Perhaps just for the ladies."

Constance, who would rather have had the brandy, did not argue.

"Fitting," Sarah said, clattering cups and crockery, "that he comes back here in that barrow. It's what he used to carry Frances Niall in before he dumped her into Willow Lake."

Murray sat suddenly down on the floor. "*Laing* killed her? For God's sake, Laing, deny it!"

Laing shrugged wearily. "What is the point? I thought I could get away with it. I even believed it was best that I did, because of the good work I do here. But I was lying to myself. I broke my oath. I did harm. I killed and I lied. And you, Murray, are already a better physician than I would ever be."

"But why?" Elizabeth asked, bewildered. "Why did you kill her?"

Laing closed his eyes and was silent. But Constance saw the tears running down his nose.

"He was her lover," she said. "Not in an evil seducer kind of way, or at least I don't think so. You really did love her, didn't you, doctor?"

Laing nodded. Since he had no free hands, he swiped his face against his shoulder with indifferent results.

"Then why on earth did you kill her?" Murray demanded.

"Because she was evil!" Laing burst out, and then groaned. "Because she didn't love me. It was always Maule. She talked about him all the time, mostly to wind me up, to hurt me as the representative of all men. I think she wanted to hurt Maule, although she never could, because he never really looked at her, not before she went to India, and certainly not when she returned. She said such awful things that night…"

And she had no empathy, Constance thought, no concept that people could snap with enough provocation and act outside their usual character.

"I couldn't stand it anymore," Laing all but whispered. "I didn't mean to kill her. At least, I don't think I did. I just had to shut her up, stop the terrible words just for a moment."

"So you put the pillow over her face and she stopped," Constance said.

He nodded dumbly.

"*My* pillow?" Sarah said in outrage.

"Yours?" Humphrey said, startled. He'd seemed stunned since Laing's revelations about Frances's feelings.

Sarah placed two cups on the table with some force, shoving them toward Constance and Elizabeth.

Constance said, "Mrs. Phelps let them meet in her house." In a lower voice, she added. "You don't need to tell us how she compelled you, just that she did."

"It's my silence that led to her death," Sarah said fiercely, "and nearly led to yours and his too. I should never have let her in the house, never have added to her silly belief that she was invincible, untouchable. But I could tell she was headed for a fall, and I was *glad* of it, God forgive me." She sat down abruptly on the nearest rickety chair. "She said I'd killed my husband, that Dr. Laing knew and would back her up."

Everyone stared at her, even Laing, who'd seemed to lose interest in the proceedings.

"Of course you didn't kill Phelps," Humphrey said forcefully. "You looked after him devotedly, nursed him…"

"I gave him digitalis for his heart," Sarah said miserably. "I got the dose wrong. If I hadn't, he wouldn't have died."

The appalled silence almost crushed Constance. The utter misery and despair of the woman to have committed such a mistake against the man she loved... No wonder she had embraced her reduced circumstances. She worked so hard to punish herself.

"He would," Laing said. "His heart was too weak. Your digitalis kept him alive for years, and you never got it wrong. We talked about it. I never mentioned him or his illness to Frances."

"She made it up," Constance said slowly. "Like she made up stories about everyone, including Sir Humphrey and Lady Maule, just to get her own way. This was the perfect place to meet, close to Dr. Laing's cottage and to Fairfield Grange, yet hidden from the road and from prying eyes. So she found a way to eject you whenever she wanted to be here, a way that would also keep you silent. Just part of her network of lies and petty power."

"And I loved her," Laing said hoarsely. "How could I love someone so hateful, so *evil*..."

Constance waved that aside. "She wasn't all evil any more than she was the saint everyone made her out to be when she died." Frances had just needed someone to stand up to her, to give her the shock of reality she needed—and the freedom to follow her own dreams. *She should have come to me.*

How ridiculous. Frances had never heard of Constance. And Constance could only ever save a handful of the lost souls swarming the great, ugly city...

Something drew her eyes to Solomon, who was gazing at her with his dark, steady eyes, eyes that were too sharp and too beautiful for anyone's peace.

The cottage door opened without warning and Constable Napier almost fell in, the inspector more leisurely and, for once, more grateful to be behind him.

"DIDN'T YOU SUSPECT him?" Solomon asked Murray as the policemen took Laing away. They stood with Constance in the road, next to Sarah's gap in the hedge. Sarah herself was bathing Betsy's shot ear and murmuring comforting nonsense that seemed to soothe the animal.

"I was too wrapped up, too smug about thinking myself the better doctor than my master, even though he worked admirably long hours. It never entered my head that he was not seeing patients but was instead totally distracted by love." Murray gave a short, bitter laugh. "Maddened by it, I should say. How can he have imagined he could get away with shooting you here in cold blood, yards from our cottage?"

"I think he suspected we had broken into the Grange," Solomon said. "I presume he meant to silence us and blame our deaths on the same mythical thieves."

"While destroying the evidence of the lantern," Constance added. "I hope there is more proof in his cottage."

"It doesn't matter," Solomon said. "He confessed to killing Frances before a room full of witnesses, and later to the police, too. Also to assaulting us." Without warning, he lifted Constance by the waist and put her on Betsy's broad back, then placed his hand beneath her foot to keep it steady.

Sarah gave the mare's nose a last pat and exchanged curt nods with Solomon and Constance before she strode back into the yard.

"This will wreck Colonel Niall," Elizabeth said, coming out a moment later with Humphrey.

"Laing has said he'll plead guilty," Humphrey said. "All the fight has gone out of him. No more needs to come out than that Laing killed her for love and is paying the price. Which he is. I suspect death will be a relief to him."

"What will you do?" Solomon asked Murray.

"Take over the practice here, if I am allowed to. And if Laing hasn't given everyone a disgust of doctors."

Humphrey put a hand on his shoulder and squeezed. "We'll support you all we can. Goodnight, Dr. Murray. I'll send Betsy and another vehicle up to you in the morning."

It seemed a very prosaic way to part, yet it reminded Constance only too well of her previous parting with the doctors only a hundred yards farther up the road. As Betsy moved beneath her toward The Willows, she found herself glancing over her shoulder and peering into the darkness of the hedges and fields.

The pain in her ankle had settled down to a dull ache. The desultory conversation around her seemed far away as her mind drifted. She was aware only of Besty's plodding, of the warmth of Solomon's hand beneath her bandaged foot, and the touch of his arm at her waist to keep her steady. It couldn't have been very comfortable for him. Constance liked it, though. Awareness of him kept her awake when she was tired enough to fall asleep on Betsy's back.

At The Willows, one of the returned stable lads was there to collect and care for the mare, while Solomon carried Constance into the house and upstairs to their bedchamber, the goodnights of their hosts ringing distantly in her ears.

"Why, Solomon," she said sleepily, "this is so unexpected."

"You know it isn't," he said, "so don't try to bamboozle me."

Smiling, she let her head fall against his shoulder. She must, she thought, be very tired indeed. She was relishing her own vulnerability in the arms of the man she was about to share a bed with. She remembered the touch of his lips in that Norfolk inn. She could not think, just *feel*, all warm and fuzzy and sweet...

He set her down on the bed gently enough, though he immediately stepped back. She twisted around to give him access to the fastenings of her gown, and as he had done several times before, he dealt with them for her.

Why did it feel different? Why was she *so* aware of his fingers at her nape, brushing the tingling skin of her back? Because he must be hurt too by his fight with Laing? No, although he was... But she could barely breathe, and her heart was pounding so hard he should have heard it.

His fingers fell away.

She closed her eyes. *Now, Solomon. Now...* What was she even hoping for?

"Can you manage?" he asked distantly. "Or shall I ask Lady Maule to help you? Our cover is shattered, after all."

His words felt like a blast of cold water. "Of course I can manage."

She didn't even wait for him to turn his back before she began to tug off her gown. Her heart lurched when she heard him move, but he only walked to the window, looking out on the night while she changed into her nightgown.

Only when she stood and, holding on to the bed, hopped in the direction of the washstand did he stride back to her, and with his arm at her waist all but lifted her over the distance.

No doubt it was laughable, but her whole body blushed at the intimacy. The thin lawn of her gown was no protection from his heat, his movement against her, his very scent... But again, he moved quickly away from her, turning back the bedcovers while she splashed water over her hands and face, then brushed her teeth.

He was there again to support her back to the bed, his touch electric. His hand at her waist was long and slender, his body pleasingly hard and muscled and—

"I shall be back in five minutes and douse the lights then," he said coolly, releasing her as soon as she sat on the bed. He walked out of the room.

I disgust him. I still disgust him as a woman, even if he tolerates me as a friend. Can I live with this?

Five minutes later, when he returned, she was lying down in the bed, turned away from him, willing herself to unconsciousness. After all, half an hour ago, she had almost been asleep on Besty's back. Now, when she could and should have slept, her nerves were all coiled up like springs.

After the usual rustling of clothes and movements she had got ridiculously used to, he snuffed out the candles and the mattress dipped as he got into bed. He lay down well away from her.

"Goodnight, Solomon."

"Goodnight, Constance." There was a pause, then, "Does your ankle pain you? Do you need something for—"

"No, it's fine, thank you."

He did not reply.

She said, "We solved the mystery. We did very well, considering, did we not?"

"I think we did."

"Are you in pain?" she asked. "Your throat—"

"I am not in pain."

"Then why are you so unhappy?"

She felt him turn over. Was he peering at her through the darkness?

"I am not unhappy." He sounded surprised. "Are you?"

She thought about it. "No. We proved Elizabeth's innocence, and she and Humphrey seem closer. And there is no real evil, is there? Just bad behavior and consequences and tragedy. Would you mind very much holding me? Just until we fall asleep."

Oh God, where had that come from? She just felt so small and alone…

If he had sprung out of bed and bolted, he would have surprised her less. Instead, he moved nearer.

"Constance," he murmured as his arm came around her.

She did not turn into him, but she clung to his hand in gratitude. He snuggled her, and within seconds the tragedy had slipped away, leaving only warmth and comfort and *him*. And then she drifted into sleep.

CHAPTER NINETEEN

S OLOMON WOKE BLEARILY at the first light of dawn. He usually did, but he was not usually too tired to get up. Nor was he usually plastered against the delectable form of Constance Silver. Desire had wakened him, and it raged through him now, not least because his hand was cupped around her breast.

The exotic floral and spiced scent of her hair, her skin, filled his senses. She was so soft and warm, her curves open to his caresses, and from there… Temptation clamored, all the more powerful because it was joined to a much more novel tenderness.

Last night's vulnerability had moved him. He had been glad to give her what comfort and care she wanted and sought nothing in return. But if he turned her now, if he kissed her mouth, would his own conflagration not consume her? She was not indifferent. Neither of them had ever been. Together, they would burn so brightly he would never be the same. And she…

She trusted him.

It was that, and the tenderness in his heart, that saved them both. Very gently, he disengaged his hand and his arm and rolled away from her to the cold side of the bed. Ice would have been better. But in truth, he was so tired that with that small physical distance from her allurement, he could simply close his eyes and let his imagination drift. Much, much safer. And he fell once more into slumber.

CONSTANCE WAS NOT asleep. She had wakened to the wonder of his intimate touch, to the hardness of his fully aroused body at her back, his heart pounding against her. She felt heavy and weak and wonderful.

He *did* want her. At least in his sleep. All she could do was enjoy the moment and wait for him to wake. What then?

Excitement mounted. She lay perfectly still, her whole being alive and yearning... It had come to her some time ago, during the Greenforth mystery, that even if he didn't know it, Solomon needed her. It seemed she needed him too, in ways that went far beyond mere loneliness, or even this wild, fierce desire.

Before she could dwell on what that really meant, he moved. Not just a little, but right away from her, leaving her cold and hurt and frustrated.

I cannot bear this. Animal instincts are not enough. To him, I will always be Constance Silver and therefore out of bounds. He would be appalled by the intimacy, if he were awake...

All the same, something had changed in his awareness of her. It had been there last night, even before they left the house, though he hid too well for her to know what was going on in his mind or his heart. His manner had varied wildly between cool aloofness and...something else, drat the man. If she had to guess, their growing closeness troubled him. And he would not allow it.

She knew suddenly that he would leave in the morning without her, just as he had done in Norfolk this summer.

Drearily, she supposed it was for the best.

No, it damned well isn't! Where is your pride, Constance Silver?

She summoned it and planned, and when she was sure he really was asleep, she slipped out of bed. This time, *she* would be the one to leave.

SOLOMON WOKE WITH a beam of autumnal sunlight on his face and a tenderness around his throat where Laing had tried to strangle him. His fists stung a bit too.

He had slept for longer than he meant to, and he knew instinctively that Constance was not in bed beside him. A cup of coffee stood on the table near the door, so the maid had already been in.

He threw off the bedclothes and rose, ignoring the stiffness in his bruised body. While he washed, shaved, and dressed, he tried to find the balance to face her. They would be clearing up the final points of the mystery, of course, probably making statements to the police, so that would help. But he should not insult her by shutting her out. And he should apologize for being so overfamiliar last night. At least then, he would know whether or not she had even noticed. And if she had, he could gauge how she felt about it.

Something was changing in a relationship he had always valued. It was fragile and precious, and he would not push it. But nor would he push it away.

With growing excitement, he straightened his necktie, finished his coffee, and went down to the breakfast parlor.

Sir Humphrey and Lady Maule were there, lingering over tea. Constance must have already eaten, he thought with peculiarly sharp disappointment.

"Good morning," Elizabeth said brightly. "I trust you are none the worse for your adventures?"

"No, I'm perfectly well. Forgive my lateness."

"Let me ring for fresh eggs."

"No, don't trouble. This is excellent." He took some toast and a few slices of ham and sat down at the table before asking casually, "Where is Constance?"

There was a pause. He looked up quickly to find the Maules exchanging glances.

"Gone," Maule said in surprise. "Didn't you know? She said not to wake you. John Coachman took her to the railway station in time to catch the early train."

Time stood still.

She was awake. I offended her. All hands and lust like all the other men she's ever met... He took a breath, remembering to veil his expression.

"If she told me, I was too sound asleep to hear," he said.

The door opened and the butler entered. "Colonel Niall has called, my lady. Shall I show him to the drawing room?"

Maule crumpled his napkin and laid it on the table. "No," he said firmly. "Ask him to join us here." As the butler bowed and departed, Maule met his wife's eyes. "There will be no more pandering to his insulting suspicions. He will meet us both, or neither of us."

Well said, thought Solomon.

But Colonel Niall, when he entered, looked neither fierce nor outraged to find Elizabeth there. Although his bow was certainly rather stiff and his face oddly rigid.

"Forgive the informality, colonel," Elizabeth said. "We were up late with a little excitement last night, and everything this morning is thrown back. Will you join us in a cup of tea? Some toast?"

"No, I won't, though I thank you," Niall said stiffly. "I just came to say my piece, and then I'll leave you to it." He looked Elizabeth in the eye. "I spoke this morning to Inspector Omand, who told me the truth of my daughter's death. I hope you can forgive my quite unjustified behavior toward you. I was entirely wrong and I beg your pardon. Yours too, Maule—I must have made your life very difficult. Both your lives. I can only be grateful for your forbearance. I'm sorry."

"You are grieving, sir," Elizabeth said quickly. "There should be no grudges or anger between neighbors."

"We accept your very handsome apology," Maule said. "And you are welcome to join us."

The colonel sat in the chair that should have been Constance's. He accepted a cup of tea with thanks, but did not touch it, then said abruptly, "I don't know what to do, what to say to people."

"Don't say anything," Maule advised. "Just thank them for their kindness. Dr. Laing's arrest will be a nine-day wonder. The village will gossip, of course; we can't change that. But we'll make sure people remember the good work Frances did, the way she made people laugh and lit up whatever room she entered."

"Very good of you," Niall said hoarsely. "I could never control her. She was worse after my wife died, got ridiculous ideas like wanting to be a doctor. *A doctor!*"

"If that had been possible," Solomon said, "things might have been different for all of you." He was sure Constance would think so, and he agreed with her. To ignore one's own nature, one's vocation, only led to unhappiness and frustration.

He could not and should not try to take Constance from hers. But perhaps he could distract her a little with one thing they had in common. She had gone, for now, but this time, *he* would make the first move…

SHE HAD LEFT him a brief note, handed to him by Mrs. Haslett after breakfast. It said that matters at her establishment in London required her attention. She asked that Elizabeth's maids pack the rest of her bags, if he wouldn't mind taking them back to Town for her. Her footmen would call for them next week, if that was convenient.

"Is it?" Elizabeth asked, reading over his shoulder.

"Convenient?" Solomon said vaguely. "Of course. I shall leave you in peace today. And apologize for our lack of honesty with you, Maule."

"Humph knows that was my fault," Elizabeth said. She tapped the note with one fingertip. "That's a very cool note for a friend. Have you quarreled?"

"No," Solomon said. He gave a lopsided smile. "It would be easier if we had. Merely, we don't quite understand each other."

"I think you understand each other well enough," Elizabeth said shrewdly. "It's yourselves you don't understand."

Solomon blinked at that stunning piece of insight and decided to put it away for later.

"Honesty," Maule growled. "That's what you need. And if I've learned anything, it's that the past does not matter, only the present."

He was wrong, but Solomon did not tell him so, for Maule had taken his wife's hand, and she was smiling mistily up at him.

A mad clattering on the stairs, accompanied by shouts of laughter, warned them that the children had been freed from the schoolroom, and Maule stalked out to read them the riot act.

"Would you believe me," Elizabeth asked Solomon, "if I told you Constance is the best person I know?"

"Yes," he said briefly. With a bow, he left her to pack his own baggage. And Constance's.

THREE DAYS LATER, Constance sat in her private sitting room at the front of the London establishment. She had just gone over the books for the month and was counting out the final wages due to Hildie, who had been offered the position of under-housemaid in a respectable house over toward Knightsbridge.

She was interrupted by Janey, who tended to erupt into a room rather than enter.

"Your bags have turned up, ma'am, and there's a gent in the downstairs salon. Bloody handsome gent too, even if he sounds like a sodding reformer."

"Who let a reformer into the house?" Constance demanded, letting the bad language go on order to address the greater crime. "Whoever did so can be rid of him again."

"Says he's a friend of yours," Janey said, and dropped a card on the desk in front of Constance.

Her breath stopped. *Solomon Grey, Esquire.* "Here?"

"When have I ever brought anyone here in my life?" Janey said indignantly, taking *here* as meaning this very room. "And it's only his *name* sounds suspicious. Walks like one of them haughty cats. Lovely coat and eyes that melt you at a hundred yards. Do you want him thrown out?"

She sounded disappointed, but she would have done it, probably without the aid of the footmen.

"No," Constance said, rising abruptly as panic set in. Why had he come here? To tell her not to bother him again? Wouldn't a letter have done? Perhaps he was just being friendly or making sure she was well after her bolt from The Willows. Then she remembered the maps on his table when she had gone to his flat. The fact that he was easing out of personal involvement in his various businesses. He was going away. He had come to say goodbye.

The ache in her heart grew sharper, but she ignored it as she always did. "I'll go down and see him. While I do, ask around and see if the girls know anyone who might want to replace Hildie."

She walked out of the room, still limping slightly, though her ankle was much better today. Her heart beat foolishly fast. She even touched her hair with one hand to be sure it was tidy. At least her gown was decent. In her line of work, she couldn't afford anyone to see her in an unbecoming dress.

Her hand shook slightly on the banister as she descended the stairs, but she schooled her face to an expression of polite welcome. Nodding briefly to Anthony, the liveried footman in the hall—who basically guarded any visitors left alone and remained at his post until Constance dismissed him—she entered the salon with all the practiced composure she could muster.

Solomon stood with his back to her, examining the porcelain figurine on the inlaid walnut table. She wondered if he was surprised by the quiet elegance of her salon. Had he expected something vulgar and plush, like stained red-velvet sofas trimmed with gold?

He turned quickly as she entered, and her mouth went dry—not just because of the way he looked but because he was *here*, and because for an instant before he veiled his eyes, something very like hope blazed there.

What did he hope for?

He replaced the figurine on the table and bowed. "Constance."

"Solomon. I am surprised to see you in such unhallowed halls."

"I'm not a prig, Constance."

"You wish to apply for an invitation?" *Stupid, stupid, why did I say that?*

"Don't be silly. I could have done that by letter. How is your ankle?"

"Still healing, as you can no doubt tell, but much better. Thank you for asking."

"I don't suppose you helped it bolting off by train at the crack of dawn."

"I did not bolt," she said icily.

"Yes, you did. I don't ask your reasons. They're your own. I just want to be sure you are well."

"Perfectly." She swallowed. "Thank you for returning my bags. How did you leave the Maules?"

"Finding their way. She told him everything and he is coming to terms with it, but I believe their marriage is strong. He still loves her."

"And she has always loved him." She walked across the room to cover her restlessness, adjusting the arrangement of chrysanthemums in the vase by the window. "Is the neighborhood in uproar?"

"Somewhat stunned by Dr. Laing's fall. Oh, do you remember the silver bracelet in Frances's treasure drawer? The police found a matching one in Laing's bedchamber, so there is proof of their relationship if the police need it. He gave her one as a love token. He was saving the other for a wedding gift."

"Poor Laing," she said. "He truly was besotted. The real tragedy is that she would probably have made an excellent doctor's wife, being of real use to the whole community and perhaps finding her own fulfillment. But she had fixed on Humphrey and could not see what was in front of her face."

He shrugged. "People don't choose whom to love. They just do. Besides, it is facile to blame everything he did on Frances. He held the pillow over her face for long enough to kill her, and she must have struggled. After which, he deliberately covered up his crime and was quite prepared to let others suffer for it. Including Elizabeth. And you and me, of course, when we found him out."

She shuddered, remembering the burning gig, the shots that missed their targets by mere whiskers, and then the fury of Laing's attack on Solomon. And he had been complicit in driving Sarah from her home whenever he and Frances trysted. It was all hard to forgive, impossible to justify.

She paced back toward Solomon, fixing her gaze on the region of his collar and necktie. "Is your throat still bruised?"

He touched it. "A bit. Though I feel we should try not to end all our cases with fire. It is becoming a bad habit."

Her breath caught. "You have another case?" she blurted.

"Not precisely, or not yet." His eyes, animated during their discussion, grew veiled once more. "But I have a proposition for you."

Oh, don't. Please don't. Her disappointment was ludicrous. Why should she be offended that he took her for what she was? That, given his own personal fastidiousness, he was prepared to overlook her past?

At The Willows, she would have given herself to him with joy. But this kind of transactional arrangement between them was just *wrong.* She could not do it, not for whatever pleasure she would find in his arms or he in hers. Not for anything.

"Come this evening," she said off-handedly, though her voice sounded oddly brittle to her own ears. "I shall introduce you to some charming ladies."

He blinked, as if in confusion. Then, to her amazement, his cheekbones darkened. "You misunderstand the nature of my proposition," he said coldly. "Do you really imagine I would come to you to meet *charming ladies?*"

"You could do worse," she drawled, holding his fierce gaze.

For a moment, she feared he would walk out. Then, unexpectedly, a breath of laughter escaped him, clearing his face.

"Constance, you are a shocking minx. I should know better than to let you provoke me. Listen to my proposition."

Somewhat belatedly, she indicated he should sit down, and primly took the chair opposite. Intrigued, she waited, her heart thumping for what would come next.

"We have solved two mysteries together now," he began. "Three, if we count Lord James's matter, which was largely the Tizsas' doing, even if we were there at the end."

"We can certainly allow ourselves two."

"We work well together. Do you think we are good enough to solve more such cases?"

"Perhaps, but we are not guaranteed to encounter more." *Sadly.*

"We would have more chance if we set our partnership on a business footing."

"Business?" she said, uncomprehending. She only knew one business, and this was it. She couldn't imagine his having anything to do with it.

"Silver and Grey," he said. "Agents of Inquiry."

Her mouth fell open. Hastily, she closed it again.

"Think about it," he said. "I'm sure this place all but runs itself with your hand only very lightly on the reins. I seem to have reduced my businesses to a similar degree. We have time and talent, and we might even make money at it."

Constance spun into a whirl of conjecture. What chiefly stood out for her was that he was not leaving. That he did not despise her. That he wanted to work with her, her name openly beside his in partnership. It might not be the kind of partnership she secretly craved, but perhaps neither of them was ready for that.

But to be together...

"I have taken you by surprise," he remarked.

"Yes." She frowned at him. "I won't give up my establishment here."

"I know."

She licked her lips, trying to think through her daze and the sudden, blazing happiness surging up from her toes. It would be *fun*...

He rose to his feet. "Think about it. Write or call. You know where I am."

"Thank you," she said, watching him cross the room to the door. He reached for the handle, and she caught her breath. "Solomon?"

He glanced back, his expression still masked. How much had it cost him to come here and propose this venture? He had truly been afraid of her answer, of rejection. "Yes?"

"I *have* thought. We should do it. Let us be Silver and Grey."

About the Author

Mary Lancaster lives in Scotland with her husband, three mostly grown-up kids and a small, crazy dog.

Her first literary love was historical fiction, a genre which she relishes mixing up with romance and adventure in her own writing. Her most recent books are light, fun Regency romances written for Dragonblade Publishing: *The Imperial Season* series set at the Congress of Vienna; and the popular *Blackhaven Brides* series, which is set in a fashionable English spa town frequented by the great and the bad of Regency society.

Connect with Mary on-line – she loves to hear from readers:

Email Mary:
Mary@MaryLancaster.com

Website:
www.MaryLancaster.com

Newsletter sign-up:
http://eepurl.com/b4Xoif

Facebook:
facebook.com/mary.lancaster.1656

Facebook Author Page:
facebook.com/MaryLancasterNovelist

Twitter:
@MaryLancNovels

Amazon Author Page:
amazon.com/Mary-Lancaster/e/B00DJ5IACI

Bookbub:
bookbub.com/profile/mary-lancaster

www.ingramcontent.com/pod-product-compliance
Ingram Content Group UK Ltd.
Pitfield, Milton Keynes, MK11 3LW, UK
UKHW020828150225
455111UK00011B/476